PE

Evelyn Waugh was born in Hampstead in 1903, second son of Arthur Waugh, publisher and literary critic, and brother of Alec Waugh, the popular novelist. He was educated at Lancing and Hertford College, Oxford, where he read Modern History. In 1928 he published his first work, a life of Dante Gabriel Rossetti, and his first novel, *Decline and Fall*, which was soon followed by *Vile Bodies* (1930), *Black Mischief* (1932), *A Handful of Dust* (1934) and *Scoop* (1938). During these years he travelled extensively in most parts of Europe, the Near East, Africa and tropical America, and published a number of travel books, including *Labels* (1930), *Remote People* (1931), *Ninety-Two Days* (1934) and *Waugh in Abyssinia* (1936). In 1939 he was commissioned in the Royal Marines and later transferred to the Royal Horse Guards, serving in the Middle East and in Yugoslavia. In 1942 he published *Put Out More Flags* and then in 1945 *Brideshead Revisited. When the Going was Good* and *The Loved One* preceded *Men at Arms*, which came out in 1952, the first volume of *The Sword of Honour* trilogy, and won the James Tait Black Memorial Prize. The other volumes, *Officers and Gentlemen* and *Unconditional Surrender*, followed in 1955 and 1961. *The Ordeal of Gilbert Pinfold* appeared in 1957, the *Life of Ronald Knox* in 1959 and *A Little Learning*, Waugh's last book and the first volume of a projected autobiography in 1964. Evelyn Waugh was received into the Roman Catholic Church in 1930 and his biography of the Elizabethan Jesuit martyr, *Edmund Campion*, was awarded the Hawthornden Prize in 1936. For many years he lived with his wife and six children in the West Country. He died in 1966.

Waugh said of his work: 'I regard writing not as investigation of character but as an exercise in the use of language, and with this I am obsessed. I have no technical psychological interest. It is drama, speech and events that interest me.' Mark Amory called Evelyn Waugh 'one of the five best novelists in the English language this century', while Harold Acton described him as having 'the sharp eye of a Hogarth alternating with that of the Ancient Mariner'.

Christopher Hitchens was born in 1949 and graduated from Balliol College, Oxford, in 1970. An author and journalist, he is a regular columnist for *Vanity Fair* and the *Nation*, and also contributes to the *New York Review of Books*, the *London Review of Books* and *The Times Literary Supplement*. His books include *Blood, Class and Nostalgia: Anglo-American Ironies* (1990); *For the Sake of Argument: Selected Essays* (1993); *When the Borders Bleed: The Struggle of the Kurds* (1994); *The Missionary Position: Mother Teresa in Theory and Practice* (1995); and, most recently, *No One Left to Lie To: The Triangulations of William Jefferson Clinton* (1998). He was Mellon Professor of English at the University of Pittsburgh for the year 1997 and is currently Professor of Liberal Studies at the New School for Social Research in New York. Christopher Hitchens lives in Washington, DC.

SCOOP

A NOVEL ABOUT JOURNALISTS

EVELYN WAUGH

With an Introduction by Christopher Hitchens

PENGUIN BOOKS

Published by the Penguin Group
Penguin Books Ltd, 80 Strand, London WC2R ORL, England
Penguin Group (USA) Inc., 375 Hudson Street, New York, New York 10014, USA
Penguin Group (Canada), 90 Eglinton Avenue East, Suite 700, Toronto, Ontario, Canada M4P 2Y3
(a division of Pearson Penguin Canada Inc.)
Penguin Ireland, 25 St Stephen's Green, Dublin 2, Ireland (a division of Penguin Books Ltd)
Penguin Group (Australia), 250 Camberwell Road, Camberwell, Victoria 3124, Australia
(a division of Pearson Australia Group Pty Ltd)
Penguin Books India Pvt Ltd, 11 Community Centre, Panchsheel Park, New Delhi – 110 017, India
Penguin Group (NZ), 67 Apollo Drive, Rosedale, North Shore 0632, New Zealand
(a division of Pearson New Zealand Ltd)
Penguin Books (South Africa) (Pty) Ltd, 24 Sturdee Avenue,
Rosebank, Johannesburg 2196, South Africa

Penguin Books Ltd, Registered Offices: 80 Strand, London WC2R ORL, England

www.penguin.com

First published by Chapman & Hall 1938
Published in Penguin Books 1943
Published with a new Introduction in Penguin Classics 2000

1

This edition produced for The Book People Ltd,
Hall Wood Avenue, Haydock, St Helens, WA11 9UL

Copyright 1938 by Evelyn Waugh
Introduction copyright © Christopher Hitchens 2000
All rights reserved

Printed in England by Clays Ltd, St Ives plc
Set in Monotype Baskerville

ISBN 978-1-856-13276-3

www.greenpenguin.co.uk

Penguin Books is committed to a sustainable future
for our business, our readers and our planet.
The book in your hands is made from paper
certified by the Forest Stewardship Council.

INTRODUCTION

Three years before his death in 1966, Evelyn Waugh wrote, in *Basil Seal Rides Again*, a prefiguration of his own literary obituary:

His voice was not the same instrument as of old. He had first assumed it as a conscious imposture; it had become habitual to him; the antiquated, worldly-wise moralities which, using that voice, he had found himself obliged to utter, had become his settled opinions.

The very rotundity here is its own cumbrous self-criticism: if Evelyn Waugh later became a byword for port-sodden Blimpery it was because his face shaped itself to fit a mask. Yet let us not forget the face, and the voice, that predated that heavy, bilious terminus. In the pages of *Scoop*, we encounter Waugh at the mid-season point of his perfect pitch; youthful and limber and light as a feather. In fact:

Feather-footed through the plashy fen passes the questing vole ...

No sooner has one imbibed this journalistic 'intro', from the fertile yet innocent pen of 'William Boot, Countryman', the editor of 'Lush Places', than one enters or re-enters a world of delight and imagination, freighted in its depiction with just enough of the sinister and the cynical to escape the charge of sentimentality.

The figure of the innocent abroad, or the Candide or Pinocchio, is such a familiar device as to require the most delicate handling. Waugh solves this problem brilliantly, and from the first page, by having not one but two inno- cents abroad, and by focusing initial attention on the wrong one. In a seriously heartless sentence he introduces John Boot, conceited citizen of the Republic of Letters:

He had published eight books (beginning with a life of Rimbaud written when he was eighteen, and concluding, at the moment, with *Waste of Time*, a studiously modest description of some harrowing months among the Patagonian Indians), of which most people who lunched with Lady Metroland could remem- ber the names of three or four.

I personally can never scan that passage without thinking of the vastly overrated society traveller Bruce Chatwin: there has always been someone in London who fits the description and as Waugh cleverly intuited, there always will be. This Boot – pale and ineffectual and sycophantic – flaps his gossamer wing in peevish discontent and, all unknowing, creates a typhoon in far-off Boot Magna and in even remoter Ishmaelia.

It's quite permissible to read the entire Waugh canon as an original use of original sin. When he decides to play with an innocent character, that character stays played with. The Book of Job is an over-ornate trifle when set beside the caprice visited on poor little Lord Tangent, for example, in *Decline and Fall*. But the other John Boot, the timid and bucolic near-herbivore who is forcibly mutated into 'Boot of the *Beast*', is the most satisfying and, in every sense of the term, the most 'finished' of Waugh's fictional victims.

Were I asked to reminisce and expatiate at one of Lord Copper's infamous dinners, I could become suitably bor- ing and prosaic about the brave days of Fleet Street. I could enlarge on the origins of its three colloquial names: 'The Street of Adventure'; 'The Street of Broken Dreams' and 'The Street of Shame'. As one who briefly held the title of Foreign Correspondent at the old *Daily Express*, and who still held it when the Aitken family sold out to some property developer or other, I can argue with room-emptying conviction that my own broken person represents that of the last Beaverbrook 'fireman'. I remember that pseudo-deco dark-glassed palazzo, so near to Ludgate Circus and the plaque to Edgar Wallace; a building known half-admiringly as 'The Black Lubyanka'. And I remember the thrill of its lobby and its commissionaires, as well as the surge that went through my system when taking a taxi from there to Heathrow airport; a wad of traveller's cheques at the ready and an exotic visa stamp in the old blue-and-gold hardback that was then our passport.

Was it true that the standby slogan of the *Express* foreign desk, for any hack stumbling on to a scene of carnage and misery, was: 'Anyone here been raped and speaks English?' I regret to say that it was. Is it true than an *Express* scribe in some hellhole, his copy surpassed by a *Daily Mail* man who had received an honourable flesh-wound, received a cable: 'MailMan shot. Why you unshot?' I never saw the cable itself, but I did see an entire front-page, complete with dashing photograph of the embattled correspondent, confected from whole cloth about a world-shaking event which the intrepid hack had irretrievably missed. And there wasn't anyone at the bar – the 'mahogany ridge' from which so many fine stories were filed – who did not have his version of the following:

Why, once Jakes went out to cover a revolution in one of the Balkan capitals. He overslept in his carriage, woke up at the wrong station, didn't know any different, got out, went straight to a hotel, and cabled off a thousand-word story about barricades in the streets, flaming churches, machine guns answering the rattle of his typewriter as he wrote, a dead child, like a broken doll, spreadeagled in the deserted roadway before his window – you know.

The 'you know' there is positioned to perfection. Yes, indeed we did know. There was also the matter of alcoholic etiquette:

The bunch now overflowed the hotel. There were close on fifty of them. All over the lounge and dining-room they sat and stood and leaned; some whispered to each other in what they took to be secrecy; others exchanged chaff and gin. It was their employers who paid for all this hospitality, but the conventions were decently observed – 'My round, old boy.' 'No, no, my round!' 'Have this one on me.' 'Well, the next is mine!' – except by Shumble, who, from habit, drank heartily and without return wherever it was offered.

At gatherings in the Europa in Belfast, in the Commodore in Beirut, at Meikles in old Rhodesia, and even in the Holiday Inn in Sarajevo I have heard this banter repeated, sometimes self-consciously. The names of Waugh's morally hollowed-out hacks are perhaps a bit Dickensian, but that can be overlooked in a near-flawless sentence like this one:

Shumble, Whelper and Pigge knew Corker; they had loitered of old on many a doorstep and forced an entry into many a stricken home.

I once met a man, in the Punch Tavern opposite the old *Beast* building, who fondly explained to me that one required a solid colleague when calling on the recently bereaved. 'They'll always offer a cup of tea, see, and want to talk about the crash or the accident or the murder. So your mate offers to help in the kitchen and that'll give you nice time to go in the drawing-room and swipe the photos from the mantelpiece.' But, you notice, it takes me three times as long to explain as it did for Waugh to con-jure the scene. His little story is replete with exquisite asides of the same sort, some of them short ('One native whom they questioned fled precipately at the word "police"') and some requiring a longer run-up to attain the pressure-point where mirth explodes:

They were bowling up the main street of Jacksonburg. A strip of tarmac ran down the middle; on either side were rough tracks for mules, men, cattle and camels: beyond these the irregular outline of the commercial quarter; a bank, in shoddy concrete, a Greek provisions store in timber and tin, the Cafe de la Bourse, the Carnegie Library, the Cine-Parlant, and numerous gutted sites, relics of an epidemic of arson some years back when an Insurance Company had imprudently set up shop in the city.

The last clause, with its answer-back between 'insurance' and 'prudence', both completes the scene and collapses the scenery. We are in Absurdistan.

The first chapter of Book Two is probably the finest evocation of Absurdistan ever composed. One yearns to quote or excerpt the whole of it, from which I select the fate of those missionaries who ventured into Ishmaelia:

They were eaten, every one of them: some raw, others stewed and seasoned – according to local usage and the calendar (for the better sort of Ishmaelites have been Christian for many centuries and will not publicly eat human flesh, uncooked, in Lent, without special and costly dispensation from their bishop.)

A lesser writer might have made more of the rhythm that is furnished by the remorseless succession of public ... human ... uncooked ... in Lent. But here we touch on a sensitive ganglion. Is Mr Waugh, by employing the 'stereotype' of the cannibal stewpot, not reaching for the baser instincts of his readers? Do his characters not also use words like 'darky' and 'coon' and even 'nigger' without evident compunction? Well, there's no real point in trying to acquit Mr Waugh in front of the sort of modern jury he would have despised or ignored. But he himself employs no term of hatred or contempt; his main fools and dolts are English or Swedish or German, and his villain – the memorably-sketched Dr Benito – is a suave and elegant and fluent black man. The most subhuman portrayals are of British youths back in southern England (a theme to which I want to return). One might add that the only authentic cannibal in Waugh's fiction is Basil

Seal and – a detail from Absurdistan, but a true detail none the less – that in the 1960s the exiled leaders of the Pan-African Congress wrote to Waugh at his Somerset home in Combe Florey, asking if they could annex the name 'Azania', from his novel *Black Mischief,* for the future liberated South Africa! (The title 'Azania' survives now in lapidary form on the gravestone of Steve Biko.)

I've done the best I can: Evelyn Waugh was a re-actionary and that's that. But he combined in the same person an attachment to modernism. (Lines from *The Waste Land* occur in the title of one of his novels, and in the text of another one.) Like Eliot, his prejudices were in some way his muse: how brilliant of him to have awarded Bloomsbury names to the leaders of Ishmaelia's Jackson dynasty:

It had been found expedient to merge the functions of national defence and inland revenue in an office then held in the capa-ble hands of General Gollancz Jackson; his forces were in two main companies, the Ishmaelite Mule Tax-gathering force and the Rifle Excisemen, with a small Artillery Death Duties Corps for use against the heirs of powerful noblemen.

These fine detachments are described as returning from their expeditions 'laden with the spoils of the less nimble' – a deft and near-perfect anticipation of what would later be called 'kleptocracy' in post-colonial Africa.

The manners and *mores* of the press, however, are the recurrent motif of the book and the chief reason for its enduring magic:

William and Corker went to the Press Bureau. Dr Benito, the director, was away but his clerk entered their names in his ledger and gave them cards of identity. They were small orange documents, originally printed for the registration of prostitutes.

Later:

'Once and for all, Salter, I will not have a barrier erected between me and my staff. I am as accessible to the humblest . . .'

Lord Copper paused for an emphatic example ... 'the humblest book reviewer as I am to my immediate entourage.'

This world of callousness and vulgarity and philistinism (who was it who called aloud in those days for Providence to 'drain the Rother Mere and dam the Beaver Brook'?) also introduces us to yet a third Candide of the action. Mr Salter, the hapless underling of the hateful Lord Copper, is never even given a first name. He is the plaything of fate. Best-known perhaps as the nervous utterer of the over-used phrase 'Up to a point, Lord Copper,' he deserves more recognition than he has so far received. To William Boot, it is the big city that represents *partibus infidelium*, and once there and installed against his will in a vile modern hotel he asks for a toothbrush 'and presently a page with a face of ageless evil brought it on a tray.' This hideous boy is further described as 'the knowing midget'. To Mr Salter, it is the rural dominion that suggests terror and cruelty; upon arrival at the despond-infested platform of Boot Magna Halt he encounters 'a cretinous native youth who stood on the further side of the paling, leant against it and picked at the dry paint-bubbles with a toe-like thumb. When Mr Salter looked at him, he glanced away and grinned wickedly at his boots.' Converse proves arduous: 'Mr Salter's voice sounded curiously flutey and querulous in contrast to the deep tones of the moron.' This interlude of what I would describe as life-affirming heartlessness is rounded off deliciously when the idiot lad overturns his truck, burying Mr Salter's hand-luggage in an avalanche of slag. The butler brings the news:

> 'He overturned the vehicle in the back drive.'
> 'Was he hurt?'
> 'Oh, yes, sir; gravely.'

I have always thought Sam Peckinpah's *Straw Dogs* to be the finest counterpoint to the apple-blossom propaganda of the countryside idyll. It is followed closely by *Withnail and I*, in which two Londoners go 'on holiday by mistake'. ('Stop saying that, Withnail! *Of course* he's the fucking farmer.') But Evelyn Waugh had both of these two hellish expeditions mapped out in advance:

There was something un-English and not quite right about 'the country', with its solitude and self-sufficiency, its bloody recreations, its darkness and silence and sudden, inexplicable noises; the kind of place where you never know from one minute to the next that you may not be tossed by a bull or pitchforked by a yokel or rolled over and broken up by a pack of hounds.

Indeed, Waugh seems to confirm this *noir* version at the close. 'Maternal rodents pilot their furry brood through the stubble,' writes William Boot in his resumed *Lush Places* column. 'Outside the owls hunted maternal rodents and their furry brood', notes the author in laying down his pen. And are not Shumble and Whelper and Corker and Pigge, in the last instance, peasant names? William at this point has lately emerged from a reverie about Katchen, the entirely unsuitable girl to whom he had lost his heart in Jacksonburg. Frailty, it might be said, thy name is Katchen. (Though the divine Julia Stitch can also play a pretty devious hand when it suits her.) The German girl's utter and transparent and mercenary indifference to all interests save her own, and her complete disregard for William's tender feelings, demonstrate how flayed Waugh still felt where women were concerned, and how easily a few careless words can first inflict pain and then generate bitterness. As with the owls and the rodents, and the poor, enthusiastic cub reporter who greets the returning Boot at Victoria station, life is random and unfair, and sin, however original, largely unpunished.

Perhaps aware that he might be in danger of letting cynicism or despair pollute his most sprightly fiction, Waugh summons the most literal *deus ex machina*. 'Mr Baldwin', first encountered on an aeroplane, alights again like an angel from the skies over the endangered shanties of Jacksonburg, and allows William to confirm his accidentally-acquired status as 'Boot of the *Beast*.' And from then on, the reign of good humor is restored. Even William's depraved Uncle Theodore, with his 'dark and costly expeditions to London', ends the book with a reasonable chance of getting laid.

Lest I offend by the above vulgarism, I should point out that *Scoop*, though written by one who affected infinite contempt for America, pays its own tribute to modernity and Americanism. For all the dated 'Bright Young Thing' slang ('Wasters' for *Waste of Time*: 'Foregonners' for 'foregone conclusion' – the same trick or tic that made Rugby Football into 'rugger' and Association Football into 'soccer') the New World is visible over the horizon. Lord Copper in Chapter Two finds that he has 'gotten a new angle' on Mrs Stitch's charisma. The expression 'poor hick' is used early on to describe William, who is further depicted as a potential 'sucker' when visiting General Cruttwell (in my opinion a potential original for Ian Flemin's boffin-like 'Q') for his legendary outfitting. Most amazing of all, 'When Corker and his friends' make a certain discovery about a ticket collector on their Ishmaelite train, 'they felt very badly about this.' Felt very badly? This may be one of the earliest usages of this barbarous neoligism, and I felt ungood about it, as I did on noticing the novel's one other stylistic blemish: the repetition of 'chafing dish and spirit lamp' at Boot's first dinner with Mr Salter and at Mr Salter's first and last dinner *chez* Boot.

These are spots on the sun. For all its marvellous fantasies and intricacies, *Scoop* endures because it is a novel of pitiless realism; the mirror of satire held up to catch the Caliban of the press corps, as no other narrative has ever done save Hecht and MacArthur's *Front Page* and, to a smaller extent, Michael Frayn's *Towards the End of the Morning*. 'Staunchly anti-interventionist', mutters Corker in robotic journalese after being reviled by an Ishmaelite landlady. 'Doyenne of Jacksonburg hostesses pans police project as unwarrantable interference with sanctity of Ishmaelite home.' In Moscow in the waning days of Communist rule, colleagues of mine discovered that the pre-Gorbachev ruler Konstantin Chernenko had died. But they got the tip from the cleaning ladies appointed to prepare the hall for the lying-in-state. Unwilling to give such lowly sources for their scoop, and deciding that everyone in the Soviet Union ultimately worked for the regime, they attributed the rumor to 'low level government employees.' While only the other day, the Toronto press reported that the wife of Conrad Black, himself a Megalopolitan type, had summoned a female reporter to her home. After some brisk questioning, she exclaimed: 'But you're not the one I asked for.' And so Elena Cherney discovered in time that she had been mistaken for Louisa Chialkowska ('the other one'). It still goes on, all right.

For
LAURA

BOOK I

THE STITCH SERVICE

*

ONE

I

WHILE still a young man, John Courteney Boot had, as his publisher proclaimed, 'achieved an assured and enviable position in contemporary letters.' His novels sold 15,000 copies in their first year and were read by the people whose opinion John Boot respected. Between novels he kept his name sweet in intellectual circles with unprofitable but modish works on history and travel. His signed first editions sometimes changed hands at a shilling or two above their original price. He had published eight books – beginning with a life of Rimbaud written when he was eighteen, and concluding, at the moment, with *Waste of Time*, a studiously modest description of some harrowing months among the Patagonian Indians – of which most people who lunched with Lady Metroland could remember the names of three or four. He had many charming friends, of whom the most valued was the lovely Mrs Algernon Stitch.

Like all in her circle John Boot habitually brought his difficulties to her for solution. It was with this purpose, on a biting-cold mid-June morning, that he crossed the Park and called at her house (a superb creation by Nicholas Hawksmoor modestly concealed in a cul-de-sac near Saint James's Palace).

Algernon Stitch was standing in the hall; his bowler

hat was on his head; his right hand, grasping a crimson, royally emblazoned dispatch case, emerged from the left sleeve of his overcoat; his other hand burrowed petulantly in the breast pocket. An umbrella under his left arm further inconvenienced him. He spoke indistinctly, for he was holding a folded copy of the morning paper between his teeth.

'Can't get it on,' he seemed to say.

The man who had opened the door came to his assistance, removed the umbrella and dispatch case and laid them on the marble table; removed the coat and held it behind his master. John took the newspaper.

'Thanks. Thanks very much. Much obliged. Come to see Julia, eh?'

From high overhead, down the majestic curves of the great staircase, came a small but preternaturally resonant voice.

'Try not to be late for dinner, Algy; the Kents are coming.'

'She's upstairs,' said Stitch. He had his coat on now and looked fully an English cabinet minister; long and thin, with a long, thin nose, and long, thin moustaches; the ideal model for continental caricaturists. 'You'll find her in bed,' he said.

'Your speech reads very well this morning.' John was always polite to Stitch; everybody was; Labour members loved him.

'Speech? Mine? Ah. Reads well, eh? Sounded terrible to me. Thanks all the same. Thanks very much. Much obliged.'

So Stitch went out to the Ministry of Imperial Defence and John went up to see Julia.

As her husband had told him, she was still in bed although it was past eleven o'clock. Her normally mobile face encased in clay was rigid and menacing as an Aztec mask. But she was not resting. Her secretary, Miss Holloway, sat at her side with account books, bills, and correspondence. With one hand Mrs Stitch was signing cheques;

with the other she held the telephone to which, at the moment, she was dictating details of the costumes for a charity ballet. An elegant young man at the top of a step ladder was painting ruined castles on the ceiling. Josephine, the eight-year-old Stitch prodigy, sat on the foot of the bed construing her day's passage of Virgil. Mrs Stitch's maid, Brittling, was reading her the clues of the morning crossword. She had been hard at it since half past seven.

Josephine rose from her lesson to kick John as he entered. '*Boot*,' she said savagely, '*Boot*,' catching him first on one kneecap, then on the other. It was a joke of long standing.

Mrs Stitch turned her face of clay, in which only the eyes gave a suggestion of welcome, towards her visitor.

'Come in,' she said, 'I'm just going out. Why twenty pounds to Mrs Beaver?'

'That was for Lady Jean's wedding present,' said Miss Holloway.

'I must have been insane. About the lion's head for the centurion's breastplate; there's a beautiful one over the gate of a house near Salisbury, called Twisbury Manor; copy that as near as you can; ring up *Country Life* and ask for "back numbers"; there was a photograph of it about two years ago. You're putting too much ivy on the turret, Arthur; the owl won't show up unless you have him on the bare stone, and I'm particularly attached to the owl. *Munera*, darling, like tumtiddy; always a short a in neuter plurals. It sounds like an anagram: see if "Terracotta" fits. I'm *delighted* to see you, John. Where have you been? You can come and buy carpets with me; I've found a new shop in Bethnal Green, kept by a very interesting Jew who speaks no English; the most extraordinary things keep happening to his sister. Why should I go to Viola Chasm's Distressed Area; did she come to my Model Madhouse?'

'Oh, yes, Mrs Stitch.'

'Then I suppose it means two guineas. I absolutely

loved *Waste of Time*. We read it aloud at Blakewell. The headless abbot is grand.'

'Headless abbot?'

'Not in Wasters. On Arthur's ceiling. I put it in the Prime Minister's room.'

'Did he read it?'

'Well, I don't think he *reads* much.'

'Terracotta is too long, madam, and there is no r.'

'Try hottentot. It's that kind of word. I can never do anagrams unless I can see them. No, *Twisbury*, you must have heard of it.'

'Floribus Austrum,' Josephine chanted, 'perditus et liquidis immisi fontibus apros; having been lost with flowers in the South and sent into the liquid fountain; apros is wild boars, but I couldn't quite make sense of that bit.'

'We'll do it tomorrow. I've got to go out now. Is "hottentot" any use?'

'No h, madam,' said Brittling with ineffable gloom.

'Oh, dear. I must look at it in my bath. I shall only be ten minutes. Stay and talk to Josephine.'

She was out of bed and out of the room. Brittling followed. Miss Holloway collected the cheques and papers. The young man on the ladder dabbed away industriously. Josephine rolled to the head of the bed and stared up at him.

'It's very banal, isn't it, Boot?'

'I like it very much.'

'Do you? I think all Arthur's work is banal. I read your book *Waste of Time*.'

'Ah.' John did not invite criticism.

'I thought it very banal.'

'You seem to find everything banal.'

'It is a new word whose correct use I have only lately learnt,' said Josephine with dignity. 'I find it applies to nearly everything; Virgil and Miss Brittling and my gymnasium.'

'How is the gymnasium going?'

'I am by far the best of my class, although there are several girls older than me and two middle-class boys.'

When Mrs Stitch said ten minutes, she meant ten minutes. Sharp on time she was back, dressed for the street; her lovely face, scraped clean of clay, was now alive with interest.

'Sweet Josephine, has Mr Boot been boring you?'

'It was all right really. I did most of the talking.'

'Show him your imitation of the Prime Minister.'

'No.'

'Sing him your Neapolitan song.'

'No.'

'Stand on your head. Just once for Mr Boot.'

'No.'

'Oh, dear. Well, we must go at once if we are to get to Bethnal Green and back before luncheon. The traffic's terrible.'

Algernon Stitch went to his office in a sombre and rather antiquated Daimler; Julia always drove herself, in the latest model of mass-produced baby car; brand-new twice a year, painted an invariable brilliant black, tiny and glossy as a midget's funeral hearse. She mounted the kerb and bowled rapidly along the pavement to the corner of St James's, where a policeman took her number and ordered her into the road.

'Third time this week,' said Mrs Stitch. 'I wish they wouldn't. It's such a nuisance for Algy.'

Once embedded in the traffic block, she stopped the engine and turned her attention to the crossword.

'It's "detonated",' she said, filling it in.

East wind swept the street, carrying with it the exhaust gas of a hundred motors and coarse particles of Regency stucco from a once decent Nash façade that was being demolished across the way. John shivered and rubbed some grit further into his eye. Eight minutes' close application was enough to finish the puzzle. Mrs Stitch folded the paper and tossed it over her shoulder into the back seat; looked about her resentfully at the stationary traffic.

'This is too much,' she said; started the engine, turned sharp again on to the kerb and proceeded to Piccadilly, driving before her at a brisk pace, until he took refuge on the step of Brooks's, a portly, bald young man; when he reached safety, he turned to remonstrate, recognized Mrs Stitch, and bowed profoundly to the tiny, black back as it shot the corner of Arlington Street. 'One of the things I like about these absurd cars,' she said, 'is that you can do things with them that you couldn't do in a real one.'

From Hyde Park Corner to Piccadilly Circus the line of traffic was continuous and motionless, still as a photograph, unbroken and undisturbed save at a few strategic corners where barricaded navvies, like desperate outposts of some proletarian defence, were rending the road with mechanical drills, mining for the wires and tubes that controlled the life of the city.

'I want to get away from London,' said John Boot.

'So it's come to that? All on account of your American girl?'

'Well, mostly.'

'I warned you, before you began. Is she being frightful?'

'My lips are sealed. But I've got to get far away or else go crazy.'

'To my certain knowledge she's driven three men into the bin. Where are you going?'

'That's just what I wanted to talk about.'

The line of cars jerked forwards for ten yards and again came to rest. The lunch-time edition of the evening papers was already on the streets; placards announcing

ISHMAELITE CRISIS

and

STRONG LEAGUE NOTE

were fluttering in the east wind.

'I.hmaelia seems to be the place. I was wondering if Algy would send me there as a spy.'

'Not a chance.'

'No?'

'Foregonners. Algy's been sacking ten spies a day for weeks. It's a grossly overcrowded profession. Why don't you go as a war correspondent?'

'Could you fix it?'

'I don't see why not. After all, you've been to Patagonia. I should think they would jump at you. You're sure you really want to go?'

'Quite sure.'

'Well, I'll see what I can do. I'm meeting Lord Copper at lunch today at Margot's. I'll try and bring the subject up.'

2

When Lady Metroland said half past one she meant ten minutes to two. It was precisely at this time, simultaneously with her hostess, that Mrs Stitch arrived (having been obliged by press of traffic to leave her little car in a garage half-way to Bethnal Green, and return to Curzon Street by means of the Underground railway). Lord Copper, however, who normally lunched at one, was waiting with some impatience. Various men and women who appeared to know one another intimately and did not know Lord Copper, had been admitted from time to time and had disregarded him. His subordinates at the Megalopolitan Newspaper Corporation would have been at difficulties to recognize the uneasy figure which stood up each time the door was opened and sat down again unnoticed. He was a stranger in these parts; it was a thoughtless benefaction to one of Lady Metroland's charities that had exposed him, in the middle of a busy day, to this harrowing experience; he would readily, now, have doubled the sum to purchase his release. Thus when Mrs Stitch directed upon him some of her piercing shafts of charm she found him first numb, then dazzled, then extravagantly receptive.

From the moment of her entrance the luncheon party

was transformed for Lord Copper; he had gotten a new angle on it. He knew of Mrs Stitch; from time to time he had seen her in the distance; now for the first time he found himself riddled through and through, mesmerized, inebriated. Those at the table, witnessing the familiar process, began to conjecture in tones which Lord Copper was too much entranced to overhear, what Julia could possibly want of him. 'It's her model madhouse,' said some; 'She wants the caricaturists to lay off Algy,' said others; 'Been losing money,' thought the second footman (at Lady Metroland's orders he was on diet and lunchtime always found him in a cynical mood); 'a job for someone or other,' came nearest the truth, but no one thought of John Courteney Boot until Mrs Stitch brought him into the conversation. Then they all played up loyally.

'You know,' she said, after coaxing Lord Copper into an uncompromising denunciation of the Prime Minister's public and private honesty, 'I expect he's all you say, but he's a man of far more taste than you'd suppose. He always sleeps with a Boot by his bed.'

'A boot?'' asked Lord Copper, trustful but a little bewildered.

'One of John Boot's books.'

The luncheon party had got their cue.

'Dear John Boot,' said Lady Metroland, '*so* clever and amusing. I wish I could get him to come and see me more often.'

'Such a divine style,' said Lady Cockpurse.

The table buzzed with praise of John Boot. It was a new name to Lord Copper. He resolved to question his literary secretary on the subject. He had become Boot-conscious.

Mrs Stitch changed her ground and began to ask him in the most flattering way about the chances of peace in Ishmaelia. Lord Copper gave it as his opinion that civil war was inevitable. Mrs Stitch remarked how few of the famous war correspondents still survived.

'Isn't there one called Sir Something Hitchcock?' asked Lady Cockpurse. (This was a false step since the knight in question had lately left Lord Copper's service, after an acrimonious dispute about the date of the Battle of Hastings, and had transferred to the *Daily Brute* camp.)

'Who will you be sending to Ishmaelia?' asked Mrs Stitch.

'I am in consultation with my editors on the subject. We think it a very promising little war. A microcosm, as you might say, of world drama. We propose to give it fullest publicity. The workings of a great newspaper,' said Lord Copper, feeling at last thoroughly Rotarian, 'are of a complexity which the public seldom appreciates. The citizen little realizes the vast machinery put into motion for him in exchange for his morning penny.' ('O God,' said Lady Metroland, faintly but audibly.) 'We shall have our naval, military, and air experts, our squad of photographers, our colour reporters, covering the war from every angle and on every front.'

'Yes,' said Mrs Stitch. 'Yes, yes. I suppose you will ... If I were you I should send someone like Boot. I don't suppose you could persuade *him* to go, but someone like him.'

'It has been my experience, dear Mrs Stitch, that the *Daily Beast* can command the talent of the world. Only last week the Poet Laureate wrote us an ode to the seasonal fluctuation of our net sales. We splashed it on the middle page. He admitted it was the most poetic and highly-paid work he had ever done.'

'Well, of course, if you *could* get him, Boot is your man. He's a brilliant writer, he's travelled everywhere and knows the whole Ishmaelite situation inside out.'

'Boot would be divine,' said Lady Cockpurse loyally.

*

Half an hour later Mrs Stitch rang up to say 'O.K., John. I think it's fixed. Don't take a penny less than fifty pounds a week.'

'God bless you, Julia. You've saved my life.'
'It's just the Stitch Service,' said Mrs Stitch cheerfully.

3

That evening, Mr Salter, foreign editor of *The Beast*, was summoned to dinner at his chief's country seat at East Finchley. It was a highly unwelcome invitation; Mr Salter normally worked at the office until nine o'clock. That evening he had planned a holiday at the opera; he and his wife had been looking forward to it with keen enjoyment for some weeks. As he drove out to Lord Copper's frightful mansion he thought sadly of those care-free days when he had edited the Woman's Page, or, better still, when he had chosen the jokes for one of Lord Copper's comic weeklies. It was the policy of the Megalopolitan to keep the staff alert by constant changes of occupation. Mr Salter's ultimate ambition was to take charge of the Competitions. Meanwhile he was Foreign Editor and found it a dog's life.

The two men dined alone. They ate parsley soup, whiting, roast veal, cabinet pudding; they drank whisky and soda. Lord Copper explained Nazism, Fascism, and Communism; later, in his ghastly library, he outlined the situation in the Far East. '*The Beast* stands for strong mutually antagonistic governments everywhere,' he said. 'Self-sufficiency at home, self-assertion abroad.'

Mr Salter's side of the conversation was limited to expressions of assent. When Lord Copper was right he said, 'Definitely, Lord Copper'; when he was wrong, 'Up to a point.'

'Let me see, what's the name of the place I mean? Capital of Japan? Yokohama, isn't it?'

'Up to a point, Lord Copper.'

'And Hong Kong belongs to us, doesn't it?'

'Definitely, Lord Copper.'

After a time: 'Then there's this civil war in Ishmaelia.

I propose to feature it. Who did you think of sending?'

'Well, Lord Copper, the choice seems between sending a staff reporter who will get the news but whose name the public doesn't know, or to get someone from outside with a name as a military expert. You see, since we lost Hitchcock. . . .'

'Yes, yes. He was our only man with a European reputation. *I know*. Zinc will be sending him. *I know*. But he was wrong about the Battle of Hastings. It *was* 1066. I looked it up. I won't employ a man who isn't big enough to admit when he's wrong.'

'We might share one of the Americans?'

'No, I tell you who I want; Boot.'

'Boot?'

'Yes, Boot. He's a young man whose work I'm very much interested in. He has the most remarkable style and he's been in Patagonia and the Prime Minister keeps his books by his bed. Do *you* read him?'

'Up to a point, Lord Copper.'

'Well, get on to him tomorrow. Have him up to see you. Be cordial. Take him out to dinner. Get him at any price. Well, at any reasonable price,' he added, for there had lately been a painful occurrence when instructions of this kind, given in an expansive mood, had been too literally observed and a trick cyclist who had momentarily attracted Lord Copper's attention had been engaged to edit the Sports Page on a five years' contract at five thousand a year.

4

Mr Salter went to work at midday. He found the Managing Editor cast in gloom.

'It's a terrible paper this morning,' he said. 'We paid Professor Jellaby thirty guineas for the feature article and there's not a word in it one can understand. Beaten by *The Brute* in every edition on the Zoo Mercy Slaying story. And *look at the Sports Page*.'

Together, in shame, the two men read the trick cyclist's Sports Page.

'Who's Boot?' asked Mr Salter at last.

'I know the name,' said the Managing Editor.

'The chief wants to send him to Ishmaelia. He's the Prime Minister's favourite writer.'

'Not the chap I was thinking of,' said the Managing Editor.

'Well, I've got to find him.' He listlessly turned the pages of the morning paper. 'Boot,' he said. 'Boot. Boot. Boot. Why! *Boot* – here he is. Why didn't the chief say he was a staff man?'

At the back of the paper, ignominiously sandwiched between Pip and Pop, the Bedtime Pets, and the recipe for a dish called 'Waffle Scramble,' lay the bi-weekly half-column devoted to Nature:

LUSH PLACES, edited by William Boot, Countryman.

'Do you suppose that's the right one?'

'Sure of it. The Prime Minister is nuts on rural England.'

'He's supposed to have a particularly high-class style: *"Feather-footed through the plashy fen passes the questing vole"* . . . would that be it?'

'Yes,' said the Managing Editor. 'That must be good style. At least it doesn't sound like anything else to me. I know the name well now you mention it. Never seen the chap. I don't think he's ever been to London. Sends his stuff in by post. All written out in pen and ink.'

'I've got to ask him to dinner.'

'Give him cider.'

'Is that what countrymen like?'

'Yes, cider and tinned salmon are the staple diet of the agricultural classes.'

'I'll send him a telegram. Funny the chief wanting to send him to Ishmaelia.'

TWO

I

'CHANGE and decay in all around I see,' sang Uncle Theodore, gazing out of the morning-room window.

Thus, with startling loudness, he was accustomed to relieve his infrequent fits of depression; but decay, rather than change, was characteristic of the immediate prospect.

The immense trees which encircled Boot Magna Hall, shaded its drives and rides, and stood (tastefully disposed at the whim of some forgotten, provincial predecessor of Repton), singly and in groups about the park, had suffered, some from ivy, some from lightning, some from the various malignant disorders that vegetation is heir to, but all principally from old age. Some were supported with trusses and crutches of iron, some were filled with cement; some, even now, in June, could show only a handful of green leaves at their extremities. Sap ran thin and slow; a gusty night always brought down a litter of dead timber.

The lake was moved by strange tides. Sometimes, as at the present moment, it sank to a single, opaque pool in a wilderness of mud and rushes; sometimes it rose and inundated five acres of pasture. There had once been an old man in one of the lodges who understood the workings of the water system; there were sluice gates hidden among the reeds, and manholes, dotted about in places known only to him, furnished with taps and cocks; that man had been able to control an ornamental cascade and draw a lofty jet of water from the mouth of the dolphin on the South terrace. But he had been in his grave fifteen years and the secret had died with him.

The house was large but by no means too large for the Boot family, which at this time numbered eight. There were in the direct line: William who owned the house and estate, William's sister Priscilla who claimed to own the horses, William's widowed mother who owned the contents of the house and exercised ill-defined rights over the flower garden, and William's widowed grandmother who was said to own 'the money'. No one knew how much she possessed; she had been bedridden as long as William's memory went back. It was from her that such large cheques issued as were from time to time necessary for balancing the estate accounts and paying for Uncle Theodore's occasional, disastrous visits to London. Uncle Theodore, the oldest of the male collaterals, was by far the gayest. Uncle Roderick was in many ways the least eccentric. He had managed the estates and household throughout William's minority and continued to do so with a small but regular deficit which was made up annually by one of grandmamma's cheques. The widowed Lady Trilby was William's Great-Aunt Anne, his father's elder sister; she owned the motor-car, a vehicle adapted to her own requirements; it had a horn which could be worked from the back seat; her weekly journey to church resounded through the village like the Coming of the Lord. Uncle Bernard devoted himself to a life of scholarship but had received little general recognition, for his researches, though profound, were narrow, being connected solely with his own pedigree. He had traced William's descent through three different lines from Ethelred the Unready and only lack of funds fortunately prevented him from prosecuting a claim to the abeyant barony of de Butte.

All the Boots, in one way or another, had about a hundred a year each as pocket money. It was therefore convenient for them to live together at Boot Magna where wages and household expenses were counted in with Uncle Roderick's annual deficit. The richest member of the household, in ready cash, was Nannie Bloggs, who had been bedridden for the last thirty years; she kept her savings in a red flannel bag under the bolster. Uncle Theodore made attempts on them from time to time, but she was a sharp old girl and, since she combined a long-standing aversion to Uncle Theodore with a preternatural aptitude for bringing off showy doubles during the flat racing season, her hoard continued to grow. The Bible and the Turf Guide were her only reading. She got great delight from telling each member of the family, severally and secretly, that he or she was her heir.

In other rooms about the house reposed: Nannie Price, ten years the junior of Nannie Bloggs, and bedridden from about the same age. She gave her wages to Chinese Missions and had little influence in the house; Sister Watts, old Mrs Boot's first nurse, and Sister Sampson, her second; Miss Scope, Aunt Anne's governess, veteran invalid, of some years seniority in bed to old Mrs Boot herself: and Bentinck the butler: James, the first footman, had been confined to his room for some time, but he was able on warm days to sit in an arm-chair at the window. Nurse Granger was still on her feet, but as her duties included the charge of all eight sick-rooms, it was thought she would not long survive. Ten servants waited upon the household and upon one another, but in a desultory fashion, for they could spare very little time from the five meat meals which tradition daily allowed them. In the circumstances the Boots did not entertain and were indulgently spoken of in the district as being 'poor as church mice'.

The fashionable John Courteney Boot was a remote cousin, or, as Uncle Bernard preferred, the member of a cadet branch. William had never met him; he had met very few people indeed. It was not true to say, as the Managing Editor of *The Beast* had said, that he had never been to London, but his visits had been infrequent enough for each to be distinct and perennially horrifying in his memory.

'Change and decay in all around I see,' sang Uncle Theodore. It was his habit to sing the same line over and over again. He was waiting for the morning papers. So

were William and Uncle Roderick. They were brought
by the butcher, often blotched with red, any time between eleven and midday, and then, if not intercepted,
disappeared among the sick-rooms to return at tea-time
hopelessly mutilated, for both Bentinck and old Mrs Boot
kept scrap-books, and Sister Sampson had the habit of
cutting out coupons and losing them in the bedclothes.
This morning they were late. It was a matter of great
anxiety to William.

He had never been to the Megalopolitan offices or met
anyone connected with *The Beast*. His job as author of
Lush Places had been passed on to him by the widow on
the death of its previous holder, the Rector of Boot
Magna. He had carefully modelled his style on the late
Rector's, at first painfully, now almost without effort.
The work was of the utmost importance to him: he was
paid a guinea a time and it gave him the best possible
excuse for remaining uninterruptedly in the country.

And now it was in danger. On the previous Thursday
a very dreadful thing had happened. Drawing on the
observations of a lifetime and after due cross-examination
of the head keeper and half an hour with the encyclo-
pedia, William had composed a lyrical but wholly
accurate account of the habits of the badger; one of his
more finished essays. Priscilla in a playful mood had
found the manuscript and altered it, substituting for
'badger' throughout 'the crested grebe'. It was not until
Saturday morning when, in this form, it appeared in *The
Beast*, that William was aware of the outrage.

His mail had been prodigious; some correspondents
were sceptical, others derisive; one lady wrote to ask
whether she read him aright in thinking he condoned the
practice of baiting these rare and beautiful birds with
terriers and deliberately destroying their earthy homes;
how could this be tolerated in the so-called twentieth
century? A major in Wales challenged him categorically
to produce a single authenticated case of a great crested
grebe attacking young rabbits. It had been exceedingly

painful. All through the week-end William had awaited his dismissal, but Monday and Tuesday passed without a word from *The Beast*. He composed and despatched a light dissertation on water voles and expected the worst. Perhaps the powers at *The Beast* were too much enraged even to send back his manuscript; when Wednesday's paper came he would find another tenant of *Lush Places*. It came. He hunted frantically for his half-column. It was there, a green oasis between Waffle Scramble and the Bed-time Pets. '*Feather-footed through the plashy fens passes the questing vole. . . .*' It was all right. By some miracle Saturday's shame had been covered.

His uncles peevishly claimed the paper; he surrendered it readily. He stood at the french window blinking at the summer landscape; the horses at grass beyond the ha-ha skipped and frolicked.

'Confound the thing,' said Uncle Roderick behind him. 'Can't find the cricket anywhere. Whole page seems to be given up to some damn-fool cycling championship at Cricklewood Stadium.'

William did not care. In the fullness of his gratitude he resolved to give rodents a miss that Saturday (though he was particularly attached to them) and write instead of wild flowers and birdsong. He might even risk something out of the poets.

> '*Nay not so much as out of bed?*
> *When all the birds have Matins said,*'

he sang, in his heart, to the recumbent figures above him. And then, wheezing heavily, with crumbs on his mouth, ponderously straddling across the morning-room, came Troutbeck, the aged boy, bearing a telegram. Curiosity and resentment contended for mastery in Troutbeck's demeanour; curiosity because telegrams were of rare occurrence at Boot Magna; resentment at the interruption of his 'elevenses' – a lavish and ruminative feast which occupied the servants' hall from ten-thirty until noon. William's face quickly reassured him that he had not been called from the table on any frivolous pretext. 'Bad news,' he was able to report. 'Shocking bad news for Master William.'

'It couldn't hardly be a death,' said the third house-maid. 'All the family's here.'

'Whatever it was we shall soon know,' said Troutbeck. 'It struck Master William all of a heap. Might I thank you to pass the chutney.'

Bad news indeed! Oblivious to the sunshine and the grazing horses and the stertorous breathing of his Uncle Theodore, William re-read the frightful doom that had fallen on him.

REQUEST YOUR IMMEDIATE PRESENCE HERE URGENT LORD COPPERS PERSONAL DESIRE SALTER BEAST.

'Nothing serious, I hope!' said Uncle Theodore, to whom telegrams, in the past, had from time to time brought news as disquieting as to any man living.

'Yes,' said William, 'I have been called to London.'

'Have you, my boy? That's interesting. I was thinking of running up for a night myself...'

But Uncle Theodore was speaking to the air. William was already at work, setting into motion the elaborate household machinery which would, too soon, effect his departure.

2

After an early luncheon, William went to say good-bye to his grandmother. She looked at him with doleful, mad eyes. 'Going to London, eh? Well, I hardly suppose I shall be alive when you return. Wrap up warm, dear.' It was eternal winter in Mrs Boot's sunny bedroom.

All the family who had the use of their legs attended on the steps to see William off; Priscilla bathed in tears of penitence. Nannie Bloggs sent him down three golden sovereigns. Aunt Anne's motor-car was there to take him away. At the last moment Uncle Theodore attempted to get in at the offside, but was detected and deterred. 'Just wanted to see a chap in Jermyn Street about some business,' he said wistfully.

It was always a solemn thing for a Boot to go to London; solemn as a funeral for William on this afternoon. Once or twice on the way to the station, once or twice as the train stopped on the route to Paddington, William was tempted to give up the expedition in despair. Why should he commit himself to this abominable city merely to be railed at and, for all he knew of Lord Copper's temperament, physically assaulted? But sterner counsels prevailed. He might bluff it out. Lord Copper was a townsman, a provincial townsman at that, and certainly did not know the difference between a badger and a great crested grebe. It was William's word against a few cantankerous correspondents, and people who wrote to the newspapers were proverbially unbalanced. By the time he reached Westbury he had sketched out a little scene for himself, in which he stood resolutely in the board-room defying the doctrinaire zoology of Fleet Street; every inch a Boot, thrice descended from Ethelred the Unready, rightful 15th Baron de Butte, haughty as a chieftain, honest as a peasant. 'Lord Copper,' he was saying, 'no man shall call me a liar unchastised. The great crested grebe *does* hibernate.'

He went to the dining-car and ordered some whisky. The steward said, 'We're serving teas. Whisky after Reading.' After Reading he tried again. 'We're serving dinners. I'll bring you one to your carriage.' When it came, William spilled it down his tie. He gave the steward one of Nannie Bloggs' sovereigns in mistake for a shilling. It was contemptuously refused and everyone in the carriage stared at him. A man in a bowler hat said, 'May I look? Don't often see one of them nowadays. Tell you what I'll do, I'll toss you for it. Call.'

William said, 'Heads.'

'Tails it is,' said the man in the bowler hat, putting it

in his waistcoat pocket. He then went on reading his paper and everyone stared harder at William. His spirits began to sink; the mood of defiance passed. It was always the way; the moment he left the confines of Boot Magna he found himself in a foreign and hostile world. There was a train back at ten o'clock that night. Wild horses would not keep him from it. He would see Lord Copper, explain the situation fully and frankly, throw himself upon his mercy and, successful or defeated, catch the train at ten. By Reading he had worked out this new and humble policy. He would tell Lord Copper about Priscilla's tears; great men were proverbially vulnerable to appeals of that kind. The man opposite him looked over the top of his paper. 'Got any more quids?'

'No,' said William.

'Pity.'

At seven he reached Paddington and the atrocious city was all around him.

3

The Megalopolitan building, numbers 700–853 Fleet Street, was disconcerting. At first William thought that the taxi-driver, spotting a bumpkin, had driven him to the wrong address.

His acquaintance with offices was very small. At the time of his coming of age he had spent several mornings with the family solicitor in King's Bench Walk. At home he knew the local Estate Agents and Auctioneers, the Bank and the Town Hall. He had once seen in Taunton a barely intelligible film about newspaper life in New York where neurotic men in shirt sleeves and eye-shades had rushed from telephone to tape machines, insulting and betraying one another in surroundings of unredeemed squalor. From these memories he had a confused expectation that was rudely shocked by the Byzantine vestibule and Sassanian lounge of Copper House. He thought at first that he must have arrived at some new and less exclusive rival of the R.A.C. Six lifts seemed to be in perpetual motion; with dazzling frequency their doors flew open to reveal now left, now right, now two or three at a time, like driven game, a series of girls in Caucasian uniform. 'Going up,' they cried in Punch-and-Judy accents and, before anyone could enter, snapped their doors and disappeared from view. A hundred or so men and women of all ranks and ages passed before William's eyes. The sole stationary objects were a chryselephantine effigy of Lord Copper in coronation robes, rising above the throng, on a polygonal malachite pedestal, and a concierge, also more than life size, who sat in a plate-glass enclosure, like a fish in an aquarium, and gazed at the agitated multitude with fishy, supercilious eyes. Under his immediate care were a dozen page boys in sky-blue uniforms, who between errands pinched one another furtively on a long bench. Medals of more battles than were ever fought by human arms or on earthly fields glittered on the porter's chest. William discovered a small vent in his tank and addressed him diffidently. 'Is his Lordship at home?'

'We have sixteen peers on the staff. Which was you referring to?'

'I wish to see Lord Copper.'

'Oh! Cyril, show this gentleman to a chair and give him a form.'

A minute blue figure led William to a desk and gave him a piece of paper. William filled it in. '*Mr Boot wishes to see Lord Copper. Subject: great crested grebes.*'

Cyril took the paper to the concierge, who read it, looked searchingly at William and mouthed, 'Fetch the gentleman.'

William was led forward.

'You wish to see Lord Copper?'

'Yes, please.'

'Oh! no you don't. Not about great crested grebes.'

'And badgers too,' said William. 'It is rather a long story.'

'I'll be bound it is. Tell you what, you go across the street and tell it to Lord Zinc at *The Daily Brute* office. That'll do just as well, now won't it?'

'I've got an appointment,' said William, and produced his telegram.

The concierge read it thoughtfully, held it up to the light, and said 'Ah!'; read it again and said: 'What you want to see is Mr Salter. Cyril, give the gentleman another form.'

Five minutes later William found himself in the office of the foreign editor.

It was an encounter of great embarrassment for both of them. For William it was the hour of retribution; he advanced, heavy with guilt, to meet whatever doom had been decreed for him. Mr Salter had the more active part. He was under orders to be cordial and spring Lord Copper's proposal on the poor hick when he had won his confidence by light conversation and heavy hospitality.

His knowledge of rural life was meagre. He had been born in West Kensington and educated at a large London day-school. When not engaged in one or other capacity in the vast Megalopolitan organization he led a life of blameless domesticity in Welwyn Garden City. His annual holiday was, more often than not, spent at home; once or twice when Mrs Salter complained of being run down, they had visited prosperous resorts on the East Coast. 'The country,' for him, meant what you saw in the train between Liverpool Street and Frinton. If a psychoanalyst, testing his associations, had suddenly said to Mr Salter the word 'farm,' the surprising response would have been 'Bang,' for he had once been blown up and buried while sheltering in a farm in Flanders. It was his single intimate association with the soil. It had left him with the obstinate though admittedly irrational belief that agriculture was something alien and highly dangerous. Normal life, as he saw it, consisted in regular journeys by electric train, monthly cheques, communal amusements and a cosy horizon of slates and chimneys; there was something unEnglish and not quite right about 'the country', with its solitude and self-sufficiency, its bloody recreations, its darkness and silence and sudden, inexplicable noises; the kind of place where you never knew from one minute to the next that you might not be tossed by a bull or pitch-forked by a yokel or rolled over and broken up by a pack of hounds.

He had been round the office canvassing opinions about the subjects of conversation proper to countrymen. 'Mangel-wurzels are a safe topic,' he had been told, 'only you mustn't call them that. It's a subject on which farmers are very touchy. Call them roots...'

He greeted William with cordiality. 'Ah, Boot, how are you? Don't think I've had the pleasure before. Know your work well of course. Sit down. Have a cigarette or' – had he made a floater? – 'or do you prefer your church-warden?'

William took a cigarette. He and Mr Salter sat opposite one another. Between them, on the desk, lay an open atlas in which Mr Salter had been vainly trying to find Reykjavik.

There was a pause, during which Mr Salter planned a frank and disarming opening. 'How are your roots, Boot?' It came out wrong.

'How are your boots, root?' he asked.

William, glumly awaiting some fulminating rebuke, started and said, 'I beg your pardon?'

'I mean brute,' said Mr Salter.

William gave it up. Mr Salter gave it up. They sat staring at one another, fascinated, hopeless. Then:

'How's hunting?' asked Mr Salter, trying a new line. 'Foxes pretty plentiful?'

'Well, we stop in the summer, you know.'

'Do you? Everyone away, I suppose?'

Another pause: 'Lot of foot and mouth, I expect,' said Mr Salter hopefully.

'None, I'm thankful to say.'

'Oh!'

Their eyes fell. They both looked at the atlas before them.

'You don't happen to know where Reykjavik is?'

'No.'

'Pity. I hoped you might. No one in the office does.'

'Was that what you wanted to see me about?'

'Oh, no, not at all! Quite the contrary.'

Another pause.

William saw what was up. This decent little man had been deputed to sack him and could not get it out. He came to the rescue. 'I expect you want to talk about the great crested grebe.'

'Good God, no,' said Mr Salter, with instinctive horror, adding politely, 'At least not unless *you* do.'

'No, not at all,' said William, 'I thought *you* might want to.'

'Not at all,' said Mr Salter.

'That's all right, then.'

'Yes, that all right . . .' Desperately: 'I say, how about some zider?'

'Zider?'

'Yes. I expect you feel like a drop of zider about this time, don't you? We'll go out and have some.'

The journalists in the film had been addicted to straight rye. Silent but wondering, William followed the foreign editor. They shared the lift with a very extraordinary man, bald, young, fleshless as a mummy, dressed in brown and white checks, smoking a cheroot. 'He does the Sports Page now,' said Mr Salter apologetically, when he was out of hearing.

In the public house at the corner, where *The Beast* reporters congregated, the barmaid took their order with surprise. 'Cider? I'll see.' Then she produced two bottles of sweet and fizzy liquid. William and Mr Salter sipped suspiciously.

'Not quite what you're used to down on the farm, I'm afraid.'

'Well, to tell you the truth, I don't often drink it. We give it to the haymakers, of course, and I sometimes have some of theirs.' Then, fearing that this might sound snobbish, he added, 'My Uncle Bernard drinks it for his rheumatism.'

'You're sure you wouldn't sooner have something else?'

'No.'

'You mean you wouldn't?'

'I mean I would.'

'Really?'

'Really; much sooner.'

'Good for you, Garge,' said Mr Salter, and from that moment a new, more human note was apparent in their relationship; conversation was still far from easy, but they had this bond in common, that neither of them liked cider.

Mr Salter clung to it strenuously. 'Interesting you don't like cider,' he said. 'Neither do I.'

'No,' said William. 'I never have since I was sick as a small boy, in the hay field.'

'It upsets me inside.'

'Exactly.'

'Now whisky never did anyone any harm.'

'No.'

Interest seemed to flag. Mr Salter tried once more. 'Make much parsnip wine down your way?'

'Not much . . .' It was clearly his turn now. He sipped and thought and finally said: 'Pretty busy at the office, I expect?'

'Yes, very.'

'Tell me – I've often wondered – do you keep a machine of your own or send out to the printers?'

'We have machines of our own.'

'Do you? They must work jolly fast.'

'Yes.'

'I mean, you have to get it written and printed and corrected and everything all on the same day, otherwise the news would become stale. People would have heard it on the wireless, I mean.'

'Yes.'

'D'you do much of the printing yourself?'

'No. You see, I'm the foreign editor.'

'I suppose that's why you wanted to find Reykjavik?'

'Yes.'

'Jolly difficult knowing where all these places are.'

'Yes.'

'So many of them I mean.'

'Yes.'

'Never been abroad myself.'

This seemed too good an opening to be missed. 'Would you like to go to Ishmaelia?'

'No.'

'Not at all?'

'Not at all. For one thing I couldn't afford the fare.'

'Oh, we would pay the fare,' said Mr Salter, laughing indulgently.

So that was it. Transportation. The sense of persecution which had haunted William for the last three hours took palpable and grotesque shape before him. It was too much. Conscious of a just cause and a free soul he rose and defied the nightmare. 'Really,' he said, in ringing tones, 'I call that a bit thick. I admit I slipped up on the great crested grebe, slipped up badly. As it happened, it was not my fault. I came here prepared to explain, apologize and, if need be, make reparation. You refused to listen to me. "Good God, no", you said, when I offered to explain. And now you calmly propose to ship me out of the country because of a trifling and, in my opinion, justifiable error. Who does Lord Copper think he is? The mind boggles at the vanity of the man. If he chooses to forget my eighteen months' devoted and unremitting labour in his service, he is, I admit, entitled to dismiss me . . .'

'Boot, Boot, old man,' cried Mr Salter, 'you've got this all wrong. With the possible exception of the Prime Minister, you have no more ardent admirer than Lord Copper. He wants you to *work* for him in Ishmaelia.'

'Would he pay my fare back?'

'Yes, of course.'

'Oh, that's rather different . . . Even so it seems a silly sort of scheme. I mean, how will it look in *Lush Places* when I start writing about sandstorms and lions and whatever they have in Ishmaelia? Not *lush*, I mean.'

'Let me tell you about it at dinner.'

They took a taxicab down Fleet Street and the Strand to the grill room where *The Beast* staff always entertained when they were doing so at the paper's expense.

'Do you *really* want tinned salmon?'

'No.'

'Sure?'

'Quite sure.'

Mr Salter regarded his guest with renewed approval and handed him the menu.

The esteem William had won by his distaste for cider and tinned salmon survived the ordering of dinner. William did not, as had seemed only too likely, demand pickled walnuts and Cornish pasties; nor did he, like the Budapest correspondent whom Mr Salter had last entertained in his room, draw attention to himself by calling for exotic Magyar dishes, and, on finding no one qualified to make them, insist on preparing for himself, with chafing dish and spirit lamp, before a congregation of puzzled waiters, a nauseous sauce of sweet peppers, honey, and almonds. He ordered a mixed grill, and, while he was eating, Mr Salter attempted, artfully, to kindle his enthusiasm for the new project.

'See that man there, that's Pappenhacker.'

William looked, and saw.

'Yes?'

'The cleverest man in Fleet Street.'

William looked again. Pappenhacker was young and swarthy, with great horn goggles and a receding stubbly chin. He was having an altercation with some waiters.

'Yes?'

'He's going to Ishmaelia for the *Daily Twopence*.'

'He seems to be in a very bad temper.'

'Not really. He's always like that to waiters. You see, he's a communist. Most of the staff of the *Twopence* are – they're University men, you see. Pappenhacker says that every time you are polite to a proletarian you are helping bolster up the capitalist system. He's very clever, of course, but he gets rather unpopular.'

'He looks as if he were going to hit them.'

'Yes, he does sometimes. Quite a lot of restaurants won't have him in. You see, you'll meet a lot of interesting people when you go to Ishmaelia.'

'Mightn't it be rather dangerous?'

Mr Salter smiled; to him, it was as though an Arctic explorer had expressed a fear that the weather might turn cold. 'Nothing to what you are used to in the country,' he said. 'You'll be surprised to find how far the war correspondents keep from the fighting. Why Hitchcock reported the whole Abyssinia campaign from Asmara and gave us some of the most colourful, eye-witness stuff we ever printed. In any case your life will be insured by the paper for five thousand pounds. No, no, Boot, I don't think you need worry about risk.'

'And you'd go on paying me my wages?'

'Certainly.'

'*And* my fare there *and* back, *and* my expenses?'

'Yes.'

William thought the matter over carefully. At length he said: 'No.'

'No?'

'No. It's very kind of you, but I think I would sooner not go. I don't like the idea at all.' He looked at his watch. 'I must be going to Paddington soon to catch my train.'

'Listen,' said Mr Salter. 'I don't think you have fully understood the situation. Lord Copper is particularly interested in your work and, to be frank, he insists on your going. We are willing to pay a very fair salary. Fifty pounds a month was the sum suggested.'

'*Fifty pounds a month!*' said William, goggling.

'A week,' said Mr Salter hastily.

'Gosh,' said William.

'And think what you can make on your expenses,' urged Mr Salter. 'At least another twenty. I happened to see Hitchcock's expense sheet when he was working for us in Shanghai. He charged three hundred pounds for camels alone.'

'But I don't think I shall know what to do with a camel.'

Mr Salter saw he was not making his point clear. 'Take a single example,' he said. 'Supposing you want to have dinner. Well, you go to a restaurant and do yourself proud, best of everything. Bill perhaps may be two pounds. Well, you put down five pounds for entertainment on your expenses. You've had a slap-up dinner, you're three pounds to the good, and everyone is satisfied.'

'But you see I don't like restaurants and no one pays for dinner at home, anyway. The servants just bring it in.'

'Or supposing you want to send flowers to your girl. You just go to a shop, send a great spray of orchids and put them down as ''Information''.'

'But I haven't got a girl and there are heaps of flowers at home.' He looked at his watch again. 'Well, I'm afraid I must be going. You see, I have a day-return ticket. I tell you what I'll do. I'll consult my family and let you know in a week or two.'

'Lord Copper wants you to leave tomorrow.'

'Oh, I couldn't do that, anyway, you know. I haven't packed or anything. And I daresay I should need some new clothes. Oh, no, that's out of the question.'

'We might offer a larger salary.'

'Oh, no, thank you. It isn't that. It's just that I don't want to go.'

'Is there *nothing* you want?'

'D'you know, I don't believe there is. Except to keep my job in *Lush Places* and go on living at home.'

It was a familiar cry: during his fifteen years of service with the Megalopolitan Company Mr Salter had heard it upon the lips of countless distressed colleagues; upon his own. In a moment of compassion he remembered the morning when he had been called from his desk in *Clean Fun*, never to return to it. The post had been his delight and pride; one for which he believed he had a particular aptitude . . . First he would open the morning mail and sort the jokes sent him by the private contributors (one man sent him thirty or forty a week) into those that were familiar, those that were indecent, and those that deserved the half-crown postal order payable upon publication. Then he would spend an hour or two with the bound *Punches* noting whatever seemed topical. Then the ingenious game began of fitting these legends to the funny illustrations previously chosen for him by the Art Editor. Serene and delicate sunrise on a day of tempest! From this task of ordered discrimination he had been thrown into the ruthless, cut-throat, rough-and-tumble of *The Beast* Woman's Page. From there, crushed and bedraggled, he had been tossed into the editorial chair of the Imperial and Foreign News . . . His heart bled for William, but he was true to the austere traditions of his service. He made the reply that had silenced so many resentful novices in the past.

'Oh, but Lord Copper expects his staff to work wherever the best interests of the paper call them. I don't think he would employ anyone of whose loyalty he was doubtful, *in any capacity*.'

'You mean if I don't go to Ishmaelia I get the sack?'

'Yes,' said Mr Salter. 'In so many words that is exactly what I – what Lord Copper means . . . Won't you have a glass of port before we return to the office?'

THREE

I

AN oddly-placed, square window rising shoulder high from the low wainscot, fringed outside with ivy, brushed by the boughs of a giant monkey-puzzle; a stretch of faded wallpaper on which hung a water-colour of the village churchyard painted in her more active days by Miss Scope, a small shelf of ill-assorted books and a stuffed ferret, whose death from rat-poisoning had overshadowed the whole of one Easter holiday from his private school – these, according as he woke on his right or left side, greeted William daily at Boot Magna.

On the morning after his interview with Mr Salter, he opened his eyes, relieved from a night haunted by Lord Copper in a hundred frightful forms, to find himself in black darkness; his first thought was that there were still some hours to go before daylight; then, as he remembered the season of the year and the vast, semi-conscious periods through which he had passed, in the intervals of being pursued down badger runs in the showy plumage of the great crested grebe, he accepted the more harrowing alternative that he had been struck blind; then that he was mad, for a bell was ringing insistently a few inches, it seemed, from his ear. He sat up in bed and found that he was bare to the waist; totally bare, he learned by further researches. He stretched out his arm and found a telephone; as he lifted it, the ringing stopped; a voice said, 'Mr Salter on the line.' Then he remembered the awful occurrence of the previous evening.

'Good morning,' said Mr Salter. 'I thought I'd better get you early. I expect you've been up and about for hours, eh? Used to milking and cubbing and so on?'

'No,' said William.

'No? Well, I don't get to the office much before eleven or twelve. I wondered if everything was clear about your

journey or are there one or two little things you'd like to
go into first?'

'Yes.'

'Ah, I thought there might be. Well, come round to
the office as soon as you're ready.'

Groping, William found one of the dozen or so switches
which controlled the lighting of various parts of the bedroom. He found his watch and learned that it was ten
o'clock. He found a row of bell-pushes and rang for valet
and waiter.

The evening before he had been too much surfeited
with new impressions to pay particular attention to the
room to which eventually he had been led. It was two
o'clock when Mr Salter left him; they had returned to
the Megalopolitan office after dinner; William had been
led from room to room; he had been introduced to the
Managing Editor, the Assistant Managing Editor, the
Art Editor (who had provided the camera), the Accounts
Manager, the Foreign Contacts Adviser, and a multitude
of men and women with visible means of support but no
fixed occupation who had popped in from time to time on
the various officials with whom William was talking. He
had signed a contract, an application for Life Insurance,
receipts for a camera, typewriter, a portfolio full of
tickets, and a book of traveller's cheques to the value of
£1,000. He had reached the hotel in a daze; the manage-
ment had been told to expect him; they had led him to a
lift, then, aloft, along a white, unnaturally silent passage
and left him in his room with no desire except to sleep
and awake from his nightmare in the familiar, shabby
surroundings of Boot Magna.

The room was large and faultless. A psychologist, hired
from Cambridge, had planned the decorations – magenta
and gamboge; colours which – it had been demonstrated
by experiments on poultry and mice – conduce to a mood
of dignified gaiety. Every day carpet, curtains, and
upholstery were inspected for signs of disrepair. A gentle
whining note filled the apartment emanating from a

plant which was thought to 'condition' the atmosphere. William's crumpled clothes lay on the magenta carpet; his typewriter and camera had been hidden from him by the night porter. The dressing table was fitted with a 'daylight' lamp so that women, before retiring to sleep, could paint their faces in a manner that would be becoming at dawn; but it was bare of brushes.

Presently a valet entered, drew back four or five layers of curtain and revealed the window – a model of ingenuity, devised to keep out the noise of traffic and admit the therapeutic elements of common daylight. He picked up William's clothes, inclined gracefully towards the bed in a High Anglican compromise between nod and genuflexion and disappeared from the room, leaving it bereft of any link with William's previous existence. Presently a waiter came with a bill of fare and William ordered breakfast.

'And I want a toothbrush.'

The waiter communicated this need to the hall porter and presently a page with a face of ageless evil brought it on a tray. 'It was five shillings,' he said. 'And two bob for the cabfare.'

'That's too much.'

'Oh, come on,' said the knowing midget. 'It isn't you that pays.'

William indicated some loose change on the table. The boy took it all. 'You want some pyjamas too,' he said. 'Shall I get you some?'

'No.'

'Please yourself,' said this vile boy leaving the room.

William ate his breakfast and rang for the valet.

'I want my clothes, please.'

'Here are your shoes and cuff-links, sir. I have sent the shirt and underclothes to the laundry. The suit is being cleaned. Your tie is being ironed by one of the ironing maids.'

'But I never told you to do that.'

'You gave no instructions to the contrary, sir. We

naturally send *everything* away *always* unless we are speci-
fically asked not to . . . Would that be all, sir?'

'I want something to wear, now.'

'No doubt the hall porter will be able to arrange
something.'

Some time later the same abominable child brought
him a series of parcels.

'Reach-me-downs,' he said. 'Not what I'd care to wear
myself. But it's the best I could get. Twenty quid. Shall I
have it put down?'

'Yes.'

'Nice job journalism. May take to it myself one day.'

'I'm sure you'd be very good at it.'

'Yes, I think I should. I didn't get you a razor. The
barber is six floors down.'

2

The bells of St Bride's were striking twelve when
William reached Copper House. He found Mr Salter in
a state of agitation. 'Oh dear, oh dear, you're late, Boot,
and Lord Copper himself has asked for you twice. I must
go and see if he is still accessible.'

William was left standing in the passage. Metal doors
snapped in and out: 'Going up,' 'Going down,' cried the
Caucasian lift girls; on all sides his colleagues in the great
concern came and went, bustling past him – haggard
men who had been up all night, elegant young ladies
bearing trays of milk, oily figures in overalls bearing bits
of machinery. William stood in a daze, fingering the stiff
seams of his new suit. After a time he heard himself
addressed: 'Hi, you,' said a voice, 'wake up.'

'If only I could,' said William.

'Eh?'

'Nothing.'

The man speaking to him was exactly the type William
recognized as belonging to the film he had seen in

Taunton; a short, shock-headed fellow in shirt sleeves, dicky, and eyeshade, waistcoat pocket full of pencils, first finger pointing accusingly.

'You. You're the new man, aren't you?'

'Yes, I suppose I am.'

'Well, here's a chance for you.' He pushed a type-written slip into William's hand. 'Cut along there quick. Take a taxi. Don't bother about your hat. You're in a newspaper office now.'

William read the slip. '*Mrs Stitch. Gentlemen's Lavatory, Sloane Street.*'

'We've just had this phoned through from the police-man on duty. Find out what she is doing down there. Quick!'

A lift door flew open at their side. 'Going down,' cried a Caucasian.

'In there.'

The door snapped shut; the lift shot down; soon William was in a taxi making for Sloane Street.

There was a dense crowd round the public lavatory. William bobbed hopelessly on the fringe; he could see nothing above the heads except more heads, hats giving way to helmets at the hub. More spectators closed in behind him; suddenly he felt a shove more purposeful than the rest and a voice said, 'Way, please. Press. Make way for the Press.' A man with a camera was forging a way through. 'Press, please, Press. Make way for the Press.'

William joined in behind him and followed those narrow, irresistible shoulders on their progress towards the steps. At last they found themselves at the railings, among the policemen. The camera man nodded pleas-antly to them and proceeded underground. William followed.

'Hi,' said a sergeant, 'where are *you* going?'

'Press,' said William. 'I'm on *The Beast*.'

'So am I,' said the sergeant. 'Go to it. She's down there. Can't think how she did it, not without hurting herself.'

At the foot of the steps, making, for the photographer, a happy contrast to the white tiles about it, stood a little black motor-car. Inside, her hands patiently folded in her lap, sat the most beautiful woman William had ever seen. She was chatting in a composed and friendly manner to the circle of reporters and plain-clothes men.

'I can't think what you're all making such a fuss about,' she said. 'It's simply a case of mistaken identity. There's a man I've been wanting to speak to for weeks and I thought I saw him popping in here. So I drove down after him. Well, it was someone quite different, but he behaved beautifully about it, and now I can't get out; I've been here nearly half an hour and I've a *great* deal to do. I do think some of you might help, instead of standing there asking questions.'

Six of them seized the little car and lifted it, effortlessly, on their shoulders. A cheer rose from the multitude as the jet black rose above the spikes of the railings. William followed, his hand resting lightly on the running board. They set Mrs Stitch back on the road; the police began to clear a passage for her. 'A very nice little story,' said one of William's colleagues. 'Just get in nicely for the evening edition.'

The throng began to disperse; the policemen pocketed their tips; the camera men scampered for their dark rooms. 'Boot, Boot,' cried an eager, slightly peevish voice. 'So there you are. Come back at once.' It was Mr Salter. 'I came to fetch you for Lord Copper and they told me you had gone out. It was only by sheer luck that I found where you had gone. It's been a terrible mistake. Some-one will pay for this; I know they will. Oh dear, oh dear, get into the cab quickly.'

3

Twenty minutes later William and Mr Salter passed the first of the great doors which divided Lord Copper's personal quarters from the general office. The carpets were thicker here, the lights softer, the expressions of the inhabitants more careworn. The typewriters were of a special kind; their keys made no more sound than the drumming of a bishop's fingertips on an upholstered prie-dieu; the telephone buzzers were muffled and purred like warm cats. The personal private secretaries padded through the ante-chambers and led them nearer and nearer to the presence. At last they came to massive double doors, encased in New Zealand rose-wood which by their weight, polish, and depravity of design, proclaimed unmistakably, 'Nothing but Us stands between you and Lord Copper.' Mr Salter paused, and pressed a little bell of synthetic ivory. 'It lights a lamp on Lord Copper's own desk,' he said reverently. 'I expect we shall have a long time to wait.'

But almost immediately a green light overhead flashed their permission to enter.

Lord Copper was at his desk. He dismissed some satellites and rose as William came towards him.

'Come in, Mr Boot. This is a great pleasure. I have wanted to meet you for a long time. It is not often that the Prime Minister and I agree, but we see eye to eye about your style. A very nice little style indeed . . . You may sit down too, Salter. Is Mr Boot all set for his trip?'

'Up to a point, Lord Copper.'

'Excellent. There are two invaluable rules for a special correspondent – Travel Light and Be Prepared. Have nothing which in a case of emergency you cannot carry in your own hands. But remember that the unexpected always happens. Little things we take for granted at home like . . .' he looked about him, seeking a happy example; the room, though spacious, was almost devoid of furniture; his eye rested on a bust of Lady Copper; that would not do; then, resourcefully, he said '. . . like a coil of rope or a sheet of tin, may save your life in the wilds. I should take some cleft sticks with you. I remember Hitchcock – Sir Jocelyn Hitchcock, a man who used to work for me once; smart enough fellow in his way, but *limited*, very little historical backing – I remember him saying that in Africa he always sent his dispatches in a cleft stick. It struck me as a very useful tip. Take plenty.

'With regard to Policy, I expect you already have your own views. I never hamper my correspondents in any way. What the British public wants first, last, and all the time is News. Remember that the Patriots are in the right and are going to win. *The Beast* stands by them four-square. But they must win quickly. The British public has no interest in a war which drags on indecisively. A few sharp victories, some conspicuous acts of personal bravery on the Patriot side and a colourful entry into the capital. That is *The Beast* Policy for the war.

'Let me see. You will get there in about three weeks. I should spend a day or two looking around and getting the background. Then a good, full-length dispatch which we can feature with your name. That's everything, I think, Salter?'

'Definitely, Lord Copper.' He and William rose.

It was not to be expected that Lord Copper would leave his chair twice in the morning, but he leant across the desk and extended his hand. 'Good-bye, Mr Boot, and the best of luck. We shall expect the first victory about the middle of July.'

When they had passed the final ante-room and were once more in the humbler, frequented by-ways of the great building, Mr Salter uttered a little sigh. 'It's an odd thing,' he said, 'that the more I see of Lord Copper, the less I feel I really know him.'

The affability with which William had been treated was without precedent in Mr Salter's experience. Almost with diffidence he suggested, 'It's one o'clock; if you are going to catch the afternoon aeroplane, you ought to be getting your kit, don't you think?'

'Yes.'

'I don't suppose that after what Lord Copper has said there is anything more you want to know.'

'Well, there is one thing. You see, I don't read the

papers very much. Can you tell me who is fighting who in Ishmaelia?'

'I think it's the Patriots and the Traitors.'

'Yes, but which is which?'

'Oh, I don't know *that*. *That's* Policy, you see. It's nothing to do with me. You should have asked Lord Copper.'

'I gather it's between the Reds and the Blacks.'

'Yes, but it's not quite as easy as that. You see, they are all Negroes. And the Fascists won't be called black because of their racial pride, so they are called White after the White Russians. And the Bolshevists *want* to be called black because of *their* racial pride. So when you *say* black you mean red, and when you *mean* red you say white and when the party who call themselves blacks say traitors they mean what *we* call blacks, but what *we* mean when *we* say traitors I really couldn't tell you. But from your point of view it will be quite simple. Lord Copper only wants Patriot victories and both sides call themselves patriots, and of course both sides will claim all the victories. But, of course, it's really a war between Russia and Germany and Italy and Japan who are all against one another on the patriotic side. I hope I make myself plain?'

'Up to a point,' said William, falling easily into the habit.

4

The Foreign Contacts Adviser of *The Beast* telephoned the emporium where William was to get his kit and warned them of his arrival; accordingly it was General Cruttwell, F.R.G.S., himself who was waiting at the top of the lift shaft. An imposing man: Cruttwell Glacier in Spitsbergen, Cruttwell Falls in Venezuela, Mount Cruttwell in the Pamirs, Cruttwell's Leap in Cumberland marked his travels; Cruttwell's Folly, a waterless and

indefensible camp near Salonika, was notorious to all
who had served with him in the war. The shop paid him
six hundred a year and commission, out of which, by
contract, he had to find his annual subscription to the
R.G.S. and the electric treatment which maintained the
leathery tan of his complexion.

Before either had spoken, the General sized William
up; in any other department he would have been recognized as a sucker; here, amid the trappings of high
adventure, he was, more gallantly, a greenhorn.

'Your first visit to Ishmaelia, eh? Then perhaps I can
be of some help to you. As no doubt you know, I was
there in '97 with poor "Sprat" Larkin...'

'I want some cleft sticks, please,' said William firmly.

The General's manner changed abruptly. His leg had
been pulled before, often. Only last week there had been
an idiotic young fellow dressed up as a missionary . . .
'What the devil for?' he asked tartly.

'Oh, just for my dispatches, you know.'

It was with exactly such an expression of simplicity
that the joker had asked for a tiffin gun, a set of chota
pegs and a chota mallet. 'Miss Barton will see to you,' he
said, and turning on his heel he began to inspect a newly-
arrived consignment of rhinoceros hide whips in a
menacing way.

Miss Barton was easier to deal with. 'We can have
some cloven for you,' she said brightly. 'If you will make
your selection I will send them down to our cleaver.'

William, hesitating between polo sticks and hockey
sticks, chose six of each; they were removed to the work-
shop. Then Miss Barton led him through the departments
of the enormous store. By the time she had finished with
him, William had acquired a well-, perhaps rather over-,
furnished tent, three months' rations, a collapsible canoe,
a jointed flagstaff and Union Jack, a hand-pump and
sterilizing plant, an astrolabe, six suits of tropical linen
and a sou'wester, a camp operating table and set of
surgical instruments, a portable humidor, guaranteed to

preserve cigars in condition in the Red Sea, and a Christmas hamper complete with Santa Claus costume and a
tripod mistletoe stand, and a cane for whacking snakes.
Only anxiety about time brought an end to his marketing.
At the last moment he added a coil of rope and a sheet of
tin; then he left under the baleful stare of General
Cruttwell.

5

It had been arranged for him that William should fly
to Paris and there catch the Blue Train to Marseilles. He
was just in time. His luggage, which followed the taxi in
a small pantechnicon, made him a prominent figure at
the office of the Air Line.

'It will cost you one hundred and three pounds supplement on your ticket,' they said, after it had all been
weighed.

'Not *me*,' said William cheerfully, producing his travellers' cheques.

They telephoned to Croydon and ordered an addi-
tional aeroplane.

Mr Pappenhacker of the *Twopence* was a fellow passenger. He travelled as a man of no importance; a typewriter and a single 'featherweight' suitcase constituted
his entire luggage; only the unobtrusive *Messageries Mari-
times* labels distinguished him from the surrounding male
and female commercial travellers. He read a little Arabic
Grammar, holding it close to his nose, oblivious to all
about him. William was the centre of interest in the
motor omnibus, and in his heart he felt a rising, wholly
pleasurable excitement. His new possessions creaked and
rattled on the roof, canoe against astrolabe, humidor
against ant-proof clothes box; the cleft sticks lay in a
bundle on the opposite seat; the gardens of South London
sped past. William sat in a happy stupor. He had never
wanted to go to Ishmaelia, or, for that matter, to any

foreign country, to earn £50 a week or to own a jointed flagstaff or a camp operating table; but when he told Mr Salter that he wanted nothing except to live at home and keep his job, he had hidden the remote and secret ambition of fifteen years or more. He did, very deeply, long to go up in an aeroplane. It was a wish so far from the probabilities of life at Boot Magna that William never spoke of it; very rarely consciously considered it. No one at home knew of it except Nannie Bloggs. She had promised him a flight if she won the Irish Sweepstake, but after several successive failures she had decided that the whole thing was a popish trick and refused to take further tickets, and with her decision William's chances seemed to fade beyond the ultimate horizon. But it still haunted his dreams and returned to him, more vividly, in the minutes of transition between sleep and wakefulness, on occasions of physical exhaustion and inner content, hacking home in the twilight after a good day's hunt, fuddled with port on the not infrequent birthdays of the Boot household. And now its imminent fulfilment loomed through the haze that enveloped him as the single real and significant feature. High over the chimneys and the giant monkey-puzzle, high among the clouds and rainbows and clear blue spaces, whose alternations figured so largely and poetically in *Lush Places*; high above the most ecstatic skylark, above earth-bound badger and great crested grebe, away from people and cities to a region of light and void and silence – that was where William was going in the Air Line omnibus; he sat mute, rapt, oblivious of the cleft sticks and the portable typewriter.

At Croydon he was received with obeisance; a special official had been detailed to attend to him. 'Good day, Mr Boot . . . This way, Mr Boot . . . The men will see to your baggage, Mr Boot.' On the concrete court in front of the station stood his aeroplane, her three engines tuning up, one screw swinging slow, one spinning faster, one totally invisible, roaring all-out. 'Good afternoon, Mr Boot,' said a man in overalls.

'Good afternoon, Mr Boot,' said a man in a peaked cap.

Pappenhacker and the commercial travellers were being herded into the service plane. William watched his crates being embarked. Men like gym instructors moved at the double behind rubber-tyred trolleys. 'All in, Mr Boot,' they said, touching their caps. William distributed silver.

'Excuse me, Mr Boot,' a little man in a seedy soft hat stood at William's elbow, 'I haven't yet had the pleasure of stamping your passport.'

FOUR

I

'OH dear, oh dear,' said Mr Salter. 'D'you know, I believe it would be as well to keep Lord Copper in ignorance of this incident. The *Twopence* will be a day ahead of us – perhaps more. Lord Copper would not like that. It might cause trouble for the Foreign Contacts Adviser or – or someone.'

William's luggage was piled in the Byzantine Hall; even there, under the lofty, gilded vaults, it seemed enormous. He and Mr Salter regarded it sadly. 'I'll have all this sent on to your hotel. It must not be seen by the Personal Staff. Here is your application form for an emergency passport. The Art Department will take your photograph and we have an Archdeacon in the Religious Department who will witness it. Then I think you had better keep away from the office until you start. I'm afraid that you've missed the Messageries ship, but there's a P. and O. next day to Aden. You can get across from there. And, officially, remember, you left this afternoon.'

It was a warm evening, heavy with the reek of petrol.

William returned sadly to his hotel and re-engaged his room. The last edition of the evening papers was on the streets. '*Society Beauty in Public Convenience*' they said. '*Mrs Stitch Again.*'

William walked to Hyde Park. A black man, on a little rostrum, was explaining to a small audience why the Ishmaelite patriots were right and the traitors were wrong. William turned away. He noticed with surprise a tiny black car bowling across the grass; it sped on, dexterously swerving between the lovers; he raised his hat but the driver was intent on her business. Mrs Stitch had just learned that a baboon, escaped from the Zoo, was up a tree in Kensington Gardens and she was out to catch it.

'Who built the Pyramids?' cried the Ishmaelite orator. 'A Negro. Who invented the circulation of the blood? A Negro. Ladies and gentlemen, I ask you as impartial members of the great British public, who discovered America?'

And William went sadly on his way to a solitary dinner and an early bed.

2

At the passport office next morning they told William that he would want a visa for Ishmaelia. 'In fact you may want two. Someone's just opened a rival legation. We haven't recognized it officially, of course, but you may find it convenient to visit them. Which part are you going to?'

'The patriotic part.'

'Ah, then you'd better get two visas,' said the official.

William drove to the address they gave him. It was in Maida Vale. He rang the bell and presently a tousled woman opened the door.

'Is this the Ishmaelite Legation?' he asked.

'No, it's Doctor Cohen's and he's out.'

'Oh... I wanted an Ishmaelite visa.'

'Well, you'd better call again. I daresay Doctor Cohen

will have one, only he doesn't come here not often except sometimes to sleep.'

The lower half of another woman appeared on the landing overhead. William could see her bedroom slippers and a length of flannel dressing-gown.

'What is it, Effie?'

'Man at the door.'

'Tell him whatever it is we don't want it.'

'He says will the Doctor give him something or other.'

'Not without an appointment.'

The legs disappeared and a door slammed.

'That's Mrs Cohen,' said Effie. 'You see how it is; they're Yids.'

'Oh dear,' said William. 'I was told to come here by the passport office.'

'Sure it isn't the nigger downstairs you want?'

'Perhaps it is.'

'Well, why didn't you say so? He's downstairs.'

William then noticed, for the first time, that a little flag was flying from the area railings. It bore a red hammer and sickle on a black ground. He descended to the basement where, over a door between two dustbins, a notice proclaimed:

REPUBLIC OF ISHMAELIA
LEGATION AND CONSULATE-GENERAL
If away leave letters with tobacconist at No. 162b

William knocked and the door was opened by the Negro whom he had seen the evening before in Hyde Park. The features, to William's undiscriminating eye, were not much different from those of any other Negro, but the clothes were unforgettable.

'Can I see the Ishmaelite consul-general, please?'

'Are you from the Press?'

'Yes, I suppose in a way I am.'

'Come in. I'm him. As you see, we are a little under-staffed at the moment.'

The consul-general led him into what had once been

the servants' hall. Photographs of Negroes in uniform and ceremonial European dress hung on the walls. Samples of tropical produce were disposed on the table and along the bookshelves. There was a map of Ishmaelia, an eight-piece office suite and a radio. William sat down. The consul-general turned off the music and began to talk.

'The patriotic cause in Ishmaelia,' he said, 'is the cause of the coloured man and of the proletariat throughout the world. The Ishmaelite worker is threatened by a corrupt and foreign coalition of capitalistic exploiters, priests and imperialists. As that great Negro Karl Marx has so nobly written . . . ' He talked for about twenty minutes. The black-backed, pink palmed, fin-like hands beneath the violet cuffs flapped and slapped. 'Who built the Pyramids?' he asked. 'Who invented the circulation of the blood? . . . Africa for the African worker; Europe for the African worker; Asia, Oceania, America, Arctic, and Antarctic for the African worker.'

At length he paused and wiped the line of froth from his lips.

'I came about a visa,' said William diffidently.

'Oh,' said the consul-general, turning on the radio once more. 'There's fifty pounds deposit and a form to fill in.'

William declared that he had not been imprisoned, that he was not suffering from any contagious or out-rageous disease, that he was not seeking employment in Ishmaelia or the overthrow of its political institutions; paid his deposit and was rewarded with a rubber stamp on the first page of his new passport.

'I hope you have a pleasant trip,' said the consul-general. 'I'm told it's a very interesting country.'

'But aren't you an Ishmaelite?'

'*Me?* Certainly not. I'm a graduate of the Baptist College of Antigua. But the cause of the Ishmaelite worker is the cause of the Negro worker of the world.'

'Yes,' said William. 'Yes. I suppose it is. Thank you very much.'

'Who discovered America?' demanded the consul-
general to his retreating back, in tones that rang high
above the sound of the wireless concert. 'Who won the
Great War?'

3

The rival legation had more spacious quarters in an
hotel in South Kensington. A gold swastika on a white
ground hung proudly from the window. The door of the
suite was opened by a Negro clad in a white silk shirt,
buckskin breeches and hunting boots who clicked his
spurs and gave William a Roman salute.

'I've come for a visa.'

The pseudo-consul led him to the office. 'I shall have
to delay you for a few minutes. You see the Legation is
only just open and we have not yet got our full equipment. We are expecting the rubber stamp any minute
now. In the meantime let me explain the Ishmaelite
situation to you. There are many misconceptions. For
instance, the Jews of Geneva, subsidized by Russian gold,
have spread the story that we are a black race. Such is the
ignorance, credulity, and prejudice of the tainted European states that the absurd story has been repeated in the
press. I must ask you to deny it. As you will see for yourself, we are pure Aryans. In fact we were the first white
colonizers of Central Africa. What Stanley and Living-
stone did in the last century, our Ishmaelite ancestors
did in the Stone Age. In the course of the years the
tropical sun has given to some of us a healthy, in some
cases almost a swarthy tan. But all responsible anthro-
pologists...'

William fingered his passport and became anxious
about luncheon. It was already past one.

'... The present so-called government bent on the des-
truction of our great heritage...' There was an interruption. The pseudo-consul went to the door. 'From the
stationer's,' said a cockney voice. 'Four and eight to pay.'

'Thank you, that is all.'

'Four and eight to pay or else I takes it away again.'
There was a pause. The pseudo-consul returned.

'There is a fee of five shillings for the visa,' he said.
William paid. The pseudo-consul returned with the rubber stamp, jingling four pennies in his breeches pocket.

'You will see the monuments of our glorious past in Ishmaelia,' he said, taking the passport. 'I envy you very much.'

'But are you not an Ishmaelite?'

'Of course; by descent. My parents migrated some generations ago. I was brought up in Sierra Leone.'

Then he opened the passport.

4

The bells of St Bride's were striking four when, after a heavy luncheon, William returned to the Megalopolitan Building.

'Boot. Oh dear, oh dear,' said Mr Salter. 'You ought to be at the aerodrome. What on earth has happened?'

'He burned my passport.'

'Who did?'

'The patriot consul.'

'Why?'

'It had a traitor visa on it.'

'I see. How very unfortunate. Lord Copper would be *most* upset if he came to hear of it. I think we had better go and ask the Foreign Contacts Adviser what to do.'

On the following afternoon, provided with two passports, William left Croydon aerodrome in his special plane.

5

He did not leave alone.

The propellers were thundering; the pilot threw away his cigarette and adjusted his helmet; the steward wrapped a rug round William's feet and tenderly laid in his lap a wad of cotton wool, a flask of smelling salts and an empty paper bag; the steps were being wheeled from the door. At that moment three figures hurried from the shelter of the office. One was heavily enveloped in a sand-coloured ulster; a check cap was pulled low on his eyes and his collar was fastened high against the blast of the engines. He was a small man in a hurry, yet, bustling and buttoned up as he was, a man of unmistakable importance, radiating something of the dignity of a prize Pekingese. This impression was accentuated by the extreme deference with which he was treated by his companions, one a soldierly giant carrying an attaché case, the other wearing the uniform of high rank in the company.

This official now approached William, and, above the engine, asked his permission to include a passenger and his servant. The name was lost in the roar of the propellers. 'Mr . . . I needn't tell you who *he* is . . . only plane available . . . request from a very high quarter . . . infinitely obliged if . . . as far as Le Bourget.'

William gave his assent and the two men bowed silently and took their places. The official withdrew. The little man delicately plugged his ears and sank deeper into his collar. The door was shut; the ground staff fell back. The machine moved forward, gathered speed, hurtled and bumped across the rough turf, ceased to bump, floated clear of the earth, mounted and wheeled above the smoke and traffic and very soon hung, it seemed motionless, above the Channel, where the track of a steamer, far below them, lay in the bright water like a line of smoke on a still morning. William's heart rose with it and gloried, lark-like, in the high places.

6

All too soon they returned to earth. The little man and his servant slipped unobtrusively through the throng and William was bayed on all sides by foreigners. The parcels and packing cases seemed to fill the shed, and the customs officers, properly curious, settled down to a thorough examination.

'Tous sont des effets personnels – tous usés,' William said gallantly, but one by one, with hammers and levers, the crates were opened and their exotic contents spread over the counter.

It was one of those rare occasions when the humdrum life of the *douanier* is exalted from the tedious traffic in vegetable silks and subversive literature to realms of adventure; such an occasion as might have inspired the jungle scenes of Rousseau. Not since an Egyptian lady had been caught cosseting an artificial baby stuffed with hashish had the customs officials of Le Bourget had such a beano.

'Comment dit-on humidor?' William cried in his distress. 'C'est une chose pour garder les cigares dans la Mer Rouge – et dedans ceci sont les affaires de l'hospitale pour couper les bras et les jambes, vous comprenez – et ça c'est pour tuer les serpents et ceci est un bateau qui collapse et ces branches de mistletoe sont pour Noël, pour baiser dessous, vous savez ...'

'Monsieur, il ne faut pas se moquer des douanes.'

The cleft sticks alone passed without question, with sympathy.

'Ils sont pour porter les dépêches.'

'C'est un Sport?'

'Oui, oui, certainement – le Sport.'

There and at the Gare de Lyon he spent vast sums; all the porters of Paris seemed to have served him, all the officials to need his signature on their sheaves of documents. At last he achieved his train, and, as they left Paris, made his way uncertainly towards the restaurant car.

7

Opposite him at the table to which he was directed sat a middle-aged man, at the moment engaged in a homily to the waiter in fluent and apparently telling argot. His head was totally bald on the top and of unusual conical shape; at the sides and back the hair was closely cut and dyed a strong, purplish shade of auburn. He was neatly, rather stiffly dressed for the time of year, and heavily jewelled; a cabochon emerald, massive and dull, adorned his tie; rubies flashed on his fingers and cuff-links as his hands rose and spread configuring the swell and climax of his argument; pearls and platinum stretched from pocket to pocket of his waistcoat. William wondered what his nationality could be and thought perhaps Turkish. Then he spoke, in a voice that was not exactly American or Levantine or Eurasian or Latin or Teuton, but a blend of them all.

'The moment they recognize an Englishman they think they can make a monkey of him,' he said in this voice. 'That one was Swiss; they're the worst; tried to make me buy mineral water. The water in the carafes is excellent. I have drunk quantities of it in my time without ever being seriously affected – and I have a particularly delicate stomach. May I give you some?'

William said he preferred wine.

'You are interested in clarets? I have a little vineyard in Bordeaux – on the opposite slope of the hill to Château Mouton-Rothschild where in my opinion the soil is rather less delicate than mine. I like to have something to give my friends. They are kind enough to find it drinkable. It has never been in the market, of course. It is a little hobby of mine.'

He took two pills, one round and white, the other elliptical and black, from a rococo snuff-box and laid them on the tablecloth beside his plate. He drew a coroneted crêpe de Chine handkerchief from his pocket, carefully wiped his glass, half-filled it with murky liquid from the water bottle, swallowed his medicine and then said:

'You are surprised at my addressing you?'

'Not at all,' said William politely.

'But it *is* surprising. I make a point of never addressing my fellow travellers. Indeed I usually prefer to dine in the coupé. But this is not our first meeting. You were kind enough to give me a place in your aeroplane this afternoon. It was a service I greatly appreciate.'

'Not at all,' said William. 'Not at all. Very glad to have been any help.'

'It was the act of an Englishman – a fellow Englishman,' said the little man simply. 'I hope that one day I shall have the opportunity of requiting it . . . I probably shall,' he added rather sadly. 'It is one of the pleasant if quite onerous duties of a man of my position to requite the services he receives – usually on a disproportionately extravagant scale.'

'Please,' said William, 'do not give the matter another thought.'

'I never do. I try to let these things slip from my mind as one of the evanescent delights of travel. But it has been my experience that sooner or later I am reminded of them by my benefactor . . . You are on your way to the Côte d'Azur?'

'No, only as far as Marseille.'

'I rejoice in the Côte d'Azur. I try to get there every year, but too often I am disappointed. I have so much on my hands – naturally – and in winter I am much occupied with sport. I have a little pack of hounds in the Midlands.'

'Oh? Which?'

'You might not have heard of us. We march with the Fernie. I suppose it is the best hunting country in England. It is a little hobby of mine, but at times, when there is a frost, I long for my little house at Antibes. My friends are kind enough to say I have made it comfortable. I expect you will one day honour me with a visit there.'

'It sounds delightful.'

'They tell me the bathing is good but that does not interest me. I have some plantations of flowering trees which horticulturists are generous enough to regard with interest, and the largest octopus in captivity. The chef too is, in his simple seaside way, one of the best I have.

Those simple pleasures suffice for me . . . You are surely not making a long stay in Marseille?'

'No, I sail tomorrow for East Africa. For Ishmaelia,' William added with some swagger.

The effect on his companion was gratifying. He blinked twice and asked with subdued courtesy:

'Forgive me; I think I must have misheard you. Where are you going?'

'To Ishmaelia. You know, the place where they say there is a war.'

There was a pause. Finally: 'Yes, the name is in some way familiar. I must have seen it in the newspapers.' And, taking a volume of pre-Hitler German poetry from the rack above him, he proceeded to read, shaping the words with his lips like a woman in prayer, and slowly turning the leaves.

Undeviating as the train itself, the dinner followed its changeless course from consommé to bombe. William's companion ate little and said nothing. With his coffee he swallowed two crimson cachets. Then he closed his book of love poems and nodded across the restaurant car.

The soldierly valet who had been dining at the next table rose to go.

'Cuthbert.'

'Sir?'

He stood attentively at his master's side.

'Did you give my sheets to the *conducteur*?'

'Yes, sir.'

'See that he has made them up properly. Then you may go to bed. You know the time in the morning?'

'Yes, sir; thank you, sir; good night, sir.'

'Good night, Cuthbert . . .' Then he turned to William and said with peculiar emphasis: 'A very courageous man that. He served with me in the war. He never left my side, so I recommended him for the V.C. He never leaves me now. And he is adequately armed.'

William returned to his carriage to lie awake, doze

fitfully and at last to raise the blinds upon a landscape of vines and olives and dusty aromatic scrub.

8

At Marseille he observed, but was too much occupied to speculate upon the fact, that his companion of the evening before had also left the train. He saw the dapper, slightly rotund figure slip past the barrier a few paces ahead of the valet, but immediately the stupendous responsibilities of his registered baggage pressed all other concerns from his mind.

FIVE

I

THE ships which William had missed had been modern and commodious and swift; not so the *Francmaçon* in which he was eventually obliged to sail. She had been built at an earlier epoch in the history of steam navigation and furnished in the style of the day, for service among the high waves and icy winds of the North Atlantic. Late June in the Gulf of Suez was not her proper place or season. There was no space on her decks for long chairs; her cabins, devoid of fans, were aired only by tiny portholes, built to resist the buffeting of an angrier sea. The passengers sprawled listlessly on the crimson plush settees of the lounge. Carved mahogany panels shut them in; a heraldic ceiling hung threateningly overhead; light came to them, dimly, from behind the imitation windows of stained, armorial glass, and, blinding white, from the open door, whence too came the sounds of the winch, the smell of cargo and hot iron, the patter of bare feet and the hoarse, scolding voice of the second officer.

William sat in a hot, soft chair, a map of Ishmaelia

open upon his knees, his eyes shut, his head lolling forwards on his chest, fast asleep, dreaming about his private school, now, he noted without surprise, peopled by Negroes and governed by his grandmother. An appalling brass percussion crashed and sang an inch or two from his ear. A soft voice said, 'Lunce pliss.' The Javanese with the gong proceeded on his apocalyptic mission, leaving William hot and wet, without appetite, very sorry to be awake.

The French colonial administrator, who had been nursing his two children in the next arm-chair to William's, rose briskly. It was the first time that day they had met face to face, so they shook hands and commented on the heat. Every morning, William found, it was necessary to shake hands with all the passengers.

'And madame?'

'She suffers. You are still studying the map of Ishmaelia...' They turned together and descended the staircase towards the dining saloon; the functionary leading a tottering child by either hand. '... It is a country of no interest.'

'No.'

'It is not rich at all. If it were rich it would already belong to England. Why do you wish to take it?'

'But I do not wish to.'

'There is no oil, there is no tin, no gold, no iron – positively none,' said the functionary, growing vexed at such unreasonable rapacity. 'What do you want with it?'

'I am going as a journalist.'

'Ah, well, to the journalist every country is rich.'

They were alone at their table. The functionary arranged his napkin about his open throat, tucked the lowest corner into his cummerbund and lifted a child on to either knee. It was always thus that he sat at meals, feeding them to repletion, to surfeit, alternately, from his own plate. He wiped his glass on the tablecloth, put ice into it, and filled it with the harsh, blue-red wine that was included free in the menu. The little girl took a deep draught. 'It is excellent for their stomachs,' he explained, refilling for his son.

There were three empty places at their table. The administrator's wife, the Captain's, and the Captain's wife's. The last two were on the bridge directing the discharge of cargo. The Captain led a life of somewhat blatant domesticity; half the boat deck was given up to his quarters, where a vast brass bedstead was visible through the portholes, and a variety of unseamanlike furniture. The Captain's wife had hedged off a little veranda for herself with pots of palm and strings of newly laundered underclothes. Here she passed the day stitching, ironing, flopping in and out of the deck-house in heelless slippers, armed with a feather brush, often emerging in a dense aura of Asiatic perfume to dine in the saloon; a tiny, hairless dog capered about her feet. But in port she was always at her husband's side, exchanging civilities with the company's agents and the quarantine inspectors, and arranging, in a small way, for the transfer of contraband.

'Even supposing there is oil in Ishmaelia,' said the administrator, resuming the conversation which had occupied him ever since, on the first night of the voyage, William had disclosed his destination, 'how are you going to get it out?'

'But I have no interest in commerce. I am going to report the war.'

'War is all commerce.'

William's command of French, just adequate, inaccurately, for the exchange of general information and the bare courtesies of daily intercourse, was not strong enough for sustained argument, so now, as at every meal, he left the Frenchman victorious, saying '*Peut-être*,' with what he hoped was Gallic scepticism, and turning his attention to the dish beside him.

It was a great, white fish, cold and garnished; the children had rejected it with cries of distress; it lay on a charger of imitation silver; the two brown thumbs of the coloured steward lay just within the circle of mayonnaise; lozenges and roundels of coloured vegetable spread symmetrically about its glazed back. William looked sadly at this fish. 'It is very dangerous,' said the administrator. 'In the tropics one easily contracts disease of the skin...'

... Far away the trout were lying among the cool pebbles, nose upstream, meditative, hesitant, in the waters of his home; the barbed fly, unnaturally brilliant overhead; they were lying, blue-brown, scarred by the grill, with white-bead eyes, in chaste silver dishes. 'Fresh green of the river bank; faded terra-cotta of the dining-room wallpaper, colours of distant Canaan, of deserted Eden,' thought William – 'are they still there? Shall I ever revisit those familiar places...?'

... 'Il faut manger, il faut vivre,' said the Frenchman, 'qu'est-ce qu'il y a comme viande?'

And at that moment, suddenly, miasmically, in the fiery wilderness, there came an apparition.

A voice said in English, 'Anyone mind if I park myself here?' and a stranger stood at the table, as though conjured there by William's unexpressed wish; as though conjured, indeed, by a djinn who had imperfectly understood his instructions.

The new-comer was British but, at first sight, unprepossessing. His suit of striped flannel had always, as its tailor proudly remarked, fitted snugly at the waist. The sleeves had been modishly narrow. Now in the midday heat it had resolved into an alternation of wrinkles and damp adherent patches; steaming visibly. The double-breasted waistcoat was unbuttoned and revealed shirt and braces.

'Not dressed for this climate,' remarked the young man, superfluously. 'Left in a hurry.'

He sat down heavily in the chair next to William's and ran his napkin round the back of his collar. 'Phew. What does one drink on this boat?'

The Frenchman who had regarded him with resentment

from the moment of his appearance, now leant forward and spoke, acidly.

The hot man smiled in an encouraging way and turned to William.

'What's old paterfamilias saying?'

William translated literally. 'He says that you have taken the chair of the Captain's lady.'

'Too bad. What's she like? Any good?'

'Bulky,' said William.

'There was a whopper upstairs with the captain. What I call the Continental Figure. Would that be her?'

'Yes.'

'Definitely no good, old boy. Not for Corker anyway.'

The Frenchman leaned towards William.

'This is the Captain's table. Your friend must not come here except by invitation.'

'I do not know him,' said William. 'It is his business.'

'The Captain should present him to us. This is a reserved place.'

'Hope I'm not butting in,' said the Englishman.

The steward offered him the fish; he examined its still unbroken ornaments and helped himself. 'If you ask me,' he said cheerfully, his mouth full, 'I'd say it was a spot off colour, but I never do care much for French cooking. Hi, you, Alphonse, comprenez pint of bitter?'

The steward gaped at him, then at the fish, then at him again. 'No like?' he said at last.

'No like one little bit, but that's not the question under discussion. Me like a big tankard of Bass, Worthington, whatever you got. Look, comme ça,' – he made the motions of drinking – 'I say, what's the French for bitter?'

William tried to help.

The steward beamed and nodded.

'Whisky-soda?'

'All right, Alphonse, you win. Whisky-soda it shall be. Beaucoup whisky, beaucoup soda, tout-de-suite. The truth is,' he continued, turning to William, 'my French is a bit rusty. You're Boot of *The Beast*, aren't you?

Thought I might run into you. I'm Corker of the U.N. Just got on board with an hour to spare. Think of it; I was in Fleet Street on Tuesday; got my marching orders at ten o'clock, caught the plane to Cairo, all night in a car and here I am, all present and, I hope, correct. God, I can't think how you fellows can eat this fish.'

'We can't,' said William.

'Found it a bit high?'

'Exactly.'

'That's what I thought,' said Corker, 'the moment I saw it. Here, Alphonse, mauvais poisson – parfume formidable – prenez – et portez vite le whisky, you black bum.'

The Frenchman continued to feed his children. It is difficult for a man nursing two children, aged five and two and clumsy eaters at that, to look supercilious, but the Frenchman tried and Corker noticed it.

'Does the little mother understand English?' he asked William.

'No.'

'That's lucky. Not a very matey bird?'

'No.'

'Fond of la belle France?'

'Well, I can't say I've ever been there – except to catch this ship.'

'Funny thing, neither have I. Never been out of England except once, when I went to Ostend to cover a chess congress. Ever play chess?'

'No.'

'Nor do I. God, that was a cold story.' The steward placed on the table a syphon and a bottle of whisky which carried the label 'Edouard VIII: Very old Genuine Scotch Whisky: André Bloc et Cie, Saigon,' and the coloured picture of a Regency buck, gazing sceptically at the consumer through a quizzing glass.

'Alphonse,' said Corker, 'I'm surprised at you.'

'No like?'

'Bloody well no like.'

'Whisky-soda,' the man explained, patiently, almost tenderly, as though in the nursery. 'Nice.'

Corker filled his glass, tasted, grimaced, and then resumed the interrupted inquiry. 'Tell me honestly, had you ever heard of Ishmaelia before you were sent on this story?'

'Only very vaguely.'

'So had I. And the place I'd heard of was something quite different in the Suez Canal. You know, when I first started in journalism I used to think that foreign correspondents spoke every language under the sun and spent their lives studying international conditions. Brother, look at us! On Monday afternoon I was in East Sheen breaking the news to a widow of her husband's death leap with a champion girl cyclist – the wrong widow as it turned out; the husband came back from business while I was there and cut up very nasty. Next day the Chief has me in and says, "Corker, you're off to Ishmaelia." "Out of town job?" I asked. "East Africa," he said, just like that, "pack your traps." "What's the story?" I asked. "Well," he said, "a lot of niggers are having a war. I don't see anything in it myself, but the other agencies are sending feature men, so we've got to do something. We want spot news," he said, "and some colour stories. Go easy on the expenses." "What are they having a war about?" I asked. "That's for you to find out," he said, but I haven't found out yet. Have you?'

'No.'

'Well, I don't suppose it matters. Personally I can't see that foreign stories are ever news – not *real* news of the kind U.N. covers.'

'Forgive me,' said William, 'I'm afraid I know very little about journalism. What is U.N.?'

'No kidding?'

'No,' said William, 'no kidding.'

'Never heard of Universal News?'

'I'm afraid not.'

'Well, I won't say we're the biggest news agency in the

country – some of the stuffier papers won't take us – but we certainly are the hottest.'

'And what, please,' asked William, 'is a news agency?' Corker told him.

'You mean that everything that you write goes to *The Beast?*'

'Well, that's rather a sore point, brother. We've been having a row with you lately. Something about a libel action one of our boys let you in for. But you take the other agencies, of course, and I daresay you'll patch it up with us. They're featuring me as a special service.'

'Then why do they want to send me?'

'All the papers are sending specials.'

'And all the papers have reports from three or four agencies?'

'Yes.'

'But if we all send the same thing it seems a waste.'

'There would soon be a row if we did.'

'But isn't it very confusing if we all send different news?'

'It gives them a choice. They all have different policies, so of course, they have to give different news.'

They went up to the lounge and drank their coffee together.

The winches were silent; the hatches covered. The agents were making their ceremonious farewells to the Captain's wife. Corker sprawled back in his plush chair and lit a large cheroot.

'Given me by a native I bought some stuff off,' he explained. 'You buying much stuff?'

'Stuff?'

'Oriental stuff – you know, curios.'

'No,' said William.

'I'm a collector – in a small way,' said Corker. 'That's one of the reasons why I was glad to be sent on this story. Ought to be able to pick up some pretty useful things out East. But it's going to be a tough assignment from all I hear. Cut-throat competition. That's where I envy you –

working for a paper. You only have to worry about getting your story in time for the first edition. We have to race each other all day.'

'But the papers can't use your reports any earlier than ours.'

'No, but they use the one that comes in first.'

'But if it's exactly the same as the one that came in second and third and fourth and they are all in time for the same edition ... ?'

Corker looked at him sadly. 'You know, you've got a lot to learn about journalism. Look at it this way. News is what a chap who doesn't care much about anything wants to read. And it's only news until he's read it. After that it's dead. We're paid to supply news. If someone else has sent a story before us, our story isn't news. Of course there's colour. Colour is just a lot of bull's-eyes about nothing. It's easy to write and easy to read, but it costs too much in cabling, so we have to go slow on that. See?'

'I think so.'

That afternoon Corker told William a great deal about the craft of journalism. The *Francmaçon* weighed anchor, swung about, and steamed into the ochre hills, through the straits and out into the open sea while Corker recounted the heroic legends of Fleet Street; he told of the classic scoops and hoaxes; of the confessions wrung from hysterical suspects; of the innuendo and intricate misrepresentations, the luscious, detailed inventions that composed contemporary history; of the positive, daring lies that got a chap a rise of screw; how Wenlock Jakes, highest paid journalist of the United States, scooped the world with an eye-witness story of the sinking of the *Lusitania* four hours before she was hit; how Hitchcock, the English Jakes, straddling over his desk in London, had chronicled day by day the horrors of the Messina earthquake; how Corker himself, not three months back, had had the rare good fortune to encounter a knight's widow trapped by the foot between lift and landing. 'It was through that story I got sent here,' said Corker. 'The boss promised me the first big chance that turned up. I little thought it would be this.'

Many of Corker's anecdotes dealt with the fabulous Wenlock Jakes. '. . . syndicated all over America. Gets a thousand dollars a week. When he turns up in a place you can bet your life that as long as he's there it'll be the news centre of the world.

'Why, once Jakes went out to cover a revolution in one of the Balkan capitals. He overslept in his carriage, woke up at the wrong station, didn't know any different, got out, went straight to an hotel, and cabled off a thousand-word story about barricades in the streets, flaming churches, machine-guns answering the rattle of his typewriter as he wrote, a dead child, like a broken doll, spreadeagled in the deserted roadway below his window – *you* know.

'Well, they were pretty surprised at his office, getting a story like that from the wrong country, but they trusted Jakes and splashed it in six national newspapers. That day every special in Europe got orders to rush to the new revolution. They arrived in shoals. Everything seemed quiet enough, but it was as much as their jobs were worth to say so, with Jakes filing a thousand words of blood and thunder a day. So they chimed in too. Government stocks dropped, financial panic, state of emergency declared, army mobilized, famine, mutiny and in less than a week there *was* an honest to God revolution under way, just as Jakes had said. There's the power of the press for you.

'They gave Jakes the Nobel Peace Prize for his harrowing descriptions of the carnage – but that was colour stuff.'

Towards the conclusion of this discourse – William took little part beyond an occasional expression of wonder – Corker began to wriggle his shoulders restlessly, to dive his hand into his bosom and scratch his chest, to roll up his sleeve and gaze fixedly at a forearm which was rapidly becoming mottled and inflamed.

It was the fish.

2

For two days Corker's nettle-rash grew worse, then it began to subside.

William used often to see him at his open door; he sat bare to the waist, in his pyjama trousers, typing long, informative letters to his wife and dabbing himself with vinegar and water as prescribed by the ship's doctor; often his disfigured face would appear over the gallery of the dining saloon calling petulantly for Vichy water.

'He suffers,' remarked the functionary with great complacency.

Not until they were nearing Aden did the rash cool a little and allow of Corker coming down to dinner. When he did so William hastened to consult him about a radiogram which had arrived that morning and was causing him grave bewilderment. It read:

OPPOSITION SPLASHING FRONTWARD SPEEDILIEST STOP ADEN REPORTED PREPARED WARWISE FLASH FACTS BEAST.

'I can't understand it,' said William.

'No?'

'The only thing that makes any sense is Stop Aden.'

'Yes?' Corker's face, still brightly patterned, was, metaphorically, a blank.

'What d'you think I'd better do?'

'Just what they tell you, old boy.'

'Yes, I suppose I'd better.'

'Far better.'

But William was not happy about it. 'It doesn't make any sense, read it how you will. I wonder if the operator has made a muddle somewhere,' he said at last.

'I should ask him,' said Corker, scratching. 'And now if you don't mind I must get back to the vinegar bottle.'

There had been something distinctly unmatey about his manner, William thought. Perhaps it was the itch.

3

Early next morning they arrived off Steamer Point. The stewards, in a frenzy of last-minute avarice, sought to atone for ten days' neglect with a multitude of un-needed services. The luggage was appearing on deck. The companion ladder was down, waiting the arrival of the official launch. William leant on the taffrail gazing at the bare heap of clinker half a mile distant. It did not seem an inviting place for a long visit. There seemed no front-ward splashing to oppose. The sea was dead calm and the ship's refuse lay all round it – a bank-holiday litter of horrible scraps – motionless, undisturbed except for an Arab row-boat peddling elephants of synthetic ivory. At William's side Corker bargained raucously for the largest of these toys.

Presently the boy from the wireless room brought him a message. 'Something about you,' he said, and passed it on to William.

It said: CO-OPERATING BEAST AVOID DUPLICA-TION BOOT UNNATURAL.

'What does that mean?'

'It means our bosses have been getting together in London. You're taking our special service on this Ishmaelia story. So you and I can work together after all.'

'And what is unnatural?'

'That's our telegraphic name.' Corker completed his purchase, haggled over the exchange from francs to rupees, was handsomely cheated, and drew up his ele-phant on a string. Then he said casually, 'By the by, have you still got that cable you had last night?'

William showed it to him.

'Shall I tell you what this says? "Opposition splashing" means that the rival papers are giving a lot of space to this story. "Frontward speediliest" – go to the front as fast as you can – full stop – Aden is reported here to be prepared on a war-time footing – "Flash Facts" – send them the details of this preparation at once.'

'Good heavens!' said William. 'Thank you. What an extraordinary thing . . . It wouldn't have done at all if I'd stayed on at Aden, would it?'

'No, old boy, not at all.'

'But why didn't you tell me this last night?'

'Old boy, have some sense. Last night we were competing. It was a great chance, leaving you behind. Then the *Beast* would have had to take U.N. Laugh? I should have bust my pants. However, they've fixed things up without that. Glad to have you with me on the trip, old boy. And while you're working with me, don't go showing service messages to anybody else, see?'

Happily nursing his bakelite elephant Corker sauntered back to his cabin.

Passport officers came on board and sat in judgement in the first-class smoking room. The passengers who were to disembark assembled to wait their turn. William and Corker passed without difficulty. They elbowed their way to the door, through the little knot of many-coloured, many-tongued people who had emerged from the depths of the ship. Among them was a plump, dapper figure redolent of hair-wash and shaving soap and expensive scent; there was a glint of jewellery in the shadows, a sparkle of reflected sunlight on the hairless, conical scalp; it was William's dining companion from the Blue Train. They greeted one another warmly.

'I never saw you on board,' said William.

'Nor I you. I wish I had known you were with us. I would have asked you to dine with me in my little suite. I always maintain a certain privacy on the sea. One so easily forms acquaintances which become tedious later.'

'This is a long way from Antibes. What's brought you here?'

'Warmth,' said the little man simply. 'The call of the sun.'

There was a pause and, apparently, some uncertainty at the official table behind them.

'How d'you suppose this bloke pronounces his name?' asked the first passport officer.

'Search me,' said the second.

'Where's the man with the Costa-Rican passport?' said the first passport officer, addressing the room loudly.

A Hindu who had no passport tried to claim it, was detected and held for further inquiry.

'Where's the Costa-Rican?' said the officer again.

'Forgive me,' said William's friend, 'I have a little business to transact with these gentlemen,' and, accompanied by his valet, he stepped towards the table.

'Who's the pansy?' asked Corker.

'Believe it or not,' William replied, 'I haven't the faintest idea.'

His business seemed to take a long time. He was not at the gangway when the passengers disembarked, but as they hugged slowly to shore in the crowded tender a speed-boat shot past them in a glitter of sunlit spray, bouncing on the face of the sea and swamping their bulwarks in its wash. In it sat Cuthbert the valet, and his enigmatic master.

4

There were two nights to wait in Aden for the little ship which was to take them to Africa. William and Corker saw the stuffed mermaid and the wells of Solomon. Corker bought some Japanese shawls and a set of Benares trays; he had already acquired a number of cigarette boxes, an amber necklace, and a model of Tutankhamen's sarcophagus during his few hours in Cairo; his bedroom at the hotel was an emporium of Oriental Art. 'There's something about the East always gets me,' he said. 'The missus won't know the old home when I've finished with it.'

These were his recreations. In his serious hours he

attempted to interview the Resident, and was rebuffed;
tried the captain of a British sloop which was coaling for
a cruise in the Persian Gulf; was again rebuffed; and
finally spent two hours in conference with an Arab guide
who for twenty rupees supplied material for a detailed
cable about the defences of the settlement. 'No use our
both covering it,' he said to William. 'Your story had
better be British unpreparedness. If it suits them, they'll
be able to work that up into something at the office. You
know – "Aden the focal point of British security in the
threatened area still sunk in bureaucratic lethargy" –
that kind of thing.'

'Good heavens! how can I say that?'

'That's easy, old boy. Just cable ADEN UNWARWISE.'

On the third morning they sailed for the little Italian
port from which the railway led into the mountains of
independent Ishmaelia.

5

In London it was the night of the Duchess of Stayle's
ball. John Boot went there because he was confident of
finding Mrs Stitch. It was the kind of party she liked. For
half an hour he hunted her among the columns and
arches. On all sides stood dignified and vivacious groups
of the older generation. Elderly princesses sat in little
pools of deportment, while the younger generation loped
between buffet and ballroom in subdued and self-
conscious couples. Dancing was not an important part of
the entertainment; the Duchess's daughters were all
admirably married; at eleven o'clock the supper room
was full of elderly, hearty eaters.

John Boot sought Mrs Stitch high and low; soon it
would be too late, for she invariably went home at one;
she was indeed just speaking of going when he finally ran
her to earth in the Duke's dressing-room, sitting on a bed,
eating *foie-gras* with an ivory shoe-horn. Three elderly
admirers glared at him.

'John,' she said, 'how *very* peculiar to see you. I thought you were at the war.'

'Well, Julia, I'm afraid we must go,' said the three old boys.

'Wait for me downstairs,' said Mrs Stitch.

'You won't forget the Opera on Friday?' said one.

'I hope Josephine will like the jade horse,' said another.

'You *will* be at Alice's on Sunday?' said the third.

When they had gone, Mrs Stitch said: 'I must go too. Just tell me in three words what happened. The last thing I heard was from Lord Copper. He telephoned to say you had left.'

'Not a word from him. It's been very awkward.'

'The American girl?'

'Yes, exactly. We said good-bye a fortnight ago. She gave·me a lucky pig to wear round my neck – it was made of bog-oak from Tipperary. We were both very genuinely affected. Since then I haven't dared go out or answer the telephone. I only came here because I knew she wouldn't be coming.'

'Poor John. I wonder what went wrong . . . I like the bit about the pig *very* much.'

BOOK II

STONES £20

*

ONE

I

ISHMAELIA, that hitherto happy commonwealth, cannot conveniently be approached from any part of the world. It lies in the North-Easterly quarter of Africa, giving colour by its position and shape to the metaphor often used of it – 'the Heart of the Dark Continent'. Desert, forest, and swamp, frequented by furious nomads, protect its approaches from those more favoured regions which the statesmen of Berlin and Geneva have put to school under European masters. An inhospitable race of squireens cultivate the highlands and pass their days in the perfect leisure which those peoples alone enjoy who are untroubled by the speculative or artistic itch.

Various courageous Europeans, in the seventies of the last century, came to Ishmaelia, or near it, furnished with suitable equipment of cuckoo clocks, phonographs, opera hats, draft-treaties and flags of the nations which they had been obliged to leave. They came as missionaries, ambassadors, tradesmen, prospectors, natural scientists. None returned. They were eaten, every one of them; some raw, others stewed and seasoned – according to local usage and the calendar (for the better sort of Ishmaelites have been Christian for many centuries and will not publicly eat human flesh, uncooked, in Lent, without special and costly dispensation from their bishop). Punitive expeditions suffered more harm than they inflicted, and in the nineties humane counsels prevailed. The European powers independently decided that they did not want that profitless piece of territory; that the one thing less desirable than seeing a neighbour established there was the trouble of taking it themselves. Accordingly, by general consent, it was ruled off the maps and its immunity guaranteed. As there was no form of government common to the peoples thus segregated, nor tie of language, history, habit, or belief, they were called a Republic. A committee of jurists, drawn from the Universities, composed a constitution, providing a bicameral legislature, proportional representation by means of the single transferable vote, an executive removable by the President on the recommendation of both houses, an independent judicature, religious liberty, secular education, *habeas corpus*, free trade, joint stock banking, chartered corporations, and numerous other agreeable features. A pious old darky named Mr Samuel Smiles Jackson from Alabama was put in as the first President; a choice whose wisdom seemed to be confirmed by history, for, forty years later, a Mr Rathbone Jackson held his grandfather's office in succession to his father Pankhurst, while the chief posts of the state were held by Messrs Garnett Jackson, Mander Jackson, Huxley Jackson, his uncle and brothers, and by Mrs Athol (*née* Jackson) his aunt. So strong was the love which the Republic bore the family that General Elections were known as 'Jackson Ngomas' wherever and whenever they were held. These, by the constitution, should have been quinquennial, but since it was found in practice that difficulty of communication rendered it impossible for the constituencies to vote simultaneously, the custom had grown up for the receiving officer and the Jackson candidate to visit in turn such parts of the Republic as were open to travel, and entertain the neighbouring chiefs to a six days' banquet at their camp, after which the stupefied aborigines recorded their votes in the secret and solemn manner prescribed by the constitution.

It had been found expedient to merge the functions of
national defence and inland revenue in an office then
held in the capable hands of General Gollancz Jackson;
his forces were in two main companies, the Ishmaelite
Mule Taxgathering Force and the Rifle Excisemen with
a small Artillery Death Duties Corps for use against the
heirs of powerful noblemen; it was their job to raise the
funds whose enlightened expenditure did so much to
enhance President Jackson's prestige among the rare
foreign visitors to his capital. Towards the end of each
financial year the General's flying columns would lumber
out into the surrounding country on the heels of the fugi-
tive population and returned in time for budget day
laden with the spoils of the less nimble; coffee and hides,
silver coinage, slaves, livestock, and firearms would be
assembled and assessed in the Government warehouses;
salaries would be paid, and cover in kind deposited at the
bank for the national overdraft, and donations made, in
the presence of the diplomatic corps, to the Jackson Non-
sectarian Co-educational Technical Schools and other
humane institutions. On the foundation of the League of
Nations, Ishmaelia became a member.

Under this liberal and progressive régime, the republic
may be said, in some way, to have prospered. It is true
that the capital city of Jacksonburg became unduly large,
its alleys and cabins thronged with landless men of native
and alien blood, while the country immediately surrounding it became depopulated, so that General Gollancz Jackson was obliged to start earlier and march
further in search of the taxes; but on the main street there
were agencies for many leading American and European
firms; there was, moreover, a railway to the Red Sea
coast, bringing a steady stream of manufactured imports
which relieved the Ishmaelites of the need to practise
their few clumsy crafts, while the adverse trade balance
was rectified by an elastic system of bankruptcy law. In
the remote provinces, beyond the reach of General
Gollancz, the Ishmaelites followed their traditional call-

ings of bandit, slave, or gentleman of leisure, happily
ignorant of their connexion with the town of which a
few of them, perhaps, had vaguely and incredulously
heard.

Occasional travelling politicians came to Jacksonburg,
were entertained and conducted round the town, and
returned with friendly reports. Big game hunters on safari
from the neighbouring dominions sometimes strayed into
the hinterland, and if they returned at all dined out for
years to come on the experience. Until a few months
before William Boot's departure no one in Europe knew
of the deep currents that were flowing in Ishmaelite
politics; nor did many people know of them in Ishmaelia.

It began during Christmas week with a domestic row
in the Jackson family. By Easter the city, so lately a
model of internal amity, was threatened by civil war.

A Mr Smiles Soum was reputed to lead the Fascists.
He was only one-quarter Jackson (being grandson in the
female line of President Samuel Smiles Jackson), and
three-quarters pure Ishmaelite. He was thus by right of
cousinship admitted to the public pay-roll, but he ranked
low in the family and had been given no more lucrative
post than that of Assistant Director of Public Morals.

Quarrels among the ruling family were not unusual,
particularly in the aftermath of weddings, funerals, and
other occasions of corporate festivity, and were normally
settled by a readjustment of public offices. It was common knowledge in the bazaars and drink-shops that Mr
Smiles was not satisfied with his post at the Ministry of
Public Morals, but it was a breach of precedent and,
some thought, the portent of a new era in Ishmaelite
politics, when he followed up his tiff by disappearing
from Jacksonburg and issuing a manifesto, which, it was
thought by those who knew him best, he could not con-
ceivably have composed himself.

The White Shirt movement which he called into being
had little in common with the best traditions of Ishmaelite politics. Briefly his thesis was this: the Jacksons were

effete, tyrannical, and alien; the Ishmaelites were a white
race who, led by Smiles, must purge themselves of the
Negro taint; the Jacksons had kept Ishmaelia out of the
Great War and thus deprived her of the fruits of victory;
the Jacksons had committed Ishmaelia to the control of
international Negro finance and secret subversive Negro
Bolshevism, by joining the League of Nations; they were
responsible for the various endemic and epidemic diseases
that ravaged crops, livestock, and human beings; all
Ishmaelites who were suffering the consequences of im-
prudence or ill-fortune in their financial or matrimonial
affairs were the victims of international Jacksonism;
Smiles was their Leader.

The Jacksons rose above it. Life in Ishmaelia went on
as before and the Armenian merchant in Main Street
who had laid in a big consignment of white cotton shirt-
ings found himself with the stuff on his hands. In Moscow, Harlem, Bloomsbury, and Liberia, however, keener
passions were aroused. In a hundred progressive weeklies
and Left Study Circles the matter was taken up and the
cause of the Jacksons restated in ideological form.

Smiles represented international finance, the subjuga-
tion of the worker, sacerdotalism; Ishmaelia was black,
the Jacksons were black, collective security and democ-
racy and the dictatorship of the proletariat were black.
Most of this was unfamiliar stuff to the Jacksons, but
tangible advantages followed. A subscription list was
opened in London and received support in chapels and
universities; wide publicity was given to the receipt in
Ishmaelia of three unused penny stamps addressed to the
President by 'A little worker's daughter in Bedford
Square.'

In the chief cities of Europe a crop of 'patriot consulates' sprang up devoted to counter-propaganda.

Newspaper men flocked to Jacksonburg. It was the
wet season when business was usually at a standstill;
everything boomed this year. At the end of August the
rains would stop. Then, everybody outside Ishmaelia

agreed, there would be a war. But, with the happy dis-
position of their race, the Ishmaelites settled down to
exploit and enjoy their temporary good fortune.

2

The Hotel Liberty, Jacksonburg, was folded in the
peace of Saturday afternoon, soon to be broken by the
arrival of the weekly train from the coast but, at the
moment, at four o'clock, serene and all-embracing. The
wireless station was shut and the fifteen journalists were
at rest. Mrs Earl Russell Jackson padded in stockinged
feet across the bare boards of the lounge looking for a
sizeable cigar-end, found one, screwed it into her pipe, and
settled down in the office rocking-chair to read her Bible.
Outside – and, in one or two places, inside – the rain fell
in torrents. It rang on the iron roof in a continuous, rest-
ful monotone; it swirled and gurgled in the channels it
had cut in the terrace outside; it seeped under the front
door in an opaque pool. Mrs Earl Russell Jackson puffed
at her pipe, licked her thumb, and turned a page of the
good book. It was very pleasant when all those noisy
white men were shut away in their rooms; quite like old
times; they brought in good money, these journalists –
heavens, what she was charging them! – but they were a
great deal of trouble; brought in a nasty kind of customer
too – Hindus, Ishmaelites from up country, poor whites
and near-whites from the town, police officers, the off-
scourings of the commercial cafés and domino saloons,
interpreters and informers and guides, not the kind of
person Mrs Earl Russell Jackson liked to see about her
hotel. What with washing and drinking and telephoning
and driving about in the mud in taxi-cabs and developing
films and cross-questioning her old and respectable pat-
rons, there never seemed a moment's peace.

Even now they were not all idle; in their austere trade
they had forfeited the arts of leisure.

Upstairs in his room, Mr Wenlock Jakes was spending

the afternoon at work on his forthcoming book *Under the Ermine*. It was to be a survey of the undercurrents of English political and social life. '*I shall never forget,*' he typed, '*the evening of King Edward's abdication. I was dining at the Savoy Grill as the guest of Silas Shock of the* New York Guardian. *His guests were well chosen, six of the most influential men and women in England; men and women such as only exist in England, who are seldom in the news but who control the strings of the national purse. On my left was Mrs Tiffin, the wife of the famous publisher; on the other side was Prudence Blank, who has been described to me as "the Mary Selena Wilmark of Britain"; opposite was John Titmuss whose desk at the* News Chronicle *holds more secrets of state than any ambassador's . . . big business was represented by John Nought, agent of the Credential Assurance Co. . . . I at once raised the question of the hour. Not one of that brilliant company expressed any opinion. There, in a nutshell, you have* England, *her greatness – and her littleness.*'

Jakes was to be paid an advance of 20,000 dollars for this book.

In the next room were four furious Frenchmen. They were dressed as though for the cinema camera in breeches, open shirts, and brand new chocolate-coloured riding boots cross-laced from top to bottom; each carried a bandolier of cartridges round his waist and a revolver-holster on his hip. Three were seated, the fourth strode before them, jingling his spurs as he turned and stamped on the bare boards. They were composing a memorandum of their wrongs.

We the undersigned members of the French Press in Ishmaelia, they had written, *protest categorically and in the most emphatic manner against the partiality shown against us by the Ishmaelite Press Bureau and at the discourteous lack of co-operation of our so-called colleagues . . .*

In the next room, round a little table, sat Shumble, Whelper, Pigge, and a gigantic, bemused Swede. Shumble

and Whelper and Pigge were special correspondents; the
Swede was resident correspondent to a syndicate of
Scandinavian papers – and more; he was Swedish Vice-
Consul, head surgeon at the Swedish Mission Hospital, and
proprietor of the combined Tea, Bible, and Chemist shop
which was the centre of European life in Jacksonburg; a
pre-crisis resident of high standing. All the journalists
tried to make friends with him; all succeeded; but they
found him disappointing as a news source.

These four were playing cards.

'I will go four no hearts,' said Erik Olafsen.

'You can't do that.'

'Why cannot I do that? I have no hearts.'

'But we explained just now . . .'

'Will you please be so kind and explain another
time?'

They explained; the cards were thrown in and the
patient Swede collected them in his enormous hand.
Shumble began to deal.

'Where's Hitchcock today?' he asked.

'He's on to something. I tried his door. It was locked.'

'His shutters have been up all day.'

'I looked through the keyhole,' said Shumble. 'You bet
he's on to something.'

'D'you think he's found the Fascist headquarters?'

'Wouldn't put it past him. Whenever that man dis-
appears you can be sure that a big story is going to break.'

'If you please, what is Hitchcock?' asked the Swede.

Mr Pappenhacker of *The Twopence* was playing with a
toy train – a relic of College at Winchester, with which
he invariably travelled. In his youth he had delighted to
address it in Latin alcaics and to derive Greek names for
each part of the mechanism. Now it acted as a sedative
to his restless mind.

The Twopence did not encourage habits of expensive
cabling. That day he had composed a long 'turnover' on
Ishmaelite conditions and posted it in the confidence

that, long before it arrived at London, conditions would
be unrecognizable.

Six other journalists of six nationalities were spending
their day of leisure in this hotel. Time lay heavily on
them. The mail train was due some time that evening to
relieve their tedium.

Fifty yards distant in the annexe, secluded from the
main block of the hotel by a water-logged garden, lay Sir
Jocelyn Hitchcock, fast asleep. The room was in half-
darkness; door and windows were barred. On the table,
before his typewriter, stood a primus stove. There was a
small heap of tins and bottles in the corner. On the walls
hung the official, wildly deceptive map of Ishmaelia; a
little flag in the centre of Jacksonburg marked Hitchcock's present position. He slept gently; his lips under the
fine, white moustache curved in a barely perceptible
smile of satisfaction. For reasons of his own he was in
retirement.

3

And the granite sky wept.

In the rainy season it was impossible to say, within
twelve hours or so, the time of the train's arrival. Today
it had made a good journey. It was still light when the
telephone rang in Mrs Jackson's office to tell her that it
had left the last station and would soon be there.
Instantly the Hotel Liberty came to life. The hall-boy
donned his peaked cap and set out with Mrs Jackson to
look for clients. Shumble, Whelper, and Pigge left their
game and put on their mackintoshes; the Frenchmen
struggled into Spahi capes. The six other journalists
emerged from their rooms and began shouting for taxis.
Paleologue, Jakes' jackal, reported for duty and was dis-
patched to observe arrivals. The greater and more for-
bidding part of the population of Jacksonburg was
assembled on the platform to greet William's arrival.

He and Corker had had a journey of constant annoyance. For three days they had been crawling up from the
fierce heat of the coast into the bleak and sodden highlands. There were four first-class compartments on their
train; one was reserved for a Swiss ticket collector. In
the remaining three, in painful proximity, sat twenty-
four Europeans, ten of whom were the advance party of
the Excelsior Movie-Sound News of America. The others
were journalists. They had lunched, dined, and slept at
the rest houses on the line. During the first day, when
they were crossing the fiery coastal plain, there had been
no ice; on the second night, in the bush, no mosquito
nets; on the third night, in the mountains, no blankets.
Only the little Swiss official enjoyed tolerable comfort.
At every halt fellow employees brought him refreshment
– frosted beer, steaming coffee, baskets of fruit; at the
restaurants there were special dishes for him and rocking-
chairs in which to digest them; there were bedrooms with
fine brass bedsteads and warm hip-baths. When Corker
and his friends discovered that he was only the ticket
collector they felt very badly about this.

Some time during the second day's journey the luggage
van became detached from the rest of the train. Its loss
was discovered that evening when the passengers wanted
their mosquito nets.

'Here's where that little beaver can be useful,' said
Corker.

He and William went to ask his help. He sat in his
rocking-chair smoking a thin, mild cheroot, his hands
folded over his firm little dome of stomach. They stood
and told him of their troubles. He thanked them and said
it was quite all right.

'Such things often happen. I always travel with all my
possessions in the compartment with me.'

'I shall write to the Director of the Line about it,' said
Corker.

'Yes, that is the best thing to do. It is always possible
that the van will be traced.'

'I've got some very valuable curios in my luggage.'

'Unfortunate. I am afraid it is less likely to be recovered.'

'D'you know who we are?'

'Yes,' said the Swiss, with a little shudder. 'Yes, I know.'

By the end of the journey Corker had come to hate this man. And his nettle-rash was on him again. He reached Jacksonburg in a bad humour.

Shumble, Whelper, and Pigge knew Corker; they had loitered together of old on many a doorstep and forced an entry into many a stricken home. 'Thought you'd be on this train,' said Shumble. 'Your name's posted for collect facilities in the radio station. What sort of trip?'

'Lousy. How are things here?'

'Lousy. Who's with you?'

Corker told him, adding: 'Who's here already?'

Shumble told him.

'All the old bunch.'

'Yes, and there's a highbrow yid from *The Twopence* – but we don't count him.'

'No, no competition there.'

'*The Twopence* isn't what you would call a *newspaper*, is it? . . . Still, there's enough to make things busy and there's more coming. They seem to have gone crazy about this story at home. Jakes is urgenting eight hundred words a day.'

'*Jakes here?* Well, there must be something in it.'

'Who's the important little chap with the beard?' – they looked towards the customs shed through which the Swiss was being obsequiously conducted.

'You'd think he was an ambassador,' said Corker bitterly.

The black porter of the Hotel Liberty interrupted them. Corker began to describe in detail his lost elephant. Shumble disappeared in the crowd.

'Too bad, too bad,' said the porter. 'Very bad men on railway.'

'But it was registered through.'

'Maybe he'll turn up.'

'Do things often get lost on your damned awful line?'

'Most always.'

All round them the journalists were complaining about their losses. '. . . Five miles of film,' said the leader of the Excelsior Movie-Sound News. 'How am I going to get *that* through the expenses department?'

'Very bad men on railway. They like film plenty – him make good fire.'

William alone was reconciled to the disaster; his cleft sticks were behind him; it was as though, on a warm day, he had suddenly shed an enormous, fur-lined motoring-coat.

4

So far as their profession allowed them time for such soft feelings, Corker and Pigge were friends.

'. . . It was large and very artistic,' said Corker, describing his elephant, 'just the kind of thing Madge likes.'

Pigge listened sympathetically. The bustle was over. William and Corker had secured a room together at the Liberty; their sparse hand-luggage was unpacked and Pigge had dropped in for a drink.

'What's the situation?' asked William, when Corker had exhausted his information – though not his resentment – about the shawls and cigarette boxes.

'Lousy,' said Pigge.

'I've been told to go to the front.'

'That's what we all want to do. But in the first place there isn't any front, and in the second place we couldn't get to it if there was. You can't move outside the town without a permit, and you can't get a permit.'

'Then what are you sending?' asked Corker.

'Colour stuff,' said Pigge, with great disgust. 'Preparations in the threatened capital, soldiers of fortune, mystery men, foreign influences, volunteers . . . there isn't any hard news. The Fascist headquarters are up-country somewhere in the mountains. No one knows where. They're going to attack when the rain stops in about ten days. You can't get a word out of the government. They won't admit there *is* a crisis.'

'What, not with Jakes and Hitchcock here?' said Corker in wonder. 'What's this President like, anyway?'

'Lousy.'

'Where is Hitchcock, by the way?'

'That's what we all want to know.'

5

'Where's Hitchcock?' asked Jakes.

Paleologue shook his head sadly. He was finding Jakes a hard master. For over a week he had been on his payroll. It seemed a lifetime. But the pay was fabulous and Paleologue was a good family man; he had two wives to support and countless queer-coloured children on whom he lavished his love. Until the arrival of the newspaper men — that decisive epoch in Ishmaelite social history — he had been dragoman and interpreter at the British Legation, on wages which — though supplemented from time to time by the sale to his master's colleagues of any waste-paper he could find lying around the Chancery — barely sufficed for the necessaries of his household; occasionally he had been able to provide amusement for bachelor attachés; occasionally he sold objects of native art to the ladies of the compound. But it had been an exiguous living. Now he was getting fifty American dollars a week. It was a wage beyond the bounds of his wildest ambition ... but Mr Jakes was very exacting and very peremptory.

'Who was on the train?'

'No one except the newspaper gentlemen and M. Giraud.'

'Who's he?'

'He is in the Railway. He went down to the coast with his wife last week, to see her off to Europe.'

'Yes, yes, I remember. That was the "panic-stricken refugees" story. No one else?'

'No, Mr Jakes.'

'Well, go find Hitchcock.'

'Yes, sir.'

Jakes turned his attention to his treatise. *The dominant member of the new cabinet,* he typed, *was colourful Kingsley Wood...*

6

Nobody knew exactly at what time or through what channels word went round the Hotel Liberty that Shumble had got a story. William heard it from Corker who heard it from Pigge. Pigge had guessed it from something odd in Shumble's manner during dinner – something abstracted, something of high excitement painfully restrained. He confided in Whelper, 'He's been distinctly rummy ever since he came back from the station. Have you noticed it?'

'Yes,' said Whelper. 'It sticks out a mile. If you ask me, he's got something under his hat.'

'Just what I thought,' said Pigge gloomily.

And before bedtime everyone in the hotel knew it.

The French were furious. They went in a body to their Legation. 'It is too much,' they said. 'Shumble is receiving secret information from the Government. Hitchcock, of course, is pro-British, and now, at a moment like this, when as Chairman of the Foreign Press Association he should forward our protest officially to the proper quarter, he has disappeared.'

'Gentlemen,' said the Minister. 'Gentlemen, it is Saturday night. No Ishmaelite official will be available until noon on Monday.'

'The Press Bureau is draconic, arbitrary, and venal; it is in the hands of a clique; we appeal for justice.'

'Certainly, without fail, on Monday afternoon' . . .

'We'll stay awake in shifts,' said Whelper, 'and listen. He may talk in his sleep.'

'I suppose you've searched his papers?'

'Useless. He never takes a note.' . . .

Paleologue threw up his hands hopelessly.

'Have his boy bring you his message on the way to the wireless station.'

'Mr Shumble always take it himself.'

'Well, go find out what it is. I'm busy.' . . .

Shumble sat in the lounge radiating importance. Throughout the evening everyone in turn sat by his side, offered him whisky and casually reminded him of past acts of generosity. He held his own counsel. Even the Swede got wind of what was going and left home to visit the hotel.

'Schombol,' he said, 'I think you have some good news, no?'

'Me?' said Shumble. 'Wish I had.'

'But forgive me, please, everyone say you have some good news. Now I have to telegraph to my newspapers in Scandinavia. Will you please tell me what your news is?'

'I don't know anything, Erik.'

'What a pity. It is so long since I sent my paper any good news.'

And he mounted his motor cycle and drove sadly away into the rain.

7

At a banquet given in his honour, Sir Jocelyn Hitchcock once modestly attributed his great success in life to the habit of 'getting up earlier than the other fellow'. But this was partly metaphorical, partly false, and in any case wholly relative, for journalists are as a rule late risers. It

was seldom that in England, in those night-refuges they
called their homes, Shumble, Whelper, Pigge, or Corker
reached the bathroom before ten o'clock. Nor did they in
Jacksonburg, for there was no bath in the Hotel Liberty;
but they and their fellows had all been awake since dawn.

This was due to many causes – the racing heart, nausea,
dry mouth and smarting eyes, the false hangover produced by the vacuous mountain air, to the same symptoms of genuine hangover, for, with different emotions,
they had been drinking deeply the evening before in the
anxiety over Shumble's scoop; but more especially to the
structural defects of the building. The rain came on sharp
at sunrise, and every bedroom had a leak somewhere in
its iron ceiling. And with the rain and the drips came the
rattle of Wenlock Jakes's typewriter as he hammered
away at another chapter of *Under the Ermine*. Soon the
bleak passages resounded with cries of 'Boy!' 'Water!'
'Coffee!'

As early arrivals Shumble, Whelper, and Pigge might,
like the Frenchmen, have had separate rooms, but they
preferred to live at close quarters and watch one another's
movements. The cinema men had had little choice.
There were two rooms left; the Contacts and Relations
Pioneer Co-ordinating Director occupied one; the rest
of the outfit had the other.

'Boy!' cried Corker, standing barefoot in a dry spot at
the top of the stairs. 'Boy!'

'Boy!' cried Whelper.

'Boy!' cried the Frenchmen. 'It is formidable. The
types attend to no one except the Americans and the
English.'

'They have been bribed. I saw Shumble giving money
to one of the boys yesterday.'

'We must protest.'

'I have protested.'

'We must protest again. We must demonstrate.'

'Boy! Boy! Boy!' shouted everyone in that hotel, but
nobody came.

In the annexe, Sir Jocelyn Hitchcock slipped a rain-coat over his pyjamas and crept like a cat into the bushes.

8

Presently Paleologue arrived to make his morning report to his master. He met Corker at the top of the stairs. 'You got to have boy for yourself in this country,' he said.

'Yes,' said Corker. 'It seems I ought.'

'I fix him. I find you very good boy from Adventist Mission, read, write, speak English, sing hymns, everything.'

'Sounds like hell to me.'

'Please?'

'Oh, all right, it doesn't matter. Send him along.'

In this way Paleologue was able to supply servants for all the new-comers. Later the passages were clustered with moon-faced mission-taught Ishmaelites. These boys had many responsibilities. They had to report their masters' doings, morning and evening, to the secret police; they had to steal copies of their masters' cables for Wenlock Jakes. The normal wage for domestic service was a dollar a week; the journalists paid five, but Paleologue pocketed the difference. In the meantime they formulated new and ingenious requests for cash in advance – for new clothes, funerals, weddings, fines, and entirely imaginary municipal taxes: whatever they exacted, Paleologue came to know about it and levied his share.

9

Inside the bedroom it was sunless, draughty, and damp; all round there was rattling and shouting and tramping and the monotonous splash and patter and gurgle of rain. Corker's clothing lay scattered about the room. Corker sat on his bed stirring condensed milk into his tea. 'Time you were showing a leg, old boy,' he said.

'Yes.'

'If you ask me, we were all a bit tight last night.'

'Yes.'

'Feeling lousy?'

'Yes.'

'It'll soon pass off when you get on your feet. Are my things in your way?'

'Yes.'

Corker lit his pipe and a frightful stench filled the room. 'Don't think much of this tobacco,' he said. 'Home grown. I bought it off a nigger on the way up. Care to try some?'

'No, thanks,' said William, and rose queasily from his bed.

While they dressed Corker spoke in a vein of unaccustomed pessimism. 'This isn't the kind of story I'm used to,' he said. 'We aren't getting anywhere. We've got to work out a routine, make contacts, dig up some news sources, jolly up the locals a bit. I don't feel settled.'

'Is that my toothbrush you're using?'

'Hope not. Has it got a white handle?'

'Yes.'

'Then I am. Silly mistake to make; mine's green . . . but, as I was saying, we've got to make friends in this town. Funny thing, I don't get that sense of popularity I expect.' He looked at himself searchingly in the single glass. 'Suffer much from dandruff?'

'Not particularly.'

'I do. They say it comes from acidity. It's a nuisance. Gets all over one's collar, and one has to look smart in our job. Good appearance is half the battle.'

'D'you mind if I have my brushes?'

'Not a bit, old boy, just finished with them . . . Between ourselves that's always been Shumble's trouble – bad appearance. But, of course, a journalist is welcome everywhere, even Shumble. That's what's so peculiar about this town. As a rule, there is one thing you can always count on in our job – popularity. There are plenty of disadvantages, I grant you, but you *are* liked and respected. Ring people up any hour of the day or night, butt into their homes uninvited, make them answer a string of damn fool questions when they want to do something else – they like it. Always a smile and the best of everything for the gentlemen of the press. But I don't feel it here. I damn well feel the exact opposite. I ask myself, are we known, loved, and trusted? and the answer comes back, "No Corker, you are not." '

There was a knock on the door, barely audible above the general hubbub, and Pigge entered.

'Morning, chaps. Cable for Corker. It came last night. Sorry it's been opened. They gave it to me and I didn't notice the address.'

'Oh, no?' said Corker.

'Well, there's nothing in it. Shumble had that query yesterday.'

Corker read: INTERNATIONAL GENDARMERIE PROPOSED PREVENT CLASH TEST REACTIONS UN-NATURAL. 'Crumbs, they must be short of news in London. What's Gendarmerie?'·

'A sissy word for cops,' said Pigge.

'Well, it's a routine job. I suppose I must do something about it. Come round with me . . . We may make some contacts,' he added, not very hopefully.

Mrs Earl Russell Jackson was in the lounge. 'Good morning, madam,' said Corker, 'and how are you today?'

'I aches,' said Mrs Jackson with simple dignity. 'I aches terrible all round the sit-upon. It's the damp.'

'The Press are anxious for your opinion upon a certain question, Mrs Jackson.'

'Aw, go ask somebody else. They be coming to mend that roof as quick as they can, and they can't come no quicker than that not for the Press, nor nobody.'

'See what I mean, old boy – not popular.' Then, turn-

ing again to Mrs Jackson with his most elaborate manner
he said, 'Mrs Jackson, you misunderstand me. This is a
matter of public importance. What do the women of
Ishmaelia think of the proposal to introduce a force of
international police?'

Mrs Jackson took the question badly. 'I will not stand
for being called a woman in my own house,' she said.
'And I've never had the police here but once, and that
was when I called them myself for to take out a customer
that went lunatic and hanged himself.' And she swept
wrathfully away to her office and her rocking-chair.

'Staunchly anti-interventionist,' said Corker. 'Doyen
of Jacksonburg hostesses bans police project as unwarrantable interference with sanctity of Ishmaelite home ...
but it's not the way I'm used to being treated.'

They went to the front door to call a taxi. Half a
dozen were waiting in the courtyard; their drivers, com-
pletely enveloped in sodden blankets, dozed on the front
seats. The hotel guard prodded one of them with the
muzzle of his gun. The bundle stirred; a black face
appeared, then a brilliant smile. The car lurched forward through the mud.

'The morning round,' said Corker. 'Where to
first?'

'Why not the station to ask about the luggage?'

'Why not? *Station*,' he roared at the chauffeur. 'Understand – station? Puff-puff.'

'All right,' said the chauffeur, and drove off at break-
neck speed through the rain.

'I don't believe this is the way,' said William.

They were bowling up the main street of Jacksonburg.
A strip of tarmac ran down the middle; on either side
were rough tracks for mules, men, cattle, and camels;
beyond these the irregular outline of the commercial
quarter; a bank, in shoddy concrete, a Greek provisions
store in timber and tin, the Café de La Bourse, the
Carnegie Library, the Ciné-Parlant, and numerous
gutted sites, relics of an epidemic of arson some years

back when an Insurance Company had imprudently set up shop in the city.

'I'm damn well sure it's not,' said Corker. 'Hi, you! *Station*, you black booby!'

The coon turned round in his seat and smiled. 'All right,' he said.

The car swerved off the motor road and bounced perilously among the caravans. The chauffeur turned back, shouted opprobriously at a camel driver and regained the tarmac.

Armenian liquor, Goanese tailoring, French stationery, Italian hardware, Swiss plumbing, Indian haberdashery, the statue of the first President Jackson, the statue of the second President Jackson, the American Welfare Centre, the latest and most successful innovation in Ishmaelite life – Popotakis's Ping-Pong Parlour – sped past in the rain. The mule trains plodded by, laden with rock salt and cartridges and paraffin for the villages of the interior.

'Kidnapped,' said Corker cheerfully. 'That's what's happened to us. What a story.'

But at last they came to a stop.

'This isn't the station, you baboon.'

'Yes, all right.'

They were at the Swedish Consulate, Surgery, Bible and Tea Shop. Erik Olafsen came out to greet them.

'Good morning. Please to come in.'

'We told this ape to drive us to the station.'

'Yes, it is a custom here. When they have a white man they do not understand, they always drive him to me. Then I can explain. But please to come in. We are just about to start our Sunday hymn singing.'

'Sorry, old boy. Have to wait till next Sunday. We've got work to do.'

'They say Schombol has some news.'

'Not really?'

'No, not really. I asked him . . . but you can do no work here on Sunday. Everything is closed.'

So they found. They visited a dozen barred doors and

returned disconsolately to luncheon. One native whom
they questioned fled precipitately at the word 'police'.
That was all they could learn about local reactions.

'We've got to give it up for the day,' said Corker.
'Reactions are easy, anyway. I'll just say that the government will co-operate with the democracies of the world
in any measures calculated to promote peace and justice,
but are confident in their ability to maintain order without foreign intervention. This is going to be a day of rest
for Corker.'

Shumble kept his story under his hat and furtively
filed a long message – having waited for a moment when
the wireless station was empty of his colleagues.

So the rain fell and the afternoon and evening were
succeeded by another night and another morning.

10

William and Corker went to the Press Bureau. Dr
Benito, the director, was away, but his clerk entered their
names in his ledger and gave them cards of identity. They
were small orange documents, originally printed for the
registration of prostitutes. The space for thumb-print was
now filled with a passport photograph, and at the head
the word 'journalist' substituted in neat Ishmaelite
characters.

'What sort of bloke is this Benito?' Corker asked.

'Creepy,' said Pigge.

They visited their Consulate, five miles out of town in
the Legation compound. Here, too, they had to register
and, in addition, buy a guinea stamp. The Vice-Consul
was a young man with untidy ginger hair. When he took
William's passport he stared and said, 'By God, you're
Beastly.'

William said, 'Moke.'

These two had known each other at their private school. Corker was nonplussed.

'What the hell are you doing here?' said the Vice-Consul.

'I'm supposed to be a journalist.'

'God, how funny. Come to dinner?'

'Yes.'

'Tonight?'

'Yes.'

'Grand.'

Outside the door Corker said, 'He might have asked me too. Just the kind of contact I can do with.'

II

At lunch-time that day Shumble's story broke.

Telegrams in Jacksonburg were delivered irregularly and rather capriciously, for none of the messengers could read. The usual method was to wait until half a dozen had accumulated and then send a messenger to hawk them about the most probable places until they were claimed. On precisely such an errand a bowed old warrior arrived in the dining-room of the Liberty and offered William and Corker a handful of envelopes. 'Righto, old boy,' said Corker, 'I'll take charge of these.' He handed the man a tip, was kissed on the knee in return, and proceeded to glance through the bag. 'One for you, one for me, one for everyone in the bunch.'

William opened his. It read: BADLY LEFT DISGUISED SOVIET AMBASSADOR RUSH FOLLOW BEAST. 'Will you please translate?'

'Bad news, old boy. Look at mine. ECHO SPLASHING SECRET ARRIVAL RED AGENT FLASH INTERVIEW UNNATURAL. Let's see some more.'

He opened six before he was caught. All dealt with the same topic. *The Twopence* said: KINDLY INVESTIGATE AUTHENTICITY ALLEGED SPECIAL SOVIET DELEGA-

TION STOP CABLE DEFERRED RATE. Jakes's was the
fullest: LONDON ECHO REPORTS RUSSIAN ENVOY
ORGANISER ARRIVED SATURDAY DISGUISED RAIL-
WAY OFFICIAL STOP MOSCOW DENIES STOP DENY
OR CONFIRM WITH DETAILS. Shumble's said:
WORLD SCOOP CONGRATULATIONS CONTINUE
ECHO.

'D'you see now?' said Corker.

'I think so.'

'It's that nasty bit of work with the beard. I knew he
was going to give us trouble.'

'But he *is* a railway employee. I saw him in the ticket
office today when I went to ask about my luggage.'

'Of course he is. But what good does that do us?
Shumble's put the story across. Now we've got to find a
red agent or boil.'

'Or explain the mistake.'

'Risky, old boy, and unprofessional. It's the kind of
thing you can do once or twice in a real emergency, but
it doesn't pay. They don't like printing denials – naturally. Shakes public confidence in the Press. Besides, it
looks as if we weren't doing our job properly. It would be
too easy if every time a chap got a scoop the rest of the
bunch denied it. And I will hand it to Shumble, it was
a pretty idea ... the beard helped, of course ... might have
thought of it myself if I hadn't been so angry.'

Other journalists were now crowding round claiming
their radiograms. Corker surrendered them reluctantly.
He had not had time to open Pigge's. 'Here you are, old
boy,' he said. 'I've been guarding it for you. Some of
these chaps might want to see inside.'

'You don't say,' said Pigge coldly. 'Well, they're
welcome.'

It was like all the rest. BOLSHEVIST MISSION
REPORTED OVERTAKEN CONTROL RUSH FACTS.

The hunt was up. No one had time for luncheon that
day. They were combing the town for Russians.

Wenlock Jakes alone retained his composure. He ate in

peace and then summoned Paleologue. 'We're killing this story,' he said. 'Go round to the Press Bureau and have Benito issue an official *démenti* before four o'clock. See it's posted in the hotel and in the wireless station. And put it about among the boys that the story's dead.

He spoke gravely, for he hated to kill a good story.

So the word went round.

A notice was posted in French and English at all the chief European centres of the capital.

It is categorically denied that there is any Russian diplomatic representative accredited to the Republic of Ishmaelia. Nor is there any truth in the report, spread by subversive interests, that a Russian national of any description whatever arrived in Jacksonburg last Saturday. The train was occupied exclusively by representatives of the foreign press and an employee of the Railway.

> GABRIEL BENITO
> *Minister of Foreign Affairs*
> *and Propaganda.*

The Press acted in unison and Shumble's scoop died at birth. William sent his first press message from Ishmaelia:
ALL ROT ABOUT BOLSHEVIK HE IS ONLY TICKET COLLECTOR ASS CALLED SHUMBLE THOUGHT HIS BEARD FALSE BUT IT'S PERFECTLY ALL RIGHT REALLY WILL CABLE AGAIN IF THERE IS ANY NEWS VERY WET HERE YOURS WILLIAM BOOT — and went out to dinner with the British Vice-Consul.

12

Jack Bannister, known at the age of ten as 'Moke', inhabited a little villa in the Legation compound. He and William dined alone at a candle-lit table. Two silent boys, in white gowns, waited on them. Bannister's pet —

but far from tame – cheetah purred beside the log fire.
There were snipe, lately bagged by the first secretary.
They drank some sherry, and some Burgundy and some
port, and, to celebrate William's arrival, a good deal
more port. Then they settled themselves in easy chairs
and drank brandy. They talked about school and the
birds and beasts of Ishmaelia. Bannister showed his col-
lection of skins and eggs.

They talked about Ishmaelia. 'No one knows if it's got
any minerals because no one's been to see. The map's a
complete joke,' Bannister explained. 'The country has
never been surveyed at all; half of it's unexplored. Why,
look here,' he took down a map from his shelves and
opened it. 'See this place, Laku. It's marked as a town of
some five thousand inhabitants, fifty miles north of Jacksonburg. Well, there never has been such a place. Laku
is the Ishmaelite for "I don't know." When the boundary
commission were trying to get through to the Sudan in
1898 they made a camp there and asked one of their boys
the name of the hill, so as to record it in their log. He said
"Laku," and they've copied it from map to map ever
since. President Jackson likes the country to look important in the atlases, so when this edition was printed he
had Laku marked good and large. The French once appointed a Consul to Laku when they were getting active
in this part of the world.'

Finally they touched on politics.

'I can't think why all you people are coming out here,'
said Bannister plaintively. 'You've no idea how it adds to
my work. The Minister doesn't like it, either. The F.O.
are worrying the life out of him.'

'But isn't there going to be a war?'

'Well, we usually have a bit of scrapping after the
rains. There's a lot of bad men in the hills. Gollancz
usually shoots up a few when he goes out after the taxes.'

'Is that all?'

'Wish we knew. There's something rather odd going
on. Our information is simply that Smiles had a row with

the Jacksons round about Christmas time and took to the hills. That's what everyone does out here when he gets in wrong with the Jacksons. We thought no more about it. The next thing we hear is from Europe that half a dozen bogus consulates have been set up and that Smiles has declared a Nationalist Government. Well, that doesn't make much sense. There never has been any Government in Ishmaelia outside Jacksonburg, and, as you see, everything is dead quiet here. But Smiles is certainly getting money from someone, and arms, too, I expect. What's more, we aren't very happy about the President. Six months ago he was eating out of our hand. Now he's getting quite standoffish. There's a concession to a British Company to build the new coast road. It was all settled but for the signing last November. Now the Ministry of Works is jibbing, and they say that the President is behind them. I can't say I like the look of things, and having all you journalists about doesn't make it any easier.'

'We've been busy all day with a lunatic report about a Russian agent who had come to take charge of the Government.'

'Oh!' said Bannister with sudden interest. 'They've got hold of that, have they? What was the story exactly?'

William told him.

'Yes, they've got it pretty mixed.'

'D'you mean to say there's any truth in it?'

Bannister looked diplomatic for a minute and then said, 'Well, I don't see any harm in your knowing. In fact, from what the Minister said to me today, I rather think he'd welcome a little publicity on the subject. There is a Russian here, name of Smerdyakev, a Jew straight from Moscow. He didn't come disguised as a ticket collector, of course. He's been here some time – in fact, he came up by the same train as Hitchcock and that American chap. But he's lying low, living with Benito. We don't quite know what he's up to; whatever it is, it doesn't suit H.M.G.'s book. If you want a really interesting story I should look into him.'

It was half an hour's drive, at this season, from the Legation quarter to the centre of the town. William sat in the taxi, lurching and jolting, in a state of high excitement. In the last few days he had caught something of the professional infection of Corker and his colleagues, had shared their consternation at Hitchcock's disappearance, had rejoiced quietly when Shumble's scoop was killed. Now *he* had something under his hat; a tip-off straight from headquarters, news of high international importance. His might be the agency which would avert or precipitate a world war; he saw his name figuring in future history books '. . . *the Ishmaelite crisis of that year whose true significance was only realized and exposed through the resources of an English journalist, William Boot . . .*' Slightly dizzy with this prospect, as with the wine he had drunk and the appalling rigours of the drive, he arrived at the Liberty to find the lights out in the lounge and all his colleagues in bed.

He woke Corker, with difficulty.

'For Christ's sake. You're tight. Go to bed, old boy.'

'Wake up, I've got a story.'

At that electric word Corker roused himself and sat up in bed.

William told him, fully and proudly, all that he had learned at dinner. When he had finished, Corker lay back again among the crumpled pillows. 'I might have known,' he said bitterly.

'But don't you see? This really is news. And we've got the Legation behind us. The Minister wants it written up.'

Corker turned over on his side.

'That story's dead,' he remarked.

'But Shumble had it all wrong. Now we've got the truth. It may make a serious difference in Europe.'

Corker spoke again with finality. 'Now go to bed, there's a good chap. No one's going to print your story after the way it's been denied. Russian agents are off the menu, old boy. It's a bad break for Shumble, I grant you.

He got on to a good thing without knowing – and the
false beard was a very pretty touch. His story was better
than yours all round, and we killed it. Do turn out the
light.'

13

In his room in the annexe Sir Jocelyn Hitchcock covered his key-hole with stamp-paper and, circumspectly,
turned on a little shaded lamp. He boiled some water
and made himself a cup of cocoa; drank it; then he went
to the map on the wall and took out his flag, considered
for a minute, hovering uncertainly over the unscaled
peaks and uncharted rivers of that dark terrain, finally
decided, and pinned it firmly in the spot marked as the
city of Laku. Then he extinguished his light and went
happily back to bed.

TWO

I

TUESDAY morning; rain at six; Jakes's typewriter at a
quarter past; the first cry of 'Boy' soon after.

'Boy,' shouted Corker. 'Where's *my* boy?'

'Your boy in plison,' said William's boy.

'Holy smoke, what's he been up to?'

'The police were angry with them,' said William's boy.

'Well, I want some tea.'

'All right. Just now.'

*The Archbishop of Canterbury who, it is well known, is behind
Imperial Chemicals* . . . wrote Jakes.

Shumble, Whelper, and Pigge awoke and breakfasted
and dressed, but they scarcely spoke. 'Going out?' said
Whelper at last.

'What d'you think?' said Shumble.

'Not sore about anything, are you?' said Pigge.
'What d'you think?' said Shumble, leaving the room.
'He's sore,' said Pigge.
'About his story,' said Whelper.
'Who wouldn't be?' said Pigge.

Sir Jocelyn made himself some cocoa and opened a tin of tongue. He counted the remaining stores and found them adequate.

Presently William and Corker set out to look for news.
'Better try the station first,' said Corker, 'just in case the luggage has turned up.'
They got a taxi.
'Station,' said Corker.
'All right,' said the driver, making off through the rain down main street.
'Oh, Christ, he's going to the Swede again.'
Sure enough, that was where they stopped.
'Good morning,' said Erik Olafsen. 'I am very delighted to see you. I am very delighted to see all my colleagues. They come so often. Almost whenever they take a taxi. Come in, please. Have you heard the news?'
'No,' said Corker.
'They are saying in the town that there was a Russian in the train on Saturday.'
'Yes, we've heard that one.'
'But it is a mistake.'
'You don't say.'
'Yes, indeed, it is a mistake. The man was a Swiss ticket collector. I know him many years. But please to come in.'
William and Corker followed their host into his office. There was a stove in the corner, and on the stove a big coffee pot; the smell of coffee filled the room. Olafsen poured out three cupfuls.
'You are comfortable at the Liberty, yes, no?'
'No,' said William and Corker simultaneously.

'I suppose not,' said Olafsen. 'Mrs Jackson is a very religious woman. She comes every Sunday to our musical evening. But I suppose you are not comfortable. Do you know my friends Shumble and Whelper and Pigge?'

'Yes.'

'They are very nice gentlemen, and very clever. They say they are not comfortable, too.'

The thought of so much discomfort seemed to overwhelm the Swede. He gazed over the heads of his guests with huge, pale eyes that seemed to see illimitable, receding vistas of discomfort, and himself a blinded and shackled Samson with his bandages and bibles and hot, strong coffee scarcely able to shift a pebble from the vast mountain which oppressed humanity. He sighed.

The bell rang over the shop-door. Olafsen leapt to his feet. 'Excuse,' he said, 'the natives steal so terribly.'

But it was not a native. William and Corker could see the new-comer from where they sat in the office. She was a white woman; a girl. A straggle of damp gold hair clung to her cheek. She wore red gum boots, shiny and wet, spattered with the mud of the streets. Her mackintosh dripped on the linoleum and she carried a half open, dripping umbrella, held away from her side; it was short and old; when it was new it had been quite cheap. She spoke in German, bought something, and went out again into the rain.

'Who was the Garbo?' asked Corker when the Swede came back.

'She is a German lady. She has been here some time. She had a husband but I think she is alone now. He was to do some work outside the city but I do not think she knows where he is. I suppose he will not come back. She lives at the German pension with Frau Dressler. She came for some medicine.'

'Looks as though she needed it,' said Corker. 'Well, we must go to the station.'

'Yes. There is a special train this evening. Twenty more journalists are arriving.'

'Christ!'

'For me it is a great pleasure to meet so many distinguished confrères. It is a great honour to work with them.'

'Decent bloke that,' said Corker, when they again drove off. 'You know, I never feel Swedes are really foreign. More like you and me, if you see what I mean.'

2

Three hours later Corker and William sat down to luncheon. The menu did not vary at the Liberty; sardine, beef, and chicken for luncheon; soup, beef, and chicken for dinner; hard, homogeneous cubes of beef, sometimes with Worcester Sauce, sometimes with tomato ketchup; fibrous spindles of chicken with grey-green dented peas.

'Don't seem to have any relish for my food,' said Corker. 'It must be the altitude.'

Everyone was in poor spirits; it had been an empty morning; the absence of Hitchcock lay heavy as thunder over the hotel, and there was a delay of fourteen hours in transmission at the wireless station, for Wenlock Jakes had been letting himself go on the local colour.

'The beef's beastly,' said Corker. 'Tell the manageress to come here...'

At a short distance Jakes was entertaining three blacks. Everyone watched that table suspiciously and listened when they could, but he seemed to be talking mostly about himself. After a time the boy brought them chicken.

'Where's that manageress?' asked Corker.

'No come.'

'What d'you mean "no come"?'

'Manageress say only journalist him go boil himself,' said the boy more explicitly.

'What did I tell you? No respect for the Press. *Savages.*'

They left the dining-room. In the lounge, standing on one foot and leaning on his staff, was the aged warrior who delivered the telegrams. William's read:

PRESUME YOUR STEPTAKING INSURE SERVICE
EVENT GENERAL UPBREAK.

'It's no good answering,' said Corker. 'They won't
send till tomorrow morning. Come to think of it,' he
added moodily, 'there's no point in answering anyway.
Look at mine.'

CABLE FULLIER OFTENER PROMPTLIER STOP
YOUR SERVICE BADLY BEATEN ALROUND LACKING
HUMAN INTEREST COLOUR DRAMA PERSONALITY
HUMOUR INFORMATION ROMANCE VITALITY.

'Can't say that's not frank, can you?' said Corker. 'God
rot 'em.'

That afternoon he took Shumble's place at the card
table. William slept.

3

The special train got in at seven. William went to meet
it; so did everyone else.

The Ishmaelite Foreign Minister was there with his
suite. ('Expecting a nob,' said Corker.) The Minister
wore a Derby hat and ample military cape. The station-
master set a little gilt chair for him where he sat like a
daguerrotype, stiffly posed, a Victorian worthy in nega-
tive, black face, white whiskers, black hands. When the
camera men began to shoot, his Staff scrambled to get to
the front of the picture, eclipsing their chief. It was all the
same to the camera men, who were merely passing the
time and had no serious hope that the portrait would be
of any interest.

At length the little engine came whistling round the
bend, wood sparks dancing over the funnel. It stopped
and at once the second and third class passengers –
natives and near-whites – tumbled on to the platform,
greeting their relatives with tears and kisses. The station
police got in among them, jostling the levantines and
whacking the natives with swagger-canes. The first class

passengers emerged more slowly; they had already acquired that expression of anxious resentment that was
habitual to whites in Jacksonburg. They were all, every
man-jack of them, journalists and photographers.

The distinguished visitor had not arrived. The Foreign
Minister waited until the last cramped and cautious figure
emerged from the first class coach; then he exchanged
civilities with the station-master and took his leave. The
station police made a passage of a kind, but it was only
with a struggle that he regained his car.

The porters began to unload, and take the registered
baggage to the customs shed. On the head of the fore-
most William recognized his bundle of cleft sticks; then
more of his possessions – the collapsible canoe, the mistletoe, the ant-proof wardrobes. There was a cry of delight
from Corker, at his side. The missing van had arrived.
Mysteriously it had become attached to the special train;
had in fact been transposed. Somewhere, in a siding at
one of the numerous stops down the line, lay the new-
comers' luggage. Their distress deepened but Corker was
jubilant and before dinner that evening introduced his
elephant to a place of prominence in the bedroom. He
also, in his good humour, introduced two photographers
for whom he had an affection.

'Tight fit,' they said.

'Not at all,' said Corker. 'Delighted to have your
company; aren't we, Boot?'

One of them took William's newly arrived camp bed;
the other expressed a readiness to 'doss down' on the floor
for the night. Everyone decided to doss down in the
Liberty. Mrs Jackson recommended other lodgings available from friends of hers in the town. But, 'No,' they said.
'We've got to doss down with the bunch.'

The bunch now overflowed the hotel. There were close
on fifty of them. All over the lounge and dining-room
they sat and stood and leaned; some whispered to one
another in what they took to be secrecy; others exchanged chaff and gin. It was their employers who paid

for all this hospitality, but the conventions were decently observed – 'My round, old boy.' 'No, no, my round' ... 'Have this one on me.' 'Well, the next is mine' – except by Shumble who, from habit, drank heartily, and without return wherever it was offered.

'What are you all here for?' asked Corker petulantly of a new-comer. 'What's come over them at home? What's supposed to be going on, anyway?'

'It's ideological. And we're only half of it. There's twenty more at the coast who couldn't get on the train. Weren't they sick at seeing us go? It's lousy on the coast.'

'It's lousy here.'

'Yes, I see what you mean ...'

There was not much sleep that night for anyone in William's room. The photographer who was dossing down found the floor wet and draughty and, as the hours passed, increasingly hard. He turned from side to side, lay flat on his back, then on his face. At each change of position he groaned as though in agony. Every now and then he turned on the light to collect more coverings. At dawn, when the rain began to drip near his head, he was dozing uneasily, fully dressed in overcoat and tweed cap, enveloped in every available textile, including the table-cloth, the curtains, and Corker's two oriental shawls. Nor did the other photographer do much better; the camp bed seemed less stable than William had supposed when it was sold to him; perhaps it was wrongly assembled; perhaps essential parts were still missing. Whatever the reason, it collapsed repeatedly and roused William's apprehensions of the efficacy of his canoe.

Early next morning he rang up Bannister and, on his advice, moved to Frau Dressler's pension. 'Bad policy, old boy,' said Corker, 'but since you're going I wonder if you'll take charge of my curios. I don't at all like the way Shumble's been looking at them.'

4

The Pension Dressler stood in a side street and had, at
first glance, the air rather of a farm than of an hotel. Frau
Dressler's pig, tethered by one hind trotter to the jamb
of the front door, roamed the yard and disputed the
kitchen scraps with the poultry. He was a prodigious
beast. Frau Dressler's guests prodded him appreciatively
on their way to the dining-room, speculating on how soon
he would be ripe for killing. The milch-goat was allowed
a narrower radius; those who kept strictly to the cause-
way were safe, but she never reconciled herself to this
limitation and, day in, day out, essayed a series of meteoric onslaughts on the passers-by, ending, at the end of her
rope, with a jerk which would have been death to an
animal of any other species. One day the rope would
break; she knew it, and so did Frau Dressler's guests.

There was also a gander, the possession of the night
watchman, and a three-legged dog, who barked furiously
from the mouth of a barrel and was said to have belonged
to the late Herr Dressler. Other pets came and went with
Frau Dressler's guests – baboons, gorillas, cheetahs, all
inhabited the yard in varying degrees of liberty and
moved uneasily for fear of the milch-goat.

As a consequence perhaps of the vigour of the livestock, the garden had not prospered. A little bed, edged
with inverted bottles, produced nothing except, annually,
a crop of the rank, scarlet flowers which burst out everywhere in Jacksonburg at the end of the rains. Two sterile
banana palms grew near the kitchens and between them
a bush of Indian hemp which the cook tended and kept
for his own indulgence. The night watchman, too, had a
little shrub, to whose seed-pods he attributed medical
properties of a barely credible order.

Architecturally, the Pension Dressler was a mess.
There were three main buildings disposed irregularly in
the acre of ground – single-storied, tin-roofed, constructed

of timber and rubble, with wooden verandas; the two larger were divided into bedrooms; the smallest contained the dining-room, the parlour, and the mysterious, padlocked room where Frau Dressler slept. Everything of value or interest in the pension was kept in this room, and whatever was needed by anyone – money, provisions, linen, back numbers of European magazines – could be produced, on demand, from under Frau Dressler's bed. There was a hut called the bathroom, where, after due notice and the recruitment of extra labour, a tin tub could be filled with warm water and enjoyed in the half darkness among a colony of bats. There was the kitchen not far from the other buildings, a place of smoke and wrath, loud with Frau Dressler's scolding. And there were the servants' quarters – a cluster of thatched cabins, circular, windowless, emitting at all hours a cosy smell of woodsmoke and curry; the centre of a voluble round of hospitality which culminated often enough in the late evening with song and rhythmical clapping. The night watchman had his own lair where he lived morosely with two wrinkled wives. He was a tough old warrior who passed his brief waking hours in paring the soles of his feet with his dagger or buttering the bolt of his ancient rifle.

Frau Dressler's guests varied as a rule from three to a dozen in number. They were Europeans, mostly of modest means and good character. Frau Dressler had lived all her life in Africa and had a sharp nose for the unfortunate. She had drifted here from Tanganyika after the war, shedding Herr Dressler, none knew exactly where or how, on her way. There were a number of Germans in Jacksonburg employed in a humble way in the cosmopolitan commercial quarter. Frau Dressler was their centre. She allowed them to come in on Saturday evenings after the guests had dined, to play cards or chess and listen to the wireless. They drank a bottle of beer apiece; sometimes they only had coffee, but there was no place for the man who tried to get away without spending. At Christmas there was a decorated tree and a party which the German Minister attended and subsidized. The missionaries always recommended Frau Dressler to visitors in search of cheap and respectable lodgings.

She was a large shabby woman of unbounded energy. When William confronted her she was scolding a group of native peasants from the dining-room steps. The meaning of her words was hidden from William; from the peasants also; for she spoke Ishmaelite, and bad Ishmaelite at that, while they knew only a tribal patois; but the tone was unmistakable. The peasants did not mind. This was a daily occurrence. Always at dawn they appeared outside Frau Dressler's dining-room and exposed their wares – red peppers, green vegetables, eggs, poultry, and fresh local cheese. Every hour or so Frau Dressler asked them their prices and told them to be off. Always at half-past eleven, when it was time for her to begin cooking the midday dinner, she made her purchases at the price which all parties had long ago decided would be the just one.

'They are thieves and impostors,' she said to William. 'I have been fifteen years in Jacksonburg and they still think they can cheat. When I first came I paid the most wicked prices – two American dollars for a lamb; ten cents a dozen for eggs. Now I know better.'

William said that he wanted a room. She received him cordially and led him across the yard. The three-legged dog barked furiously from his barrel; the milch-goat shot out at him like a cork from a popgun and, like it, was brought up short at the end of her string; the night watchman's gander hissed and ruffled his plumage. Frau Dressler picked up a loose stone and caught him square in the chest. 'They are playful,' she explained, 'particularly the goat.'

They gained the veranda, sheltered from rain and livestock. Frau Dressler threw open a door. There was luggage in the bedroom, a pair of woman's stockings across the foot of the bed, a woman's shoes against the wall. 'We have a girl here at the moment. She shall move.'

'Oh, but please . . . I don't want to turn anyone out.'

'She shall move,' repeated Frau Dressler. 'It's my best room. There is everything you want here.'

William surveyed the meagre furniture; the meagre, but still painfully superfluous ornaments. 'Yes,' he said. 'Yes, I suppose there is.'

A train of porters carried William's luggage from the Hotel Liberty. When it was all assembled, it seemed to fill the room. The men stood on the veranda waiting to be paid. William's own boy had absented himself on the first signs of packing. Frau Dressler drove them off with a few copper coins and a torrent of abuse. 'You had better give me anything of value,' she said to William, 'the natives are all villains.'

He gave her Corker's objects of art; she carried them off to her room and stored them safely under the bed. William began to unpack. Presently there was a knock outside. The door opened. William had his back to it. He was kneeling over his ant-proof chest.

'Please,' said a woman's voice. William turned round. 'Please may I have my things?'

It was the girl he had seen the day before at the Swedish mission. She wore the same mackintosh, the same splashed gumboots. She seemed to be just as wet. William jumped to his feet.

'Yes, of course, please let me help.'

'Thank you. There's not very much. But this one is heavy. It has some of my husband's things.'

She took her stockings from the end of the bed, ran her hand into one and showed him two large holes, smiled, rolled them into a ball and put them in the pocket of her raincoat. 'This is the heavy one,' she said, pointing to a worn leather bag. William attempted to lift it. It might have been full of stone. The girl opened it. It *was* full of stone. 'They are my husband's specimens,' she said. 'He wants me to be very careful of them. They are very important. But I don't think anyone could steal them. They are so heavy.'

William succeeded in dragging the bag across the floor. 'Where to?'

'I have a little room by the kitchen. It is up a ladder. It will be difficult to carry the specimens. I wanted Frau Dressler to keep them in her room but she did not want to. She said they were of no value. You see, she is not an engineer.'

'Would you like to leave them here?'

Her face brightened. 'May I? It would be very kind. That is what I hoped, but I did not know what you would be like. They said you were a journalist.'

'So I am.'

'The town is full of journalists, but I should not have thought you were one.'

'I can't think why Frau Dressler has put me in this room,' said William. 'I should be perfectly happy anywhere else. Did you want to move?'

'I must move. You see this is Frau Dressler's best room. When I came here it was with my husband. Then she gave us the best room. But now he is at work, so I must move. I do not want a big room now I am alone. But it would be very kind if you would keep our specimens.'

There was a suitcase which belonged to her. She opened it and threw in the shoes and other woman's things that lay about the room. When it was full she looked from it to the immense pile of trunks and crates and smiled. 'It is all I have,' she said. 'Not like you.'

She went over to the pile of cleft sticks. 'How do you use these?'

'They are for sending messages.'

'You're teasing me.'

'No, indeed I'm not. Lord Copper said I was to send my messages with them.'

The girl laughed. 'How funny. Have all the journalists got sticks like this?'

'Well, no; to tell you the truth I don't believe they have.'

'How funny you are.' Her laugh became a cough. She

sat on the bed and coughed until her eyes were full of tears. 'Oh, dear. It is so long since I laughed and now it hurts me ... What is in this?'

'A canoe.'

'Now I know you are teasing me.'

'Honestly, it's a canoe. At least they said it was at the shop. Look, I'll show you.'

Together they prised up the lid of the case and filled the floor with packing. At last they found a neat roll of cane and proofed canvas.

'It is a tent,' she said.

'No, a canoe. Look.'

They spread the canvas on the floor. With great difficulty they assembled the framework of jointed cane. Twice they had to stop when the girl's laughter turned to a paroxysm of coughing. At last it was finished and the little boat rose in a sea of shavings. 'It *is* a canoe,' she cried. 'Now I will believe you about those sticks. I will believe everything you tell me. Look, there are seats. Get in, quick, we must get in.'

They sat opposite one another in the boat, their knees touching. The girl laughed, clear and loud, and this time did not cough. 'But it's beautiful,' she said. 'And so *new*. I have not seen anything so new since I came to this city. Can you swim?'

'Yes.'

'So can I. I swim *very* well. So it will not matter if we are upset. Give me one of the message sticks and I will row you ...'

'Do I intrude?' asked Corker. He was standing on the veranda outside the window, leaning into the room.

'Oh, dear,' said the girl.

She and William left the boat and stood among the shavings.

'We were just trying the canoe,' William explained.

'Yes,' said Corker. 'Whimsical. How about trying the mistletoe?'

'This is Mr Corker, a fellow journalist.'

'Yes, yes. I see he is. I must go away now.'

'Not Garbo,' said Corker. 'Bergner.'

'What does he mean'?

'He says you are like a film star.'

'Does he? Does he really say that?' Her face, clouded at Corker's interruption, beamed. 'That is how I should like to be. Now I must go. I will send a boy for the valise.'

She went, pulling the collar of her raincoat close round her throat.

'Not bad, old boy, not bad at all. I will say you're a quick worker. Sorry to barge in on the tender scene, but there's trouble afoot. Hitchcock's story has broken. He's at the Fascist headquarters scooping the world.'

'Where?'

'Town called Laku.'

'But he can't be. Bannister told me there was no such place.'

'Well, there is now, old boy. At this very moment it's bang across the front page of the *Daily Brute* and it's where we are all going or know the reason why. A meeting of the Foreign Press Association has been called for six this evening at the Liberty. Feeling is running very high in the bunch.'

The German girl came back.

'Is the journalist gone?'

'Yes. I am sorry. I'm afraid he was rather rude.'

'Was he teasing, or did he really mean I was like a film star?'

'I'm sure he meant it.'

'Do you think so too?' She leaned on the dressing-table studying her face in the mirror. She pushed back a strand of hair that had fallen over her forehead; she turned her head on one side, smiled at herself, put out her tongue. 'Do you think so?'

'Yes, very like a film star.'

'I am glad.' She sat on the bed. 'What's your name?'

William told her.

'Mine is Kätchen,' she said. 'You must put away the boat. It is in the way and it makes us seem foolish.'

Together they dismembered the frame and rolled up the canvas. 'I have something to ask,' she said. 'What do you think is the value of my husband's specimens?'

'I'm afraid I have no idea.'

'He said they were very valuable.'

'I expect they are.'

'Ten English pounds?'

'I daresay.'

'More? Twenty?'

'Possibly.'

'Then I will sell them to you. It is because I like you. Will you give me twenty pounds for them?'

'Well, you know, I've got a great deal of luggage already. I don't know quite what I should do with them.'

'I know what you are thinking – that it is wrong for me to sell my husband's valuable specimens. But he has been away for six weeks now and he left me with only eight dollars. Frau Dressler is becoming most impolite. I am sure he would not want Frau Dressler to be impolite. So this is what we will do. You shall buy them and then, when my husband comes back and says they are worth more than twenty pounds, you will pay him the difference. There will be nothing wrong in that, will there? He could not be angry?'

'No, I don't think he could possibly be angry about that.'

'Good. Oh, you have made me glad that you came here. Please, will you give me the money now? Have you an account at the bank?'

'Yes.'

'Then write a cheque. I will take it to the bank myself. Then it will be no trouble to you.'

When she had gone, William took out his expense sheet and dutifully entered the single, enigmatic item: '*Stones* ... £20.'

5

Every journalist in Jacksonburg except Wenlock Jakes,
who had sent Paleologue to represent him, attended the
meeting of the Foreign Press Association; all, in their
various tongues, voluble with indignation. The hotel boys
pattered amongst them with trays of whisky; the air was
pungent and dark with tobacco smoke. Pappenhacker
was in the chair, wearily calling for order. 'Order, gentlemen. Attention, je vous en prie. Order, *please*. Messieurs,
gentlemen ...'

'Order, order,' shouted Pigge, and Pappenhacker's
voice was drowned in cries of silence.

'... secretary to read the minutes of the last meeting.'

The voice of the secretary could occasionally be heard
above the chatter. '... held at the Hotel Liberty ... Sir
Jocelyn Hitchcock in the chair ... resolution ... unanim-
ously passed ... protest in the most emphatic manner
against ... Ishmaelite government ... militates against
professional activities ...

'... objections to make or questions to ask about these
minutes ...'

The correspondents for *Paris-Soir* and *Havas* objected
and after a time the minutes were signed. Pappenhacker
was again on his feet. 'Gentlemen, in the absence of Sir
Jocelyn Hitchcock ...'

Loud laughter and cries of 'Shame.'

'Mr Chairman, I must protest that this whole question
is being treated with highly undesirable levity.'

'Translate.'

'On traite toute la question avec une légèreté in-
désirable.'

'Thank you, Mr Porter ...'

'If you pliss to spik Sherman ...'

'Italiano ... piacere ...'

'... tutta domanda con levità spiacevole ...'

'... Sherman ...'

'Gentlemen, gentlemen, Doctor Benito has consented to meet us here in a few minutes and it is essential that I know the will of the meeting, so that I can present our demands in proper form.'

At this stage one half of the audience – those nearest to William – were distracted from the proceedings by an altercation, unconnected with the business in hand, between two rival photographers.

'Did you call me a scab?'

'I did not, but I will.'

'You will?'

'Sure, you're a scab. Now what?'

'Call me a scab outside.'

'I call you a scab here.'

'Say that outside and see what you'll get.'

Cries of 'Shame' and 'Aw, pipe down.'

'. . . gravely affecting our professional status. We welcome fair and free competition . . . obliged to enforce coercive measures...'

'Go on, sock me one and see what you get.'

'I don't want to sock you one. *You* sock *me* first.'

'Aw, go sock him one.'

'Just you give me a poke in the nose and see what you'll get.'

'. . . Notre condition professionnelle. Nous souhaitons la bienvenue à toute la compétition égale et libre.'

'Nostra condizione professionale...'

'*You* poke *me* in the nose.'

'Aw, why can't you boys sock each other and be friendly?'

'Resolution before the meeting . . . protest against the breach of faith on the part of the Ishmaelite government and demand that all restrictions on their movements be instantly relaxed. I call for a show of hands on this resolution.'

'Mr Chairman, I object to the whole tone of this resolution.'

'May I propose the amendment that facilities be withheld from Sir Jocelyn Hitchcock until we have had time to get level with him?'

'... demand an enquiry into how and from whom he received his permission to travel and the punishment of the responsible official...'

'I protest, Mr Chairman, that the whole tone is peremptory and discourteous.'

'...The motion as amended reads...'

Then Doctor Benito arrived; he came from the main entrance and the journalists fell back to make way. It was William's first sight of him. He was short and brisk and self-possessed; soot-black in face, with piercing boot-button eyes; he wore a neat black suit; his linen and his teeth were brilliantly white, he carried a little black attaché case; in the lapel of his coat he wore the button of the Star of Ishmaelia, fourth class. As he passed through them the journalists were hushed; it was as though the head-mistress had suddenly appeared among an unruly class of schoolgirls. He reached the table, shook Pappenhacker by the hand and faced his audience with a flash of white teeth.

'Gentlemen,' he said, 'I will speak first in English' (the correspondents of *Havas* and *Paris-soir* began to protest) 'after that in French.

'I have a communication to make on the part of the President. He wishes to state first that he reserves for himself absolutely the right to maintain or relax the regulations he has made for the comfort and safety of the Press, either generally or in individual cases. Secondly, that, so far, no relaxation of these regulations has been made in any case. If, as is apparently believed, a journalist has left Jacksonburg for the interior it is without the Government's consent or knowledge. Thirdly, that the roads to the interior are at the moment entirely unfit for travel, provisions are impossible to obtain and travellers would be in danger from disaffected elements of the population. Fourthly, that he has decided, in view of the wishes of the foreign Press, to relax the restrictions he has hitherto made. Those wishing to do so, may travel to the interior. They must first apply formally to my bureau where the necessary passes will be issued and steps taken for their protection. That is all, gentlemen.'

He then repeated his message in accurate French, bowed and left the meeting in deep silence. When he had, gone, Pappenhacker said, 'Well, gentlemen, I think that concludes our evening's business in a very satisfactory manner,' but it was with a dissatisfied air that the journalists left the hotel for the wireless station.

'A triumph for the power of the Press,' said Corker. 'They caved in at once.'

'Yes,' said William.

'You sound a bit doubtful, old boy.'

'Yes.'

'I know what you're thinking of – something in Benito's manner. I noticed it too. Nothing you could actually take hold of, but he seemed kind of superior to me.'

'Yes,' said William.

They sent off their service messages. William wrote: THEY HAVE GIVEN US PERMISSION TO GO TO LAKU AND EVERYONE IS GOING BUT THERE IS NO SUCH PLACE AM I TO GO TOO SORRY TO BE A BORE BOOT.

Corker, more succinctly: PERMISSION GRANTED LAKUWARD.

That night the wireless carried an urgent message in similar terms from every journalist in Jacksonburg.

William and Corker returned to the Liberty for a drink. All the journalists were having drinks. The two photographers were clinking glasses and slapping one another on the shoulder. Corker reverted to the topic that was vexing him. 'What's that blackamoor got to be superior about?' he asked moodily, 'Funny that you noticed it too.'

6

Next day Corker brought William a cable: UNPRO-CEED LAKUWARD STOP AGENCIES COVERING PATRIOTIC FRONT STOP REMAIN CONTACTING CUMREDS STOP NEWS EXYOU UNRECEIVED STOP DAILY HARD NEWS ESSENTIALEST STOP REMEMBER RATES SERVICE CABLES ONE ETSIX PER WORD BEAST.

Kätchen stood at his elbow as he read it. 'What does it mean?' she asked.

'I'm to stay in Jacksonburg.'

'Oh, I am pleased.'

William answered the cable:

NO NEWS AT PRESENT THANKS WARNING ABOUT CABLING PRICES BUT IVE PLENTY MONEY LEFT AND ANYWAY WHEN I OFFERED TO PAY WIRELESS MAN SAID IT WAS ALL RIGHT PAID OTHER END RAINING HARD HOPE ALL WELL ENGLAND WILL CABLE AGAIN IF ANY NEWS.

Then he and Kätchen went to play ping-pong at Popotakis's.

7

The journalists left.

For three days the town was in turmoil. Lorries were chartered and provisioned; guides engaged; cooks and guards and muleteers and caravan boys and hunters, cooks' boys, guards' boys, muleteers' boys, ravanboys' boys and hunters' boys were recruited at unprecedented rates of pay; all over the city, in the offices and legations, resident Europeans found themselves deserted by their servants; seminarists left the missions, male-nurses the hospital, highly placed clerks their government departments to compete for the journalists' wages. The price of benzine was doubled overnight and rose steadily until the day of the exodus. Terrific deals were done in the bazaar in tinned foodstuffs; they were cornered by a Parsee and unloaded on a Banja, cornered again by an Arab, resold and rebought, before they reached the journalists' stores. Shumble bought William's rifle and sold a half share in it to Whelper. Everyone now emulated the costume of the Frenchmen; sombreros, dungarees, jodhpurs, sunproof shirts and bullet-proof waistcoats, holsters, bandoliers, Newmarket boots, cutlasses, filled the Liberty. The men of the Excelsior Movie-Sound News, sporting horsehair capes and silk shirts of native chieftains, made camp in the Liberty garden and photographed themselves at great length in attitudes of vigilance and repose. Paleologue made his pile.

There was an evening of wild indignation when it was falsely put around that Jakes had been lent a balloon by the Government for his journey. There was an evening of anxiety when, immediately before the day fixed for their departure, the journalists were informed that the passes for their journey had not yet received the stamp of the Ministry of the Interior. A meeting of the Press Association was hastily called; it passed a resolution of protest and dissolved in disorder. Late that evening Doctor Benito delivered the passes in person. They were handsome, unintelligible documents printed in Ishmaelite and liberally decorated with rubber stamps, initials, and patriotic emblems. Benito brought one to William at the Pension Dressler.

'I'm not going, after all,' William explained.

'Not going, Mr Boot? But your pass is here, made out in order.'

'Sorry if it has caused extra work, but my editor has told me to stay on here.'

An expression of extreme annoyance came over the affable, black face.

'But your colleagues have made every arrangement. It is very difficult for my bureau if the journalists do not keep together. You see, your pass to Laku automatically cancels your permission to remain in Jacksonburg. I'm afraid, Mr Boot, it will be necessary for you to go.'

'Oh, rot,' said William. 'For one thing there is no such place as Laku.'

'I see you are very well informed about my country, Mr Boot. I should not have thought it from the tone of your newspaper.'

William began to dislike Dr Benito.

'Well, I'm not going. Will you be good enough to cancel the pass and renew my permission for Jacksonburg?'

There was a pause; then the white teeth flashed in a smile.

'But of course, Mr Boot. It will be a great pleasure. I cannot hope to offer you anything of much interest during your visit. As you have seen, we are a very quiet little community. The Academic year opens at Jackson College. General Gollancz Jackson is celebrating his silver wedding. But I do not think any of these things are of great importance in Europe. I am sure your colleagues in the interior will find far more exciting matter for their dispatches. Are you sure nothing can make you alter your decision?'

'Quite sure.'

'Very well.' Dr Benito turned to go. Then he paused. 'By the way, have you communicated to any of your colleagues your uncertainty about the existence of the city of Laku?'

'Yes, but they wouldn't listen.'

'I suppose not. Perhaps they have more experience in their business. Good night.'

8

Next morning, at dawn, the first lorry started. It was shared by Corker and Pigge. They sat in front with the driver. They had been drinking heavily and late the night before and, in the grey light, showed it. Behind, among the crates and camp furniture, lay six torpid servants.

William rose to see them off. They had kept the time of their departure a secret. Everyone, the evening before, had spoken casually of 'making a move at tennish', but when William arrived at the Liberty the whole place was astir. Others beside Pigge and Corker conceived that an advantage might come from a few hours' start; all the others. Corker and Pigge were away first, by a negligible margin. One after another their colleagues took the road behind them. Pappenhacker drove a little two-seater he had bought from the British Legation. Many of the cars flew flags of Ishmaelia and of their countries. One lorry was twice the size of any other; it rode gallantly on six wheels; its sides were armour-plated; it had been purchased, irregularly and at enormous expense, from the War Office, and bore in vast letters of still tacky paint the inscription: *EXCELSIOR MOVIE-SOUND EXPEDITIONARY UNIT TO THE ISHMAE-LITE IDEOLOGICAL FRONT.*

During these latter days the rains had notably declined, giving promise of spring. The clouds lay high over the town, revealing a wider horizon, and, as the cavalcade disappeared from view, the road to Laku lay momentarily bathed in sunshine. William waved them good-bye from the steps of the Jackson memorial and turned back towards the Pension Dressler, but as he went the sky darkened and the first drops began to fall.

He was at breakfast when his boy reported: 'All come back.'

'Who?'

'All newspaper fellows come back. Soldiers catch 'em one time and take 'em plison.'

William went out to investigate.

Sure enough the lorries were lined up outside the police station, and inside, each with an armed guard, sat the journalists. They had found the barricades of the town shut against them; the officer in charge had not been warned to expect them; he had been unable to read their passes and they were all under arrest.

At ten when Doctor Benito began his day's routine at the Press Bureau, he received them apologetically but blandly. 'It is a mistake,' he said. 'I regret it infinitely. I understood that you proposed to start at ten. If I had known that you intended to start earlier I would have made the necessary arrangements. The night-guard have orders to let no one through. You will now find the day-guard on duty. They will present arms as you pass. I have given special instructions to that effect. Good-bye, gentlemen, and a good journey.'

Once more the train of lorries set off; rain was now falling hard. Corker and Pigge still led; Wenlock Jakes came last in a smart touring car. William waved: the populace whistled appreciatively; at the gates of the city the guard slapped the butts of their carbines. William once more turned to the Pension Dressler; the dark clouds opened above him; the gutters and wet leaves sparkled in sunlight and a vast, iridescent fan of colour, arc beyond arc of splendour, spread across the heavens. The journalists had gone, and a great peace reigned in the city.

THREE

I

KÄTCHEN was smoking in a long chair on the veranda. 'Lovely,' she said. 'Lovely. In a few days now the rains will be over.'

She had been early to the hairdresser and, in place of the dank wisps of yesterday, her golden head was a tuft of curls. She had a new dress; she wore scarlet sandals and her toe-nails were painted to match them. 'The dress came yesterday,' she said. 'There is an Austrian lady who sewed it for me. I wanted to put it on last night, when we went to play ping-pong, but I thought you would like it best when my hair was done. You *do* like it?'

'Immensely.'

'And I got this,' she said. 'It is French.' She showed him an enamelled vanity case. 'The hairdresser sold it to me ... From Paris. Lipstick, powder, looking-glass, comb, cigarettes. Pretty?'

'Very pretty.'

'And now Frau Dressler is angry with me again, because of her bill. But I don't care. What business of hers is it if I sell my husband's specimens? I offered them to her and she said they were not valuable. I don't care, I don't care. Oh, William, I am so happy. Look at the rainbow. It gets bigger and bigger. Soon there will be no room in the sky for it. Do you know what I should like to do today? I should like us to take a motor-car and drive into the hills. We could get some wine and, if you ask her, Frau Dressler will make a hamper. Do not say it is for me. Let us get away from this city for a day ...'

Frau Dressler packed a hamper; Doctor Benito stamped a pass; Paleologue arranged for the hire of a motor-car. At midday William and Kätchen drove off towards the hills.

'Kätchen, I love you. Darling, darling Kätchen, I love you ...'

He meant it. He was in love. It was the first time in twenty-three years; he was suffused and inflated and tipsy with love. It was believed at Boot Magna, and jocularly commented upon from time to time, that an attachment existed between him and a neighbouring Miss Caldicote; it was not so. He was a stranger alike to the bucolic jaunts of the hayfield and the dark and costly expeditions of his Uncle Theodore. For twenty-three years he had remained celibate and heart-whole; land-bound. Now for the first time he was far from shore, submerged among deep waters, below wind and tide, where huge trees raised their spongy flowers and monstrous things without fur or feather, wing or foot, passed silently, in submarine twilight. A lush place.

2

Sir Jocelyn Hitchcock threw open the shutters of his room and welcomed the sunshine. He thrust his head out of the window and called loudly for attention. They brought him a dozen steaming jugs and filled his tub. He bathed and shaved and rubbed his head with eau de quinine until his sparse hairs were crowned with foam and his scalp smarted and glowed. He dressed carefully, set his hat at an angle and sauntered to the wireless station.

CONSIDER ISHMAELITE STORY UP-CLEANED, he wrote, SUGGEST LEAVING AGENCIES COVER UP-FOLLOWS. Then he returned to the hotel and ate a late breakfast of five lightly boiled eggs.

He packed his luggage and waited for his reply. It came before sundown, for there was little traffic at the wireless station that day. PROCEED LUCERNE COVER ECONOMIC NON-INTERVENTION CONGRESS. There was a train to the coast that night. He paid his bill at the hotel and, with three hours to spare, took a walk in the town.

The promise of the morning had been barely fulfilled. At noon the rain had started again; throughout the afternoon had streamed monotonously, and now, at sundown, ceased; for a few minutes the shoddy roofs were ablaze with scarlet and gold.

With loping steps, Erik Olafsen came down the street

towards Sir Jocelyn; his face was uplifted to the glory of the sunset and he would have walked blandly by. It was Sir Jocelyn's first impulse to let him; then, changing his mind, he stepped forward and greeted him.

'Sir Hitchcock, you are back so soon. It will disappoint our colleagues to find you not at Laku. You have had many interests in your journey, yes?'

'Yes,' said Sir Jocelyn briefly.

Across the street, deriding the splendour of the sky, there flashed the electric sign of Popotakis's Ping Pong Parlour while, from his door, an ancient French two-step, prodigiously amplified, heralded the day's end.

'Come across and have a drink,' said Sir Jocelyn.

'Not to drink, thank you so much, but to hear the interests of your journey. I was told that Laku was no such place, no?'

'No,' said Sir Jocelyn.

Even as they crossed the street, the sky paled.

Popotakis had tried a cinema, a dance hall, baccarat, and miniature golf; now he had four ping-pong tables. He had made good money, for the smart set of Jacksonburg were always hard put to get through the rainy season; the polyglot professional class had made it their rendezvous; even attachés from the legations and younger members of the Jackson family had come there. Then for a few delirious days it had been overrun with journalists; prices had doubled, quarrels had raged, the correspondent of the *Methodist Monitor* had been trussed with a net and a photographer had lost a tooth. Popotakis's old clients melted away to other, more seemly resorts; the journalists had broken his furniture and insulted his servants and kept him awake till four in the morning, but they had drunk his home-made whisky at an American dollar a glass and poured his home-made champagne over the bar at ten dollars a bottle. Now they had all gone and the place was nearly empty. Only William and Kätchen sat at the bar. Popotakis had some genuine sixty per cent absinthe; that is what they were drinking. They were in a sombre mood, for the picnic had been a failure.

Olafsen greeted them with the keenest pleasure. 'So you have not gone with the others, Boot? And you are now friends with Kätchen? Good, good. Sir Hitchcock, to present my distinguished colleague Boot of the London *Beast*.'

Sir Jocelyn was always cordial to fellow journalists, however obscure. 'Drink up,' he said. 'And have another. Sending much?'

'Nothing,' said William, 'nothing seems to happen.'

'Why aren't you with the bunch? You're missing a grand trip. Mind you, I don't know they'll get much of a story at Laku. Shouldn't be surprised if they found the place empty already. But it's a grand trip. Scenery, you know, and wild life. What are you drinking, Eriksen?'

'Olafsen. Thank you, some grenadine. That absinthe is very dangerous. It was so I killed my grandfather.'

'You killed your grandfather, Erik?'

'Yes, did you not know? I thought it was well known. I was very young at the time and had taken a lot of sixty per cent. It was with a chopper.'

'May we know, sir,' asked Sir Jocelyn sceptically, 'how old you were when this thing happened?'

'Just seventeen. It was my birthday; that is why I had so much drunk. So I came to live in Jacksonburg, and now I drink this.' He raised, without relish, his glass of crimson syrup.

'Poor man,' said Kätchen.

'Which is poor man? Me or the grandfather?'

'I meant you.'

'Yes, I am poor man. When I was very young I used often to be drunk. Now it is very seldom. Once or two time in the year. But always I do something I am very sorry for. I think, perhaps, I shall get drunk tonight,' he suggested, brightening.

'No, Erik, not tonight.'

'No? Very well, not tonight. But it will be soon. It is very long since I was drunk.'

The confession shed a momentary gloom. All four sat in silence. Sir Jocelyn stirred himself and ordered some more absinthe.

'There were parrots, too,' he said with an effort. 'All along the road to Laku. I never saw such parrots – green and red and blue and – and every colour you can think of, talking like mad. And gorillas.'

'Sir Hitchcock,' said the Swede, 'I have lived in this country ever since I killed my grandfather and I never saw or heard of a gorilla.'

'I saw six,' said Sir Jocelyn stoutly, 'sitting in a row.'

The Swede rose abruptly from his stool. 'I do not understand,' he said. 'So I think I shall go.' He paid for his grenadine and left them at the bar.

'Odd chap that,' said Sir Jocelyn. 'Moody. Men get like that when they live in the tropics. I daresay it was all a delusion about his grandfather.'

There was food of a kind procurable at Popotakis's Ping Pong Parlour. 'Will you dine with me here,' asked Sir Jocelyn, 'as it's my last evening?'

'Your last evening?'

'Yes, I've been called away. Public interest in Ishmaelia is beginning to wane.'

'But nothing has happened yet.'

'Exactly. There was only one story for a special – my interview with the Fascist leader. Of course, it's different with the Americans – fellows like Jakes. They have a different sense of news from us – personal stuff, you know. The job of an English special is to spot the story he wants, get it – then clear out and leave the rest to the agencies. The war will be ordinary routine reporting. Fleet Street have spent a lot on this already. They'll have to find something to justify it and then they'll draw in their horns. You take it from me. As soon as they get anything that smells like front page, they'll start calling back their men. Personally I'm glad to have got my work over quick. I never did like the place.'

They dined at Popotakis's and went to the station to see Hitchcock off. He had secured the single sleeping car which was reserved for official visitors and left in great good humour. 'Good-bye, Boot, remember me to them at the *Beast*. I wonder how they are feeling now about having missed that Laku story?'

The train left, and William found himself the only special correspondent in Jacksonburg.

3

He and Kätchen drove back. Kätchen said: 'Frau Dressler was very angry again this afternoon.'

'Beast.'

'William, you *do* like me.'

'I love you. I've told you so all day.'

'No, you must not say that. My husband would not allow it. I mean, as a friend.'

'No, not as a friend.'

'Oh, dear, you make me so sad.'

'You're crying.'

'No.'

'You are.'

'Yes. I am so sad you are not my friend. Now I cannot ask you what I wanted.'

'What?'

'No, I cannot ask you. You do not love me as a friend. I was so lonely, and when you came I thought everything was going to be happy. But now it is spoiled. It is so easy for you to think here is a foreign girl and her husband is away. No one will mind what happens to her . . . No, you are not to touch me. I hate you.'

William sat back silently in his corner.

'William.'

'Yes.'

'He is not going to the Pension Dressler. It is to the Swede again.'

'I don't care.'

'But I am so tired.'

'So am I.'

'Tell him to go to the Pension Dressler.'

'I told him. It's no good.'

'Very well. If you wish to be a beast . . .'

The Swede was still up, mending with patient, clumsy hands the torn backs of his hymn books. He put down the paste and scissors and came out to direct the taxi driver.

'It was not true what Sir Hitchcock said. There are no gorillas in this country. He cannot have seen six. Why does he say that?' His broad forehead was lined and his eyes wide with distress and bewilderment. 'Why did he say that, Boot?'

'Perhaps he was joking.'

'Joking? I never thought of that. Of course, it was a joke. Ha, ha, ha. I am so glad. Now I understand. A joke.' He returned to his lighted study, laughing with relief and amusement. As he settled himself to work once more, he hummed a tune. One by one the tattered books were set in order, restored and fortified, and the Swede chuckled over Sir Jocelyn's joke.

William and Kätchen drove home in complete silence. The night-watchman flung open the gates and raised his spear in salute. While William was wrangling with the taxi driver, Kätchen slipped away to her own room. William undressed and lay among his heaps of luggage. His anger softened and turned to shame, then to a light melancholy; soon he fell asleep.

4

There was one large table in the Pension dining-room. Kätchen was sitting at its head, alone; she had pushed the plate away and put her coffee in its place between her

bare elbows; she crouched over it, holding the cup in
both hands; the saucer was full and drops of coffee formed
on the bottom of the cup and splashed like tears. She did
not answer when William wished her good morning. He
went to the door and called across to the kitchen for his
breakfast. It was five minutes in coming, but still she did
not speak or leave the table. Frau Dressler bustled
through, on the way to her room, and returned laden
with folded sheets. She spoke to Kätchen gruffly in German. Kätchen nodded. The cup dripped on the tablecloth. She put her hand down to hide the spot, but Frau
Dressler saw it and spoke again. Kätchen began to cry;
she did not raise her head and the tears fell, some in the
cup, some in the saucer, some on the tablecloth.

William said, 'Kätchen . . . Kätchen, darling, what's the
matter?'

'I have no handkerchief.'

He gave her his. 'What did Frau Dressler say?'

'She was angry because I have made the tablecloth
dirty. She said why did I not help with the washing?' She
dabbed her face and the tablecloth with William's
handkerchief.

'I am afraid I was very disagreeable last night.'

'Yes, why were you like that? It had been so nice until
then. Perhaps it was the Pernod. Why were you like that,
William?'

'Because I love you.'

'I have told you you are not to say that. . . . My husband
has been away for six weeks. When he left he said he
would return in a month or at the most six weeks. It is
six weeks this morning. I am very worried what may have
become of him . . . I have been with him for two years
now.'

'Kätchen, there's something I must ask you. Don't be
angry. It's very important to me. Is he really your
husband?'

'But of course he is. It is just that he has gone away for
his work.'

'I mean, were you married to him properly in church?'

'No, not in church.'

'At a government office, then?'

'No. You see, it was not possible because of his other wife in Germany.'

'He has another wife, then?'

'Yes, in Germany, but he hates her. I am his *real* wife.'

'Does Frau Dressler know about the other wife?'

'Yes, that is why she treats me so impolitely. The German consul told her after my husband had gone away. There was a question of my papers. They would not register me at the German consulate.'

'But you are German?'

'My husband is German, so I am German, but there is a difficulty with my papers. My father is Russian and I was born in Budapest.'

'Is your mother German?'

'Polish.'

'Where is your father now?'

'I think he went to South America to look for my mother after she went away. But why do you ask me so many questions when I am unhappy? You are worse than Frau Dressler. It is not your tablecloth. You do not have to pay if it is dirty.'

She left William alone at the breakfast table.

5

Twelve miles out of town Corker and Pigge were also at breakfast.

'I never slept once,' said Corker. 'Not a wink, the whole night. Did you hear the lions?'

'Hyenas,' said Pigge.

'Hyenas laugh. These were lions or wolves. Almost in the tents.' They sat beside their lorry drinking soda water and eating sardines from a tin. The cook and the cook's boy, the driver and the driver's boy, Corker's boy and

Pigge's boy, were all heavily asleep in the lorry under a pile of blankets and tarpaulin.

'Six black bloody servants and no breakfast,' said Corker bitterly.

'They were up all night making whoopee round the fire. Did you hear them?'

'Of course I heard them. Singing and clapping. I believe they'd got hold of our whisky. I shouted to them to shut up, and they said, "Must have fire. Many bad animals."'

'Yes, hyenas.'

'Lions.'

'We've got to get the lorry out of the mud, somehow. I suppose the rest of the bunch are half-way to Laku by now.'

'I didn't think it of them,' said Corker, bitterly. 'Going past us like that without a bloody word. Shumble I can understand, but Whelper and the Excelsior Movie-News bunch. . . . With that great lorry of theirs they could have towed us out in five minutes. What have *they* got to be competitive about?... and those two photographers I gave up half my room to at the hotel – just taking a couple of shots of us and then driving off. Two white men, alone, in a savage country . . . it makes one despair of human nature...'

The preceding day had been one of bitter experience. Within a quarter of a mile of the city the metalled strip had come to an end and the road became a mud-track. For four hours the lorry had crawled along at walking pace, lurching, sticking, and skidding; they had forged through a swollen stream which washed the under-carriage; they had been thrown from side to side of the cab; the binding of the stores had broken and Pigge's typewriter had fallen into the mud behind them to be retrieved, hopelessly injured, by the grinning cook's boy. It had been an abominable journey.

Presently the track had lost all semblance of unity and split into a dozen diverging and converging camel paths, winding at the caprice of the beasts who had made them, among thorn and rock and anthills in a colourless, muddy plain. Here, without warning, the back wheels had sunk to their axles, and here the lorry had stayed while the caravan it had led disappeared from view. Tents had been pitched and the fire lighted. The cook, opening some tins at random, had made them a stew of apricots and curry powder and turtle soup and tunny fish, which in the final analysis had tasted predominantly of benzine.

In bitter cold they had sat at the tent door, while Pigge tried vainly to repair his typewriter, and Corker, struck with nostalgia, composed a letter to his wife; at eight they had retired to their sleeping-bags and lain through the long night while their servants caroused outside.

Corker surveyed the barren landscape and the gathering storm clouds, the mud-bound lorry, the heap of crapulous black servants, the pasty and hopeless face of Pigge, the glass of soda-water and the jagged tin of fish. 'It makes one despair of human nature,' he said again.

6

It was some days since William had seen Bannister, so he drove out that morning to the Consulate. There was the usual cluster of disconsolate Indians round the door. Bannister sent them away, locked the office and took William across the garden to his house for a drink.

'Looking for news?' he asked. 'Well, the Minister's got a tea-party on Thursday. D'you want to come?'

'Yes.'

'I'll get them to bung you a card. It's the worst day of the year for us. Everyone in the place comes who's got a clean collar. It's the public holiday in honour of the end of the rainy season and it always pours.'

'D'you think you could ask a German girl at my boarding-house? She's rather lonely.'

'Well, frankly, Lady G. isn't very keen on lonely
German girls. But I'll see. Is that why you didn't go off
on that wild goose chase to Laku? You're wise. I
shouldn't be at all surprised if there weren't some rather
sensational happenings here in a day or two.'

'The war?'

'No, there's nothing in that. But things are looking
queer in the town. I can't tell you more, but if you want
a hint look out for that Russian I told you about and
watch your friend Doctor Benito. What's the girl's
name?'

'Well, I'm not sure about her surname. There's some
difficulty about her papers.'

'Doesn't sound at all Lady G.'s cup of tea. Is she
pretty?'

'Lovely.'

'Then I think you can count her off the Legation list.
Paleologue's been trying to interest me in a lovely
German girl for weeks. I expect it's her. Bring her along
to dinner here one evening.'

Kätchen was delighted with the invitation. 'But we
must buy a dress,' she said. 'There is an Armenian lady
who has a very pretty one – bright green. She has never
worn it because she bought it by mail and she has grown
too fat. She asked fifty American dollars. I think if she
were paid at once it would be cheaper.' She had become
cheerful again. 'Wait,' she said, 'I have something to
show you.'

She ran to her room and returned with a sodden
square of bandana silk. 'Look, I *have* been doing some
washing after all. It is your handkerchief. I do not need
it now. I have stopped crying for today. We will go and
play ping-pong and then see the Armenian lady's green
dress.'

After luncheon Bannister telephoned. 'We've had a
cable about you from London.'

'Good God, why?'

'*The Beast* have been worrying the F.O. Apparently they think you've been murdered. Why don't you send them some news?'

'I don't know any.'

'Well, for heaven's sake invent some. The Minister will go crazy if he has any more bother with the newspapers. We get about six telegrams a day from the coast. Apparently there's a bunch of journalists there trying to get up and the Ishmaelite frontier authorities won't let them through. Two of them are British, unfortunately. And now the Liberals are asking questions in the House of Commons and are worrying his life out as it is about some infernal nonsense of a concentration of Fascist troops at Laku.'

William returned to his room and sat for a long time before his typewriter. It was over a week now since he had communicated with his employers, and his failure weighed heavily on him. He surveyed the events of the day, of all the last days. What would Corker have done?

Finally, with one finger, he typed a message. PLEASE DONT WORRY QUITE SAFE AND WELL IN FACT RATHER ENJOYING THINGS WEATHER IMPROVING WILL CABLE AGAIN IF THERE IS ANY NEWS YOURS BOOT.

7

It was late afternoon in London; at Copper House secretaries were carrying cups of tea to the more leisured departments; in Mr Salter's office there was tension and consternation.

'*Weather improving*,' said Mr Salter. '*Weather improving*. He's been in Jacksonburg ten days, and all he can tell us is that the weather is improving.'

'I've got to write a first leader on the Ishmaelite question,' said the first leader-writer. 'Lord Copper says so.

I've got to wring the withers of the Government. What do I know about it? What have I got to go on? What are special correspondents for? Why don't you cable this Boot and wake him up?'

'How many times have we cabled Boot?' asked the foreign editor.

'Daily for the first three days, Mr Salter,' said his secretary. 'Then twice a day. Three times yesterday.'

'You see.'

'And in the last message we mentioned *Lord Copper's name*,' added the secretary.

'I never felt Boot was really suited to the job,' said Mr Salter mildly. 'I was very much surprised when he was chosen. But he's all we've got. It would take three weeks to get another man out there, and by that time anything may have happened.'

'Yes, the weather may have got still better,' said the first leader-writer, bitterly. He gazed out of the window; it opened on a tiled, resonant well; he gazed at a dozen drain pipes; he gazed straight into the office opposite where the Art Editor was having tea; he gazed up to the little patch of sky and down to the concrete depths where a mechanic was washing his neck at a cold tap: he gazed with eyes of despair.

'I have to denounce the vacillation of the government in the strongest terms,' he said. 'They fiddle while Ishmaelia burns. A spark is set to the corner-stone of civilization which will shake its roots like a chilling breath. That's what I've got to say, and all I know is that Boot is safe and well and that the weather is improving...'

8

Kätchen and William dropped into the Liberty for an apéritif.

It was the first time he had been there since his change of residence.

'Do either of you happen to know a gentleman by the name of Boot?' asked Mrs Jackson.

'Yes, it's me.'

'Well, there's some cables for you somewhere.'

They were found and delivered. William opened them one by one. They all dealt with the same topic.

BADLY LEFT ALL PAPERS ALL STORIES.

IMPERATIVE RECEIVE FULL STORY TONIGHT SIX YOUR TIME WHY NO NEWS ARE YOU ILL FLASH REPLY.

YOUR CABLES UNARRIVED FEAR SUBVERSIVE INTERFERENCE SERVICE ACKNOWLEDGE RECEIPT OURS IMMEDIATELY.

There were a dozen of them in all; the earliest of the series were modestly signed SALTER; as the tone strengthened his name gave place to MONTGOMERY MOWBRAY GENERAL EDITOR BEAST, then to ELSENGRATZ MANAGING DIRECTOR MEGALOPOLITAN NEWSPAPERS. The last, which had arrived that morning, read: CONFIDENTIAL AND URGENT STOP LORD COPPER HIMSELF GRAVELY DISSATISFIED STOP LORD COPPER PERSONALLY REQUIRES VICTORIES STOP ON RECEIPT OF THIS CABLE VICTORY STOP CONTINUE CABLING VICTORIES UNTIL FURTHER NOTICE STOP LORD COPPERS CONFIDENTIAL SECRETARY.

'What are they all about?' asked Kätchen.

'They don't seem very pleased with me in London. They seem to want more news.'

'How silly. Are you upset?'

'No... Well, yes, a little.'

'Poor William. I will get you some news. Listen. I have a plan. I have lived in this town for two months. I have many friends. That is to say, I *had* them before my husband went away. They will be my friends again now that they know you are helping me. It will be a good thing for both of us. Listen – all the journalists who were here had men in the town they paid to give them news. Mr Jakes the American pays Paleologue fifty dollars a week.

You like me more than Mr Jakes likes Paleologue?'

'Much more.'

'Twice as much?'

'Yes.'

'Then you will pay me a hundred dollars a week and Frau Dressler will not be angry with me any more, so it will be a good thing for all of us. Will you think it very greedy if I ask for a hundred dollars now; you know how impolite Frau Dressler is – well, perhaps two hundred, because I shall work for you more than one week?'

'Very well,' said William.

'Look, I brought your cheque book for you from your room in case you might need it. What a good secretary I should be.'

'Do you really think you can get some news?'

'Why, yes, of course. For instance, I am very friendly with an Austrian man – it is his wife who made me this dress – and his sister is governess to the President's ch.ldren, so they know everything that goes on. I will visit them tomorrow . . . only,' she added doubtfully, 'I don't think it would be polite to go to her house and not buy anything. You are paid expenses by your paper?'

'Yes.'

'For everything? The canoe and for this vermouth and all the things in your room?'

'Yes.'

'Then I will be paid expenses too . . . the Austrian has some nightgowns she made for a lady at the French legation, only the lady's husband did not like them, so they are *very* cheap. There are four of them in crêpe-de-Chine. She would sell them for sixty American dollars. Shall I get them?'

'You don't think she would give you news if you did not?'

'It would be impolite to ask.'

'Very well.'

'And the man who cut my hair – he shaves the Minister of the Interior. He would know a great deal. Only I cannot

have my hair washed again so soon. Shall I buy some
scent from him? And I should like a rug for my room; the
floor is cold and has splinters; the Russian who sells fur is
the lover of one of the Miss Jacksons. Oh, William, what
fun we shall have working together.'

'But, Kätchen, you know, this isn't my money. You
know that if I was rich, I should give you everything
you wanted, but I can't go spending the paper's
money...'

'Silly William, it is because it is the paper's money that
I can take it. You know I could not take *yours*. My husband would not let me take money from a *man*, but from
a *newspaper* ... I think that Mr Gentakian knows a great
deal of news, too – you know his shop opposite the Ping-
Pong? ... Oh, William, I feel so happy tonight. Let us
not go back to dine at the Pension where Frau Dressler
disapproves. Let us dine again at the Ping-Pong. We can
buy some tinned caviare at Benakis, and Popotakis will
make us some toast...'

After dinner Kätchen became grave. 'I was so happy
just now,' she said. 'But now I am thinking, what is to
become of me? A few weeks and you will go away. I have
waited so long for my husband; perhaps he will not
come.'

'Do you think you could bear to live in England?'

'I have lived in England. That is where I learned to
speak. It was when I was sixteen, after my father went to
South America; I worked in a dance hall.'

'Where?'

'I don't know. It was by the sea. I met my husband
there; he was so pleased to find someone who would talk
German with him. How he talked ... Now you have made
me think of him and I am ashamed to be drinking champagne when perhaps he is in trouble.'

'Kätchen, how long must you wait for him?'

'I don't know.' She unwrapped the speckled foil from
the bottle of champagne. 'He is not a good husband to
me,' she admitted, 'to go away for so long.' She held the

foil to her face and carefully modelled it round her nose.

'Dear Kätchen, will you marry me?'

She held the false nose up to William's.

'Too long,' she said.

'Too long to wait?'

'Too long for your nose.'

'Damn!' said William.

'Now you are upset.'

'Won't you ever be serious?'

'Oh, I have been serious too much, too often.' Then she added hopefully, 'I might go with you now, and then when he comes back I will go with him. Will that do?'

'I want you to come to England with me. How long must I wait?'

'Do not spoil the evening with questions. We will play ping pong.'

That night when they reached the Pension Dressler they walked through the yard arm in arm; the livestock were asleep, and overhead the sky was clear and brilliant with stars.

'How long must I wait? How long?'

'Not long. Soon. When you like,' said Kätchen, and ran to her loft.

The three-legged dog awoke, and all over the town, in yards and refuse heaps, the pariahs took up his cries of protest.

FOUR

I

NEXT morning William awoke in a new world.

As he stood on the veranda calling for his boy, he slowly became aware of the transformation which had taken place overnight. The rains were over. The boards

were warm under his feet; below the steps the dank weeds
of Frau Dressler's garden had suddenly burst into crimson flower; a tropic sun blazed in the sky, low at present,
but with promise of a fiery noon, while beyond the tin
roofs of the city, where before had hung a blank screen
of slaty cloud, was now disclosed a vast landscape, mile
upon mile of sunlit highland, rolling green pastures, dun
and rosy terraces, villas and farms and hamlets, gardens
and crops and tiny stockaded shrines; crest upon crest
receding to the blue peaks of the remote horizon. William
called for his boy and called in vain.

'He is gone,' said Frau Dressler, crossing the yard with
a load of earthenware. 'All the boys have gone today.
They are making holiday for the end of the rains. Some
German friends have come to help me.'

And William's breakfast was eventually brought him
by a destitute mechanic who owed Frau Dressler for his
share of the last Christmas tree.

2

It was an eventful day.

At nine Erik Olafsen came to say good-bye. There was
an outbreak of plague down the line and he was off to
organize a hospital. He went without enthusiasm.

'It is stupid work,' he said. 'I have been in a plague
hospital before. How many do you think we cured?'

'I've no idea.'

'None at all. We could only catch the patients who
were too ill to move. The others ran away to the villages,
so more and more people got it. In the civilized colonies
they send soldiers, not doctors. They make a ring all
round the place where there is plague and shoot anyone
who tries to get out. Then in a few days when everyone is
dead they burn the huts. But here one can do nothing for
the poor people. Well, the Government have asked me
to go, so I leave now. Where is Kätchen?'

'She's out shopping.'

'Good. That is very good. She was sad with such old, dirty clothes. I am very glad she has become your friend. You will say good-bye to her?'

At ten she returned laden with packages. 'Darling,' she said, 'I have been so happy. Everyone is excited that the summer is come and they are all so kind and polite now they know I have a friend. Look at what I have brought.'

'Lovely. Did you get any news?'

'It was difficult. I had so much to say about the things I was buying that I did not talk politics. Except to the Austrian. The President's governess had tea with the Austrian yesterday, but I am afraid you will be disappointed. She has not seen the President for four days. You see, he is locked up.'

'Locked up?'

'Yes, they have shut him in his bedroom. They often do that when there are important papers for him to sign. But the governess is unhappy about it. You see, it is generally his family who lock him up and then it is only for a few hours. This time it is Doctor Benito and the Russian and the two black secretaries who came from America; they locked him up three days ago, and when his relatives try to see him they say he is drunk. They would not let him go to the opening of Jackson College. The governess says something is wrong.'

'Do you think I ought to report that to the *Beast?*'

'I wonder,' said Kätchen doubtfully. 'It is such a lovely morning. We ought to go out.'

'I believe Corker would make something of it . . . the editor seems very anxious for news.'

'Very well. Only be quick. I want to go for a drive.'

She left William to his work.

He sat at the table, stood up, sat down again, stared gloomily at the wall for some minutes, lit his pipe, and then, laboriously, with a single first finger and his heart heavy with misgiving, he typed the first news story of his meteoric career. No one observing that sluggish and hesitant composition could have guessed that this was a moment of history – of legend, to be handed down among the great traditions of his trade, told and retold over the milk-bars of Fleet Street, quoted in books of reminiscence, help up as a model to aspiring pupils of Correspondence Schools of Profitable Writing, perennially fresh in the jaded memories of a hundred editors; the moment when Boot began to make good.

PRESS COLLECT BEAST LONDON he wrote.
NOTHING MUCH HAS HAPPENED EXCEPT TO THE PRESIDENT WHO HAS BEEN IMPRISONED IN HIS OWN PALACE BY REVOLUTIONARY JUNTA HEADED BY SUPERIOR BLACK CALLED BENITO AND RUSSIAN JEW WHO BANNISTER SAYS IS UP TO NO GOOD THEY SAY HE IS DRUNK WHEN HIS CHILDREN TRY TO SEE HIM BUT GOVERNESS SAYS MOST UNUSUAL LOVELY SPRING WEATHER BUBONIC PLAGUE RAGING.

He got so far when he was interrupted.

Frau Dressler brought him a cable: YOUR CONTRACT TERMINATED STOP ACCEPT THIS STIPULATED MONTHS NOTICE AND ACKNOWLEDGE STOP BEAST.

William added to his message, SACK RECEIVED SAFELY THOUGHT I MIGHT AS WELL SEND THIS ALL THE SAME.

Kätchen's head appeared at the window.
'Finished?'
'Yes.'
He rolled the cable he had received into a ball and threw it into the corner of the room. The yard was bathed in sunshine. Kätchen wanted a drive. It was not a good time to tell her of his recall.

3

Twelve miles out of the town the coming of summer brought no joy to Corker and Pigge.

'Look at the flowers,' said Pigge.

'Yes. Like a bloody cemetery,' said Corker.

The lorry stood where it had sunk, buried in mud to the axles. On all sides lay evidence of the unavailing efforts of yesterday – stones painfully collected from a neighbouring water-course and bedded round the back wheels; bruised and muddy boughs dragged in the rain from the sparse woods a mile or more distant; the great boulder which they had rolled, it seemed, from the horizon to make a base for the jack – vainly; the heaps thrown up behind as the wheels, like a dog in a rabbit-hole, spun and burrowed. Listlessly helped by their boys, Pigge and Corker had worked all day, their faces blackened by exhaust smoke, their hands cut, soaked with rain, weary of limb, uncontrollable in temper.

It was a morning of ethereal splendour – such a morning as Noah knew as he gazed from his pitchy bulwarks over limitless, sunlit waters while the dove circled and mounted and became lost in the shining heavens; such a morning as only the angels saw on the first day of that rash cosmic experiment that had resulted, at the moment, in landing Corker and Pigge here in the mud, stiff and unshaven and disconsolate.

The earth-bound journalists turned hopelessly to the four quarters of the land.

'You can see for miles,' said Pigge.

'Yes,' said Corker bitterly, 'and not a bloody human being in sight.'

Their boys were dancing to celebrate the new season, clapping and shuffling and shouting a low, rhythmical song of praise. 'What the hell have they got to be cheerful about?'

'They've been at the whisky again,' said Corker.

4

That afternoon there was the party at the British Legation. Kätchen had not got her card, so William went
alone. It did not rain. Nothing marred the summer
serenity of the afternoon. Guests of all colours and nationalities paraded the gravel walks, occasionally pausing behind the flowering shrubs to blow their noses – delicately
between forefinger and thumb – as though trumpeting
against the defeated devils of winter.

'The President usually comes,' said Bannister, 'but he
doesn't seem to be here today. Odd thing, but there isn't
a single Jackson in sight. I wonder what's become of
them all.'

'I don't know about the others, but the President is
locked in his bedroom.'

'Good Lord, is he? I say, you'd better talk to the old
man about this. I'll try and get hold of him.'

The Minister was regarding the scene with an expression of alarm and despair; he stood on the top step of the
terrace, half in, half out of the french windows, in a position dimly remembered from the hide-and-seek of his
childhood as strategically advantageous; it afforded a
general survey of the dispositions of the attacking forces
and offered alternative lines of retreat, indoors or through
the rose garden.

Bannister introduced William.

The Minister gave the Vice-Consul a glance of mild
reproach and smiled bleakly, the wry smile of one heroic-
ally resisting an emotion of almost overwhelming
repulsion.

'So glad you could come,' he said. 'Being looked after
all right? Good, excellent.'

He peered over his shoulder into the shady refuge of
his study. As he did so the door opened and three obese
Indians waddled into the room; each wore a little gold
skull cap, a long white shirt, and a short black coat, each

carried a strawberry ice. 'How did they get in?' he asked petulantly. 'They've no business there at all. Get them out. Get them out.'

Bannister hurried to head them off and the Minister was left alone with William.

'You are from the *Beast*?'

'Yes.'

'Can't say I read it myself. Don't like its politics. Don't like any politics . . . Finding Ishmaelia interesting?'

'Yes, very interesting.'

'Are you? Wish I was. But, then, you've got a more interesting job. Better paid, too, I expect. I wonder, how does one get a job like that? Pretty difficult, I suppose, stiff examination, eh?'

'No, no examination.'

'No examination? My word, that's interesting. I must tell my wife. Didn't know you could get any jobs nowadays without examinations. Wretched system, ruining all the services. I've got a boy in England now, lazy fellow, can't pass any examinations, don't know what to do with him. D'you suppose they'd give him a job on your paper?'

'I expect so. It seemed quite easy to me.'

'I say, that's splendid. Must tell my wife. Here she is. My dear, Mr Boot here says he will give Archie a job on his paper.'

'I'm afraid *I* can't be much help. I got the sack this morning.'

'Did you? Did you really? Pity. Then you can't be any help to Archie.'

'No, I'm afraid not.'

'My dear,' said the Minister's wife, 'I'm very sorry indeed, but I've got to introduce a new misssionary you haven't met.'

She led him away and presented a blinking giant of a young man; the Minister nodded absently to William as he left him.

Doctor Benito was at the party, very near, very affable,

very self-possessed, smiling wickedly on all sides. He approached William.

'Mr Boot,' he said, 'you must be very lonely without your colleagues.'

'No, I much prefer it.'

'And it is dull for you,' Doctor Benito insisted, in the level patient tones of a mesmerist, 'very dull, with so little happening in the town. So I have arranged a little divertissement for you.'

'It is very kind, but I am greatly diverted here.'

'You are too kind to our simple little city. But I think I can promise you something better. Now that the summer has come there will be no difficulty. You shall have a little tour of our country and see some of its beauties – the forest of Popo, for instance, and the great waterfall at Chip.'

'It's very kind of you . . . some other time, perhaps.'

'No, no, at once. It is all arranged. I have a motor car. I cannot, alas, go with you myself, but I will send a charming young man – very cultured, a university graduate – who will be able to explain everything as well as I can. You will find my country people very hospitable. I have arranged for you to spend tonight just outside the city at the villa of the postmaster-general. Then you will be able to start early in the morning for the mountains. You will see much more than any of your colleagues, who, I hear, are not being fortunate in their trip to Laku. Perhaps you will be able to do a little lion shooting.'

'Thank you very much indeed, Doctor Benito, but I don't want to leave Jacksonburg at the moment.'

'There will be room for any companion you care to take.'

'No, thank you.'

'And you will, of course, be the guest of the Government.'

'It's not that.'

'You will see most interesting native dances, curious

customs,' he smiled more horribly than before, 'some of
the tribes are most primitive and interesting.'

'I'm very sorry, I can't go.'

'But it is all arranged.'

'I'm very sorry. You should have consulted me before
you took so much trouble.'

'My government would not like you to lose financially
by their hospitality. I quite see that you would not be
able to do your work fully during your absence, but any
reasonable recompense...'

'Look here, Doctor Benito,' said William. 'You're being
a bore. I'm not going.'

Doctor Benito suddenly stopped smiling. 'Everyone
will be very disappointed,' he said.

William told Bannister what had been said.

'Yes, they want to get you out of the way. They don't
want any journalists here when the fun starts. They even
took the trouble to shift Olafsen. They told him there was
cholera down the line.'

'Plague.'

'Some lie, anyway. I'm in communication with our
agent there by telephone. Everyone's as fit as a flea.'

'Perhaps if he knew I'd got the sack he wouldn't bother
so much.'

'He wouldn't believe it. He must have seen your cable;
all the foreign cables go to his office before they're delivered. He thinks it a trick. That's the disadvantage of
being clever in Benito's way.'

'You seem to know most things that go on in this
town.'

'It's a hobby. Must do something. If I stuck to my job
I should spend the day answering commercial question-
naires. Did you get anything interesting out of the
Minister?'

'No.'

'He sticks to his job.'

5

As William drove back from the Legation he pondered over the question of when and in what terms he should break the news of his recall to Kätchen.

He need not have worried.

In the first place he found a cable awaiting him, CON-GRATULATIONS STORY CONTRACT UNTERMINATED UPFOLLOW FULLEST SPEEDILIEST.

In the second place Kätchen was no longer at the Pension Dressler; a posse of soldiers had come for her that afternoon and taken her away in a closed motor car.

'I suppose it is because of her papers,' said Frau Dressler. 'She telephoned to the German Consulate, but they would not help her. She should not have been upset. When they put white people in prison here they are well looked after. She will be as comfortable,' she added with unprofessional candour, 'as she was here. There is one of the secret police waiting to see you. I would not let him into your room. He is in the dining-room.'

William found a natty young Negro smoking from a long cigarette holder. 'Good evening,' he said. 'I have come from Doctor Benito to take you for a little tour in the mountains.'

'I told Doctor Benito I could not go.'

'He hoped you would change your mind.'

'Why have you arrested Miss Kätchen?'

'It is a temporary measure, Mr Boot. She is being very well looked after. She is at the villa of the postmaster-general, just outside the town. She asked me to collect some luggage for her – a parcel of geological specimens that were left in your room.'

'They are my property.'

'So I understand. You paid a hundred American dollars for them, I think. Here is the money.'

William was by nature a man of mild temper; on the rare occasions when he gave way to rage the symptoms were abundantly evident. The Negro stood up, removed the cigarette end from its holder and added, 'Perhaps I should tell you that when I was at the Adventist University of Alabama I was welter-weight champion of my year ... May I repeat my offer? Doctor Benito wishes very much to examine these specimens; they are the property of the Government, for they were collected by a foreigner who came here without the formality of obtaining a prospecting licence from the Ministry of Mines – a foreigner who unfortunately is at the moment protected by the capitulations – at the moment only. Arrangements are being made about him. Since you bought these specimens under a misapprehension the Government decided very generously to make an offer of reimbursement –'

'Get out!' said William.

'Very well. You will hear of this matter again.'

He rose with dignity and swaggered into the yard.

The milch-goat looked up from her supper of waste paper; her perennial optimism quickened within her, and swelled to a great and mature confidence; all day she had shared the exhilaration of the season, her pelt had glowed under the newborn sun; deep in her heart she too had made holiday, had cast off the doubts of winter and exulted among the crimson flowers; all day she had dreamed gloriously; now in the limpid evening she gathered her strength, stood for a moment rigid, quivering from horn to tail; then charged, splendidly, irresistibly, triumphantly; the rope snapped and the welter-weight champion of the Adventist University of Alabama sprawled on his face amid the kitchen garbage.

6

The events of that day were not yet ended.

As soon as the black had gone, limping and dishevelled, and the goat, sated and peaceably disposed to retrospection, recaptured and secured, William drove back to the British Consulate with his bag of minerals.

'The party's over,' said Bannister. 'We all want a rest.'

'I've brought some luggage for you to keep an eye on.'

He explained the circumstances.

'If you knew the amount of work you were causing,' said Bannister, 'you wouldn't do this. From tomorrow onwards for the next six years I shall get a daily pile of bumf from the Ministry of Mines and in the end the Mixed Court will decide against you – God damn all capitulations. What's in the sack, anyway?'

He opened it and examined the stones. 'Yes,' he said, 'just what I expected – gold ore. The mountains in the West are stiff with it. We knew it was bound to cause international trouble sooner or later. There have been two companies after a mineral concession – German and Russian. So far as the Jacksons have any political principles it has been to make the country unprofitable for foreign investment. The President kept his end up pretty well – played one company off against the other for months. Then the Smiles trouble started. We are pretty certain that the Germans were behind it. The Russians have been harder to follow – we only learned a day or two ago that they had bought Benito and the Young Ishmaelite party. It's between Smiles and Benito now and it looks to me as if Benito had won hands down. I'm sorry – the Jacksons were a pack of rogues, but they suited the country and they suited H.M.G. We stand to lose quite a lot if they start a Soviet state here . . . Now you've stopped being a journalist I can tell you these things.'

'As a matter of fact I've just become a journalist again. D'you mind if I cable this to the *Beast*?'

'Well, don't let on that you got it from me . . . as a matter of fact a newspaper campaign at the moment might just do the trick.'

'There's another thing. Can you help me get a girl friend out of jug?'

'Certainly not,' said Bannister. 'I'm a keen supporter
of the local prison system; it's the one thing that keeps the
British Protected Persons off my doorstep. Its only weak-
ness is you can buy yourself out when you want to for a
fiver.'

7

When it was dinner-time in Jacksonburg, it was tea-
time in London.

'Nothing more from Boot,' said Mr Salter.

'Well, make up the Irish edition with his morning
cable – rewrite it and splash it. If the follow-up comes in
before six in the morning, run a special.'

8

William returned home with a mission; he was going
to do down Benito. Dimly at first, then in vivid detail, he
foresaw a spectacular, cinematographic consummation,
when his country should rise chivalrously to arms; Bengal
Lancers and kilted highlanders invested the heights of
Jacksonburg; he at their head burst open the prison
doors; with his own hands he grappled with Benito,
shook him like a kitten and threw him choking out of his
path; Kätchen fluttered towards him like a wounded bird
and he bore her in triumph to Boot Magna . . . Love,
patriotism, zeal for justice, and personal spite flamed
within him as he sat at his typewriter and began his message. One finger was not enough; he used both hands.
The keys rose together like bristles on a porcupine, jam-
med and were extricated; curious anagrams appeared on
the paper before him; vulgar fractions and marks of
punctuation mingled with the letters. Still he typed.

The wireless station closed at nine; at five minutes to
William pushed his sheaf of papers over the counter.

'Sending tomorrow,' said the clerk.

'Must send tonight; urgent,' said William.

'No tonight. Summer holiday tonight.'

William added a handful of banknotes to the typewritten sheets. 'Sending tonight,' he said.

'All right.'

Then William went round to dinner alone at Popotakis's.

9

'Two thousand words from Boot,' said Mr Salter.

'Any good?' asked the general editor.

'Look at it.'

The general editor looked. He saw '*Russian plot . . . coup d'état . . . overthrow constitutional government . . . red dictatorship . . . goat butts head of police . . . imprisoned blonde . . . vital British interest jeopardized.*' It was enough; it was news. 'It's news,' he said. 'Stop the machines at Manchester and Glasgow. Clear the line to Belfast and Paris. Scrap the whole front page. Kill the Ex-Beauty Queen's pauper funeral. Get in a photograph of Boot.'

'I don't suppose we've got a photograph of Boot in the office.'

'Ring up his relatives. Find his best girl. There must be a photograph of him somewhere in the world.'

'They took one for his passport,' said Mr Salter doubtfully, 'but I remember thinking at the time it was an extremely poor likeness.'

'I don't care if it looks like a baboon —'

'That's just how it does look.'

'Give it two columns' depth. This is the first front page foreign news we've had for a month.'

When the final edition had left the machines, carrying William's sensational message into two million apathetic homes, Mr Salter left the office.

His wife was still up when he got home.

'I've made your Ovaltine,' she said. 'Has it been a bad day?'

'Terrible.'

'You didn't have to dine with Lord Copper.'

'No, not as bad as that. But we had to remake the whole paper after it had gone to bed. That fellow Boot.'

'The one who upset you so all last week. I thought you were sacking him.'

'We did. Then we took him back. He's all right. Lord Copper knew best.'

Mr Salter took off his boots and Mrs Salter poured out the Ovaltine. When he had drunk it, he felt calmer.

'You know,' he said meditatively, 'it's a great experience to work for a man like Lord Copper. Again and again I've thought he was losing grip. But always it turns out he knew best. What made him spot Boot? It's a sixth sense... real genius.'

10

Popotakis's was empty and William was tired. He ate his dinner and strolled home. When he reached his room he found it filled with tobacco smoke; a cheroot, one of his cheroots, glowed in the darkness. A voice, with a strong German accent, said, 'Close the shutters, please, before you turn on the light.'

William did as he was asked. A man rose from the arm-chair, clicked his heels and made a guttural sound. He was a large blond man of military but somewhat dilapidated appearance. He wore khaki shorts and an open shirt, boots ragged and splashed with mud. His head, once shaven, was covered with stubble, uniform with his chin, like a clipped yew in a neglected garden.

'I beg your pardon?' said William.

The man clicked his heels again and made the same throaty sound, adding, 'That is my name.'

'Oh,' said William. Then he came to attention and said 'Boot.'

They shook hands.

'I must apologize for using your room. Once it was
mine. I did not know until I found your luggage here
that there had been a change. I left some specimens of
ore. Do you by any chance know what has become of
them?'

'I have them safe.'

'Well, it is of no importance now . . . I left a wife, too.
Have you seen her?'

'She is in prison.'

'Yes,' said the German, without surprise. 'I suppose
she is. They will put me in prison too. I have just come
from my Consulate. They say they cannot protect me. I
cannot complain. They warned me before we started that
if I failed they could not protect me . . . and I have failed
. . . if you will excuse me, I will sit down. I am very tired.'

'Have you had any dinner?'

'Not for two days. I have just returned from the interior. We could not stop to sleep or to look for food. All
the way back they were trying to kill me. They had paid
the bandits. I am very tired and very hungry.'

William took a case from the pile of stores; it was
corded and wired and lined and battened to resist all
emergencies. He struggled for some time while the German sat in a kind of melancholy stupor; then he said,
'There's some food in here if you can get it open.'

'Food.' At the word the German came to his senses.
With surprising dexterity he got the blade of his clasp
knife under the lid of the box; it fell open revealing
William's Christmas dinner.

They spread it on the table – turkey, plum pudding,
crystallized plums, almonds, raisins, champagne and
crackers. The German cried a little, nostalgically, teu-
tonically. Then he began to gorge, at first in silence, later,
with the dessert, loquaciously.

'. . . three times they shot at me on the road – but the
bandits have very old rifles. Not like the rifles we gave to
Smiles. We gave him everything, machine-guns, tanks,
consulates; we bought him two Paris newspapers, a

column a day week after week – you know what that
costs. There were five thousand volunteers ready to sail.
He could have been in Jacksonburg in a month. No one
wants the Jacksons here. They are foolish people. For a
year we have been trying to make business with them.
They said first one thing, then another. We gave them
money; we gave them all money; heavens, how many
Jacksons there are! Still, they would not make business...'

'I ought to warn you that I am a journalist.'

'That is well. When you come to write of this affair say
that it was not my fault that we failed. It was Smiles. We
gave him money and he ran away to the Sudan. He
wanted me to go with him.'

'Wouldn't that have been better?'

'I had left my wife in Jacksonburg ... besides, it is not
good for me to go to the Sudan. I was once in trouble in
Khartoum. There are many countries where it is not
good for me to go. I have often been very foolish.' At the
thought of his wife and of his former indiscretions he
seemed once more to be overcome with melancholy.
He sat in silence. William began to fear he would fall
asleep.

'Where are you going to now?' he asked. 'You can't
stay here, you know, or they will come and arrest you.'

'No,' said the German. 'I can't stay here.' And immediately he fell asleep, mouth open, head back, a crumpled cracker in his right hand, breathing uproariously.

And still that day was not ended.

Hardly had the German's preliminary, convulsive
snorts and gurgles given place to the gentler, automatic,
continuous snoring of regular sleep than William was
again disturbed.

The night watchman stood clucking in the doorway,
pointing towards the gates, smiling and nodding unin-
telligibly. The German never stirred; his snores followed
William across the yard.

At the gates a motor car was waiting. Its lights had

been turned off. The yard and the lane outside it were in
darkness. A voice, from inside the car, said, 'William, is
it you?' Kätchen scrambled out and ran to him – as he
had imagined it, like a wounded bird. 'Darling, darling,'
he said.

They clung together. In the darkness he could discern
over Kätchen's shoulder the figure of the night watchman,
stork-like, on one leg, his spear behind his shoulders.

'Darling,' said Kätchen. 'Have you got any money
with you?'

'Yes.'

'A lot?'

'Yes.'

'I promised the driver a hundred American dollars.
Was it too much?'

'Who is he?'

'The postmaster-general's chauffeur. They have arrested the postmaster-general. He was a Jackson. All the
Jacksons are being arrested. He got the key of the room
when the soldiers were having supper. I said I would give
him a hundred dollars if he brought me back.'

'Tell him to wait. I'll get the money from my room.'

The driver wrapped himself in his blanket and settled
down over the wheel. Kätchen and William stood together in the yard.

'I must go away,' said Kätchen. '*We* must go away. I
have thought about it in the motor car. You must marry
me. Then I shall be British and they will not be able to
hurt me. And we will leave Ishmaelia at once. No more
journalism. We will go to Europe together. Will you do
that?'

'Yes,' said William without hesitation.

'And will you marry me properly – in an office?'

'Yes.'

'It will be the first time I have been properly married.'
The tremendous respirations echoed across the yard.
'What is that? William, there is something making a
noise in your room.'

'Yes, I had forgotten ... you made me forget. Come and see who it is.'

They climbed the steps, hand in hand, crossed the veranda and reached the door of William's room.

Kätchen dropped his hand and ran forward with a little cry. She knelt at the German's side and held him, shook him. He stirred and grunted and opened his eyes. They spoke to one another in German; Kätchen nestled against him; he laid his cheek against her head and lapsed again into coma.

'How happy I am,' she said. 'I thought he would never come back, that he was dead or had left me. How he sleeps. Is he well? Is he hungry?'

'No,' said William. 'I don't think you need have any anxiety on that point. Within the last hour, to my certain knowledge, he has consumed an entire Christmas dinner designed for four children or six adults.'

'He must have been starving. Is he not thin?'

'No,' said William. 'Frankly I should not have called him thin.'

'Ah, you should have seen him before he went away ... How he snores. That is a good sign. Whenever he is well he snores like this.' She brooded fondly over the unconscious figure. 'But he is dirty.'

'Yes,' said William, 'very dirty indeed.'

'William, you sound so cross suddenly. Are you not glad my husband has come back to me?'

'Come back *to you?*'

'William, you are not jealous. How I despise jealousy. You could not be jealous of my husband. I have been with him for two years, before ever you and I met. I knew he would not leave me. But what are we to do now? I must think ...'

They both thought, not on the same lines.

'I have a plan,' said Kätchen at last.

'Yes?' said William gloomily.

'I think it will work nice. My husband is German, so the Ishmaelites will not be allowed to hurt him. It is

harder for me because of my papers. So I will marry you.
Then I shall be English and I and my husband can go
away together. You will give us our tickets to Europe.
It will not be expensive, we will travel in the second class.
... How is that?'

'There are several serious objections; for one thing
the German Legation are not going to protect your
friend.'

'Oh, dear. I thought if one had papers one was always
safe everywhere ... I must think of another plan ... If,
after I marry you, I marry my husband, he would then
be English, yes?'

'No.'

'Oh, dear.'

They had to speak with raised voices to make themselves heard above the German's snores. 'Would it be
very unkind to wake my husband? He is always full of
ideas. He has great experience of difficulties.'

She shook him into sensibility and they spoke together
earnestly in German.

William began to collect the distasteful remains of the
Christmas dinner; he put the crackers back in their box
and arranged the empty tins and bottles outside his door
beside his dirty shoes.

'Our only hope is the postmaster-general's chauffeur,'
said Kätchen at last. 'The town guards know him. If they
have not yet heard that the postmaster-general is in
prison he can drive through the barricades without difficulty. But he could not get to the frontier. They would
telegraph for him to be stopped. The railway is impossible.'

'There is the river,' said the German. 'It is high. We
could strike it below the cataract fifteen miles from here.
Then we could sail down to French territory – if we had
a boat.'

'How much would a boat cost?' asked Kätchen.

'Once in the Matto Grosso I made a boat,' said the
German dreamily. 'I burned out the centre of an iron-

wood tree. It took ten weeks to make, and it sank like a
stone.'

'A boat,' said Kätchen. 'But you have a boat – *our* boat.'

II

They drove through the streets of the sleeping city, the
German in front with the postmaster-general's chauffeur,
Kätchen and William at the back with the canoe. A few
hyenas flashed red eyes at them from the rubbish heaps,
then turned their mangy quarters and scuttled off into
the night.

The guards at the barrier saluted and let them pass
into the open country. They drove in silence.

'I will send you a postcard,' said Kätchen, at last, 'to
tell you we are well.'

Day was breaking as they reached the river; they came
upon it suddenly where it flowed black and swift between
low banks. There they assembled the canoe; William and
Kätchen did the work, as they had done before; it was
familiar; there was no adventure now in fitting the
sockets. The German sat on the running-board of the car,
still stupefied with the lack of sleep; his eyes were open;
his mouth also. When the boat was ready they called to
him to join them.

'It is very small,' he said.

William stood knee deep among the reeds holding it
with difficulty; the current tugged and sucked, Kätchen
climbed in, balancing precariously, with a hand on
William's arm; then the German; the boat sank almost
to the gunwales.

'We shall not have room for the stores,' said Kätchen.

'My boat in Matto Grosso was twenty feet long,' said
the German drowsily, 'it turned over and went straight
to the bottom. Two of my boys were drowned. They had
always said it would sink.'

'If we get safely to the French border,' said Kätchen,

'shall we leave the boat there for you? Will you want it again?'

'No.'

'We might sell it and send you the money.'

'Yes.'

'Or we could keep the money until we get to Europe – it will be easier to send.'

'It is an abstract speculation,' said the German, suddenly awake, and impatient. 'It is a question purely of academic interest. We shall not reach the French border. Let us start.'

'Good-bye,' said Kätchen.

The two figures sat opposite one another, knees touching, expectant, as though embarking upon the ornamental waters of a fair-ground; lovers for the day's outing, who had stood close in a queue, and now waited half reluctant to launch into the closer intimacy of the grottoes and transparencies.

William released the boat; it revolved once or twice, slowly, as it drifted into mid-stream; there it was caught in the full power of the flood, and, spinning dizzily, was swept out of sight into the dawn.

William returned to his empty room. The boy had put back the debris of the Christmas dinner, carefully ranged upon the writing-table. A cleft stick lay across the bed, bearing no message for William. He sat down at his table and with his eyes fixed on the label of the turkey tin, began to compose his dispatch.

'Take to wireless,' he ordered his boy. 'Sit on step till open. Then come back and sit on this step. Don't let anyone in. Want to sleep very much.'

But he did not sleep very much.

The boy shook him at half-past ten. 'No send,' he said, waving the typewritten message.

William painfully roused himself from his brief sleep. 'Why no send?'

'No Jacksons. No Government. No send.'

William dressed and went to the wireless bureau. A jaunty black face smiled at him through the guichet; starched collar, bow tie, long ivory cigarette-holder – the welter-weight.

'Good morning,' said William. 'I hope you are not feeling too sore after your meeting with the goat. Where is the wireless clerk?'

'He is on a little holiday. I have taken over from him.'

'My boy says that this cable has been refused.'

'That is so. We are very much occupied with government business. I think we shall be occupied all day, perhaps for several days. It would have been far better if you had gone for the tour we had planned for you. Meanwhile perhaps you would like to see the manifesto that we are issuing. I think you do not read Ishmaelite?'

'No.'

'A very barbarous language. I have never learned it. Soon we shall make Russian the official language of the country, I have a copy here in English.'

He handed William a sheet of crmson paper headed *WORKERS OF ISHMAELIA UNITE* and snapped down the trap of the guichet.

William stepped out into the sunlight. A black man on a ladder was painting out the name of Jackson Street. Someone had stencilled a sickle and hammer on the front of the post office, a red flag hung limp overhead. He read the manifesto.

. . . *development of mineral resources of the workers by the workers for the workers . . . Jacksons to be speedily brought to trial . . . arraigned for high treason to the Revolution . . . liquidated . . . New Calendar. Year One of the Soviet State of Ishmaelia . . .*

He crumpled the paper into a scarlet ball and tossed it to the goat; it went down like an oyster.

He stood on his veranda and looked across the yard to the beastly attic from which Kätchen used to greet him, at about this time in the morning, calling him to come out to Popotakis's Ping-Pong Parlour.

'Change and decay in all around I see,' he sang softly,

almost unctuously. It was the favourite tune of his uncle
Theodore.

He bowed his head.

'Oh, great crested grebe,' he prayed, 'maligned fowl,
have I not expiated the wrong my sister did you; am I
still to be an exile from the green places of my heart?
Was there not even in the remorseless dooms of antiquity
a god from the machine?'

He prayed without hope.

And then above the multitudinous noises of the Pension Dressler came a small sound, an insistent, swelling
monotone. The servants in the yard looked up. The sound
increased and high above them in the cloudless sky,
rapidly approaching, there appeared an aeroplane. The
sound ceased as the engine was cut off. The machine
circled and dropped silently. It was immediately overhead when a black speck detached itself and fell towards
them; white stuff streamed behind it, billowed and
spread. The engine sang out again; the machine swooped
up and away, out of sight and hearing. The little domed
tent paused and gently sank, as though immersed in
depths of limpid water.

'If he comes on to my roof,' said Frau Dressler. 'If he
breaks anything ...'

The parachutist came on the roof; he broke nothing.
He landed delicately on the tips of his toes; the great sail
crumpled and collapsed behind him; he deftly extricated
himself from the bonds and stood clear. He took a comb
from his pocket and settled the slightly disordered auburn
hair about his temples, glancing at his watch, bowed to
Frau Dressler and asked for a ladder, courteously in five
or six languages. They brought him one. Rung by rung,
on pointed, snake-skin toes he descended to the yard. The
milch-goat reverently made way for him. He smiled
politely at William; then recognized him.

'Why!' he exclaimed. 'It is my fellow traveller, the
journalist. How agreeable to meet a fellow Britisher in
this remote spot.'

FIVE

I

THE sun sank behind the gum trees and the first day of the Soviet of Ishmaelia ended in crimson splendour. The deserted bar-room of Popotakis's Ping-Pong Parlour glowed in the fiery sunset.

'I really do not know how to thank you,' said William.

'Please,' said his companion, laying a hand lightly on his, 'please do not embarrass me. The words you have just used seem to haunt me, wherever I go. Ever since that auspicious afternoon when you were kind enough to give me a place in your aeroplane, I have feared, sooner or later, to hear them on your lips. I suggested as much at the time, I think, if my memory does not deceive me.'

Mr Popotakis switched on the lights above the ping-pong table and asked. 'You want a game, Mr Baldwin?' for it was by this name that William's friend now preferred to be called.

('It is a convenient name,' he had explained. 'Non-committal, British and above all easily memorable. I am often obliged to pursue my business interests under an alias. My man Cuthbert chooses them for me. He has a keen sense of what is fitting, but he sometimes luxuriates a little. There have been times when his more fanciful inventions have entirely slipped my memory, at important moments. So now I am plain Mr Baldwin. I beg you to respect my confidence.')

Mr Baldwin resumed his little dissertation.

'In the rough and tumble of commercial life,' he said, 'I endeavour to requite the kindnesses I receive. The kindnesses have become more profuse and the rewards more substantial of recent years . . . however, I am sure that in you I met an entirely disinterested benefactor. I am glad to have prospered your professional career so inexpensively.

'Do you know, my first impression of you was not of a young man destined for great success in journalism? Quite the reverse. In fact, to be frank with you, I was sceptical of your identity and, when you told me of your destination, I feared you might be coming here with some ulterior object. If I seemed evasive in the early days of our – I hope I may say – friendship, you must forgive me.

'And now Mr Popotakis is offering us a game of ping-pong. For my part, I think it might be refreshing.'

Mr Baldwin removed his coat and rolled the sleeves of his crêpe-de-Chine shirt. Then he took his bat and poised himself expectantly at the end of the table. William served. Love, fifteen; love, thirty; love, forty, game; fifteen, love; thirty, love; forty, love, game. The little man was ubiquitous, ambidextrous. He crouched and bounded and skipped, slamming and volleying; now spanning the net, now five yards back, now flicking the ball from below his knees, now rocketing high among the electric lights; keeping up all the while a bright, bantering conversation in demotic Greek with Mr Popotakis.

At the end of the love set he resumed his coat and said, 'Quarter past six. No doubt you are impatient to send your second message...'

For a private wireless transmitter was one of the amenities to which William had been introduced that day.

Since Mr Baldwin's arrival Jacksonburg – or Marxville as it had been called since early that morning – had proved a town of unsuspected convenience.

'I have a little *pied à terre* here,' Mr Baldwin had explained, when William suggested their lunching at the Pension Dressler. 'My man Cuthbert has been putting it in order. I have not seen it and I fear the worst, but he is a sensitive fellow and might be put out if I lunched away from home on the day of my arrival. Will you not share the adventure of lunching with me?'

They walked, for Mr Baldwin complained that his flight had brought on a slight stiffness of the legs. He took William's arm, guiding him through the less frequented by-ways of the town and questioning him earnestly about the events of the last twenty-four hours.

'And where are your colleagues? I anticipated being vexed by them.'

'They have all gone off into the interior to look for Smiles.'

'That is excellent. You will be the sole spectator at the last act of our little drama.'

'It won't be much help. They've shut the wireless bureau.'

'It shall be opened soon. Meanwhile I have no doubt Cuthbert will be able to accommodate you. He and a Swiss associate of mine have fixed up a little makeshift which appears to work. I have been in correspondence with them daily.'

Even in the side streets there was evidence of the new régime; twice they were obliged to shelter as police lorries thundered past them laden with glaucous prisoners. The Café Wilberforce had changed its name to Café Lenin. There had been a distribution of red flags, which, ingeniously knotted or twisted, had already set a fashion in head-dresses among the women of the market.

'I ought to have come yesterday,' said Mr Baldwin peevishly. 'It would have saved a great deal of unnecessary reorganization. God bless my soul, there's another of those police vans.' They skipped for a doorway. In the centre of a machine-gun squad, William recognized the dignified figure of Mr Earl Russell Jackson.

At length their way led them to the outskirts of the city, to the nondescript railway quarter, where sidings and goods yards and warehouses stood behind a stockade of blue guns and barbed wire. They passed an iron gate and approached a bungalow.

'It is M. Giraud's,' said Mr Baldwin. 'And this is M. Giraud, but I think that introductions are superfluous.'

The bearded ticket collector greeted them deferentially from the veranda.

'M. Giraud has been in my service for some time,' said

Mr Baldwin. 'He had, in fact, been in consultation with me when you had the pleasure of travelling with him from the coast. I followed his brief period of public prominence with interest and, to be quite frank, with anxiety. If I may criticize without offence the profession you practise – at this particular moment with almost unique success – I should say that you reporters missed a good story in Mr. Giraud's little trip. I read the newspapers with lively interest. It is seldom that they are absolutely, point-blank wrong. That is the popular belief, but those who are in the know can usually discern an embryo truth, a little grit of fact, like the core of a pearl, round which have been deposited the delicate layers of ornament. In the present case, for instance, there *was* a Russian agent arranging to take over the government; M. Giraud *was* an important intermediary. But he was not the Russian. The workings of commerce and politics are very, very simple, but not quite as simple as your colleagues represent them. My man Cuthbert was also on the train with you. He should have given you a clue, but no one recognized him. He drove the engine. It was due to his ignorance of local usage that the lost luggage van was eventually recovered.'

'And may I ask,' said William diffidently, 'since you are telling me so much – whose interests do *you* represent?'

'My own,' said the little man simply. 'I plough a lonely furrow . . . Let us see what they have been able to scrape up for luncheon.'

They had scraped up fresh river fish, and stewed them with white wine and aubergines; also a rare local bird which combined the tender flavour of partridge with the solid bulk of the turkey; they had roasted it and stuffed it with bananas, almonds, and red peppers; also a baby gazelle which they had seethed with truffles in its mother's milk; also a dish of feathery Arab pastry and a heap of unusual fruits. Mr Baldwin sighed wistfully. 'Well,' he said, 'I suppose it will not hurt us to rough it for once. We shall appreciate the pleasures of civilization all the more ... but my descent in the parachute gave me quite an appetite. I had hoped for something a little more enterprising.'

He swallowed his digestive pills, praised the coffee, and then expressed a desire to sleep.

'Cuthbert will look after you,' he said. 'Give him anything you want sent to your paper.'

The wireless transmitter was in and beneath the garage; its mast rose high overhead, cleverly disguised as a eucalyptus tree. William watched the first words of his rejected dispatch sputter across the ether to Mr Salter; then he, too, decided to sleep.

At five o'clock, when Mr Baldwin reappeared, he was in a different, more conspicuous suit and the same mood of urbanity and benevolence.

'Let us visit the town,' he said, and, inevitably, they had gone to Popotakis's and they sat there at sunset in the empty bar-room.

'... No doubt you are impatient to send off your second message; I trust that the little mystery of the situation here is now perfectly clear to you.'

'Well ... No ... not exactly.'

'No? There are still gaps? Tut, tut, Mr Boot, the foreign correspondent of a great newspaper should be able to piece things together for himself. It is all very simple. There has been a competition for the mineral rights of Ishmaelia which, I may say as their owner, have been preposterously over-valued. In particular the German and the Russian Governments were willing to pay extravagantly – but in kind. Unhappily for them the commodities they had to offer – treasures from the Imperial palaces, timber, toys, and so forth – were not much in demand in Ishmaelia – in presidential circles at any rate. President Jackson had long wanted to make adequate provision for his retirement, and I was fortunately placed in being able to offer him gold for his gold concession, and my rivals found themselves faced by the alternative

of abandoning their ambitions or upsetting President
Jackson. They both preferred the latter, more romantic
course. The Germans, with a minimum of discernment,
chose to set up a native of low character named Smiles as
prospective dictator. I never had any serious fears of him.
The Russians, more astutely, purchased the Young Ishmaelite party and are, as you see, momentarily in the
ascendant.

'That, I think, should give you your material for an
article.'

'Yes,' said William. 'Thank you very much. I'm sure
Mr Salter and Lord Copper will be very grateful.'

'Dear me, how little you seem to have mastered the
correct procedure of your profession. You should ask me
whether I have any message for the British public. I have.
It is this: *Might must find a way*. Not *"Force"*, remember;
other nations use "force"; we Britons alone use "Might".
Only one thing can set things right – sudden and extreme
violence, or, better still, the effective threat of it. I am
committed to very considerable sums in this little gamble
and, alas, our countrymen are painfully tolerant, nowadays, of the losses of their financial superiors. One sighs
for the days of Pam or Dizzy. I possess a little influence in
political quarters, but it will strain it severely to provoke
a war on my account. Some semblance of popular
support, such as your paper can give, would be very
valuable . . . But I dislike embarrassing my affairs with
international issues. I should greatly prefer it, if the
thing could be settled neatly and finally, here and
now.'

As he spoke there arose from the vestibule a huge and
confused tumult; the roar of an engine which, in the tran-
quil bar-room, sounded like a flight of heavy aeroplanes,
a series of percussions like high explosive bombs, shrill,
polyglot human voices inarticulate with alarm, and
above them all a deep bass, trolling chant, half nautical,
half ecclesiastical. The flimsy structure throbbed and
shook from its shallow foundation to its asbestos roof; the

metal-bound doors flew open revealing, first, the two black commissionaires backing into the bar and, next, driving them before him, a very large man astride a motor-cycle. He rode slowly between the ping-pong tables, then put his feet to the floor and released the handle-bars. The machine shot from under him, charged the bar, and lay on its side with its back wheel spinning in a cloud of exhaust-gas, while the rider, swaying ponderously from side to side like a performing bear, surveyed the room in a puzzled but friendly spirit.

It was the Swede; but a Swede transfigured, barely recognizable as the mild apostle of the coffee pot and the sticking plaster. The hair of his head stood like a tuft of ornamental, golden grass; a vinous flush lit the upper part of his face, the high cheek bones, the blank, calf-like eyes; on the broad concavities of his forehead the veins bulged varicosely. Still singing his nordic dirge he saluted the empty chairs and ambled towards the bar.

At the first alarm Mr Popotakis had fled the building. The Swede spanned the counter and fumbled on the shelf beyond. William and Mr Baldwin watched him fascinated as he raised bottle after bottle to his nose, sniffed and tossed them disconsolately behind him. Presently he found what he wanted – the sixty per cent. He knocked off the neck, none too neatly, and set the jagged edge to his lips; his Adam's apple rose and fell. Then, refreshed, he looked about him again. The motor-cycle at his feet, churning and stinking, attracted his notice and he silenced it with a single tremendous kick.

'Might,' said Mr Baldwin reverently.

The Swede's eyes travelled slowly about him, settled on William, goggled, squinted, and betrayed signs of recognition. He swayed across the room and took William's hand in a paralysing grip : he jabbed hospitably at his face with the broken bottle and addressed him warmly and at length in Swedish.

Mr Baldwin replied. The sound of his own tongue in a strange land affected Olafsen strongly. He sat down and cried while Mr Baldwin, still in Swedish, spoke to him comfortably.

'Sometimes it is necessary to dissemble one's nationality,' he explained to William. 'I have given our friend here to believe that I am a compatriot.'

The black mood passed. Olafsen gave a little whoop and lunged in a menacing manner with the absinthe bottle.

He introduced William to Mr Baldwin.

'This is my great friend, Boot,' he said, 'a famous journalist. He is my friend though I have been made a fool. I have been made a fool,' he cried louder and more angrily, 'by a lot of blacks. They sent me down the line to an epidemic and I was laughed at. But I am going to tell the President. He is a good old man and he will punish them. I will go to his residence, now, and explain everything.'

He rose from the table and bent over the disabled motor-cycle. Mr Popotakis peeped round the corner of the service door and, seeing the Swede still in possession, popped back out of sight.

'Tell me,' said Mr Baldwin. 'Your friend here – does he become more or less pugnacious with drink?'

'I believe, more.'

'Then let us endeavour to repay his hospitality.'

With his own hands Mr Baldwin fetched a second bottle of sixty per cent from the shelf. Tolerantly conforming to the habits of the place, he snapped off the neck and took a hearty swig; then he passed the bottle to the Swede. In a short time they were singing snatches of lugubrious Baltic music, Mr Baldwin matching the Swede's deep bass, in his ringing alto. Between their songs they drank, and between drinks Mr Baldwin explained concisely, but with many repetitions, the constitutional changes of the last twenty-four hours.

'Russians are bad people.'

'Very bad.'

'They say they are Princes and they borrow money!'

'Yes.'

'President Jackson is a good old man. He gave me a harmonium for my mission. Some of the Jacksons are silly fellows, but the President is my friend.'

'Exactly.'

'I think,' said the Swede, rising, 'we will go and see my friend Jackson.'

2

The Presidential Residence, on this first, and, as it turned out, last, evening of the Soviet Union of Ishmaelia, was ceremoniously illuminated, not with the superb floods of concealed arc lamps dear to the more mature dictatorships, but, for want of better, with a multitude of 'fairy lights' with which the Jacksons were wont to festoon the veranda on their not infrequent official birthdays; all the windows of the façade, ten of them, were unshuttered and the bright lamps behind gave cosy glimpses of Nottingham lace, portières, and enlarged photographs. A red flag hung black against the night sky. Dr Benito, backed by a group of 'Young Ishmaelites', stood on the central balcony. A large crowd of Ishmaelites had assembled to see the lights.

'What is he saying?' asked William.

'He has proclaimed the abolition of Sunday and he is calling for volunteers for a ten-day, ten-hour week. I do not think he has chosen the occasion with tact.'

The Swede had left them, pushing forward on his errand of liberation. William and Mr Baldwin stood at the back of the crowd. The temper of the people was apathetic. They liked to see the place lit up. Oratory pleased them, whatever its subject; sermons, educational lectures, political programmes, panegyrics of the dead or living, appeals for charity – all had the same soporific effect. They liked the human voice in all its aspects, most particularly when it was exerted in sustained athletic effort. They had, from time to time, heard too many unfulfilled prophecies issue from that balcony to feel any particular apprehensions about the rigours of the new régime. Then, while Benito was well in his stride, a whisper of interest passed through them; necks were stretched. The Swede had appeared at the ground floor window. Benito, sensing the new alertness in his audience, raised his voice, rolled his eyes, and flashed his white teeth. The audience stood tip-toe with expectation. They could see what he could not – the Swede, in a lethargic but effective manner, liquidating the front parlour. He pulled the curtains down, he swept the fourteen ornamental vases off the chimney-piece, with a loud crash he threw a pot of fern through the window. The audience clapped enthusiastically. The 'Young Ishmaelites' behind Benito began to consult, but the speaker, oblivious to all except his own eloquence, continued to churn the night air with Marxian precepts.

To the spectators at the back of the crowd, out of earshot of the minor sounds, the sequence unfolded itself with the happy inconsequence of an early comedy film. The revolutionary committee left their leader's side and disappeared from view to return almost immediately in rout, backwards, retreating before the Swede who now came into the light of the upper drawing-room brandishing a small gilt chair over his head.

It was not ten feet drop from the balcony. The traditional, ineradicable awe of the white man combined with the obvious immediate peril of the whirling chair legs to decide the issue. With one accord they plunged over the rail on to the woolly pates below. Benito was the last to go, proclaiming class war with his last audible breath.

The Swede addressed the happy people in Ishmaelite.

'He says he is looking for his friend President Jackson,' explained Mr Baldwin.

A cheer greeted the announcement. 'Jackson' was one of the perennially exhilarating words in the Ishmaelite vocabulary; a name associated since childhood with every exciting event in Ishmaelite life. They had been

agreeably surprised to learn that the Jacksons had that
morning all been sent to prison; now, it would be a treat
to see them all again. As long as something, good or ill,
was happening to the Jacksons, the Ishmaelites felt an
intelligent interest in politics. Soon they were all crying:
'Jackson. Jackson. Jackson.'

'Jackson. Jackson,' shouted Mr Baldwin, at William's
side. 'I think we may be satisfied that the counter-revo-
lution has triumphed.'

3

An hour later William sat in his room at the Pension
Dressler and began his dispatch to *The Beast*.

From the main street a short distance away could be
heard sounds of rejoicing from the populace. President
Jackson had been found, locked in the wood shed. Now,
dazed and stiff, he was being carried shoulder high about
the city; other processions had formed about other members of the liberated family. Now and then rival processions met and came to blows. Mr Popotakis had boarded
up his café but several Indian drink shops had been
raided and the town was settling down to a night of jollity.

PRESS COLLECT URGENT MAN CALLED MISTER
BALDWIN HAS BOUGHT COUNTRY, William began.

'No,' said a gentle voice behind him. 'If you would not
resent my co-operation, I think I can compose a dispatch
more likely to please my good friend Copper.'

Mr Baldwin sat at William's table and drew the typewriter towards himself. He inserted a new sheet of paper,
tucked up his cuffs and began to write with immense
speed:

MYSTERY FINANCIER RECALLED EXPLOITS
RHODES LAWRENCE TODAY SECURING VAST EAST
AFRICAN CONCESSION BRITISH INTERESTS IN
TEETH ARMED OPPOSITION BOLSHEVIST SPIES...

'It will make about five full columns,' he said, when it

was finished. 'From my experience of newspapers I think I can safely say that they will print it in full. I am afraid we are too late for tomorrow's paper, but there is no competition to fear. Perhaps I shall have the felicity of finding you as my fellow traveller on the return journey.'

The sounds of rejoicing drew nearer and rose to a wild hubbub in the lane outside.

'Dear me,' said Mr Baldwin. 'How disconcerting. I believe they have found me out.'

But it was only General Gollancz Jackson being pulled about the town in his motor-car. The bare feet pattered away in the darkness. The cries of acclamation faded.

A knock on the door.

Cuthbert reported that, in view of the disturbed state of the town, he had taken the liberty of bringing his master's sheets to the Pension Dressler and making up a bed for him there.

'You did quite right, Cuthbert . . . And now, if you will forgive me, I will say good night. I have had an unusually active day.'

BOOK III

BANQUET

*

ONE

I

THE bells of St Bride's chimed unheard in the customary afternoon din of the Megalopolitan Building. The country edition had gone to bed; below traffic-level, in grotto-blue light, leagues of paper ran noisily through the machines; overhead, where floor upon floor rose from the dusk of the streets to the clear air of day, ground-glass doors opened and shut; figures in frayed and perished braces popped in and out; on a hundred lines reporters talked at cross purposes; sub-editors busied themselves with their humdrum task of reducing to blank nonsense the sheaves of misinformation which whistling urchins piled before them; beside a hundred typewriters soggy biscuits lay in a hundred tepid saucers. At the hub and still centre of all this animation, Lord Copper sat alone in splendid tranquillity. His massive head, empty of thought, rested in sculptural fashion upon his left fist. He began to draw a little cow on his writing pad.

Four legs with cloven feet, a ropy tail, swelling udder and modestly diminished teats, a chest and head like an Elgin marble – all this was straightforward stuff. Then came the problem – which was the higher, horns or ears? He tried it one way, he tried it the other; both looked equally unconvincing; he tried different types of ear – tiny, feline triangles, asinine tufts of hair and gristle, even, in desperation, drooping flaps remembered from a

guinea-pig in the backyard of his earliest home; he tried
different types of horn – royals, the elegant antennae of
the ibis, the vast armoury of moose and buffalo. Soon the
paper before him was covered like the hall of a hunter
with freakish heads. None looked right. He brooded over
them and found no satisfaction.

It was thus that Mr Salter found him.

Mr Salter had not wanted to come and see Lord Copper. He had nothing particular to say. He had not been
summoned. But he had the right of entry to his owner's
presence, and it was only thus, he believed, by unremitting, wholly uncongenial self-assertion, that he could
ever hope for a change of job.

'I wanted to consult you about Bucarest,' he said.

'Ah.'

'There's a long story from Jepson about a pogrom.
Have we any policy in Bucarest?'

Lord Copper roused himself from his abstraction.
'Someone on this paper must know about cows,' he said
petulantly.

'Cows, Lord Copper?'

'Don't we keep a man to write about the country?'

'Oh. That was Boot, Lord Copper.'

'Well, have him come and see me.'

'We sent him to Africa.'

'Well, have him come back. What's he doing there?
Who sent him?'

'He is on his way back now. It was Boot who brought
off the great story in Ishmaelia. When we scooped Hitchcock,' he added, for Lord Copper was frowning in a
menacing way.

Slowly the noble face lightened.

'Ah, yes, smart fellow, Boot. He was the right man for
that job.'

'It was you who discovered him, Lord Copper.'

'Of course, naturally ... had my eye on him for some
time. Glad he made good. There's always a chance for
real talent on the *Beast*, eh, Salter?'

'Definitely, Lord Copper.'

'Preparations going ahead for Boot's reception?'

'Up to a point.'

'Let me see, what was it we decided to do for him?'

'I don't think, Lord Copper, that the question was ever actually raised.'

'Nonsense. It is a matter I have particularly at heart. Boot has done admirably. He is an example to everyone on the staff – *everyone*. I wish to show my appreciation in a marked manner. When do you say he gets back?'

'At the end of next week.'

'I will thank him personally . . . You never had any faith in that boy, Salter.'

'Well . . .'

'I remember it quite distinctly. You wished to have him recalled. But I knew he had the makings of a journalist in him. Was I right?'

'Oh, definitely, Lord Copper.'

'Well, then, let us have no more of these petty jealousies. The office is riddled with them. I shall make it my concern to see that Boot is substantially rewarded . . . What, I wonder, would meet the case? . . .' Lord Copper paused, undecided. His eye fell on the page of drawings and he covered it with his blotting paper. 'Suppose,' he said at length, 'we gave him another good foreign assignment. There is this all-women expedition to the South Pole – bound to be a story in that. Do you think that would meet the case?'

'Up to a point, Lord Copper.'

'Not too lavish?'

'Definitely not.'

'I imagine that the expenses of an expedition of that kind will be heavy. Have to charter his own ship – I understand they will have no man on board.' He paused dissatisfied. 'The trouble is that it is the kind of story that may not break for two years and then we shall have to put Boot's name before the public all over again. We ought to do something *now*, while the news is still hot. I gave that illiterate fellow Hitchcock a knighthood for less.' For the first time since the question of the cow had risen to perplex him, Lord Copper smiled. 'We certainly wiped Hitchcock's eye in Ishmaelia.' He paused, and his smile broadened as he recalled the triumph of ten days ago when the *Brute* had had to remake their front page at seven in the morning and fill a special late edition with a palpable fake.

'I don't want to cheapen official honours among the staff,' he said, 'but I have a very good mind to give a knighthood to Boot. How does that strike you, Salter?'

'You don't think, Lord Copper, that he is rather an inexperienced man...?'

'No, I don't. And I deplore this grudging attitude in you, Salter. You should welcome the success of your subordinates. A knighthood is a very suitable recognition. It will not cost us a penny. As I say, honours of this kind must be distributed with discretion but, properly used, they give a proper air of authority to the paper.'

'It will mean an increase of salary.'

'He shall have it. And he shall have a banquet. Send my social secretary to me. I will make the arrangements at once.'

2

No. 10 Downing Street was understaffed; the principal private secretary was in Scotland; the second secretary was on the Lido; Parliament was in vacation but there was no rest for the Prime Minister; he was obliged to muddle along, as best he could, with his third and fourth secretaries – unreliable young men related to his wife.

'Another name for the K.C.B.'s,' he said petulantly. 'Boot – gratis.'

'Yes, Uncle Mervyn. Are you – we giving any particular reason?'

'It's someone of Copper's. Call it "Services to Litera-

ture." It's some time since Copper asked for anything –
I was getting nervous. I'll send him a personal note to tell
him it is all right. You might drop a line to Boot.'

'O.K., Uncle.'

Later his secretary said to his less important colleague:
'More birthdays. Boot – writer. Do you know anything
about him?'

'Yes, he's always lunching with Aunt Agnes. Smutty
novels.'

'Well, write, and tell him he's fixed up, will you?'

Two days later, among his bills, John Courtenay Boot
found forwarded to him a letter which said:

'*I am instructed by the Prime Minister to inform you that your
name has been forwarded to H.M. the King with the recommendation for your inclusion in the Order of Knights Commanders of
the Bath.*'

'Golly,' said Boot, 'It must be Julia.'

Mrs Stitch was staying in the same house. He went and
sat on her bed while she had breakfast. Presently he said:

'By the way, what d'you think? They're making me a
Knight.'

'Who are?'

'The King and the Prime Minister. You know . . . a
real Knight . . . Sir John Boot, I mean.'

'*Well . . .*'

'Is it your doing?'

'*Well* . . . I hardly know what to say, John. Are you
pleased about it?'

'It's hard to say yet . . . taken by surprise. But I *think* I
am . . . In fact I know I am . . . Come to think of it, I'm
very pleased indeed.'

'Good,' said Mrs Stitch. 'I'm very pleased too,' and
added, 'I suppose I did have something to do with it.'

'It was angelic of you. But why?'

'Just the Stitch service. I felt you had been disappointed
about that job on the newspaper.'

Later, when Algernon Stitch came back from a day
with the partridges, she said:

'Algie. What's come over your Prime Minister? He's
making John a Knight.'

'John Gassoway? Oh, well, he's had his tongue hanging
out for something ever since we got in.'

'No, John Boot.'

It was not often that Algernon Stitch showed surprise.
He did then.

'Boot,' he said. 'Good God!' and added after a long
pause, 'Overwork. Breaking up. Pity.'

John Boot was not sure whether to make a joke of it.
He extended his confidence to a Lady Greenidge and a
Miss Montesquieu. By dinner time the house was buzzing
with the news. There was no doubt in anyone else's mind
whether it was a joke or not.

3

'Anything to declare?'

'Nothing.'

'What, not with all this?'

'I bought it in London in June.'

'All of it?'

'More. There was a canoe . . .'

The customs officer laid hands on the nearest of the
crates which lay conspicuously among the hand luggage
of returning holiday-makers. Then he read the label and
his manner changed.

'Forgive me asking, sir, but are you by any chance Mr
Boot of the *Beast*?'

'Yes, I suppose I am.'

'Ah. Then I don't think I need trouble you, sir . . . the
missus *will* be pleased to hear I've seen you. We've been
reading a lot about you lately.'

Everyone seemed to have read about William. From

the moment he touched the fringe of the English-speaking world in the train de luxe from Marseille, William had found himself the object of undisguised curiosity. On his way round Paris he had bought a copy of the *Beast*. The front page was mainly occupied with the preparations of the Ladies' Antarctic Expedition but, inset in the middle, was a framed notice:

BOOT IS BACK

The man who made journalistic history, Boot of the Beast, *will tomorrow tell in his own inimitable way the inner story of his meteoric leap to fame. How does it feel to tell the truth to two million registered readers? How does it feel to have risen in a single week to the highest pinnacle of fame? Boot will tell you.*

That had been the paper of the day before. At Dover William bought the current issue. There, above a facsimile of his signature and a composite picture of his passport photograph surcharged on an Ishmaelite landscape, in the size which the *Beast* reserved for its most expensive contributors, stood the promised article.

'*Two months ago,*' it said, '*when Lord Copper summoned me from my desk in the* Beast *office, to handle the biggest news story of the century, I had never been to Ishmaelia, I knew little of foreign politics. I was being pitted against the most brilliant brains, the experience, and the learning of the civilized world. I had nothing except my youth, my will to succeed, and what – for want of a better word – I must call my flair. In the two months' battle of wits . . .*'

William could read no more. Overcome with shame he turned towards the train. A telegraph boy was loafing about the platform uttering monotonous, monosyllabic, plaintive, gull-like cries which, in William's disturbed mind, sounded like 'Boot. Boot. Boot.' William turned guiltily towards him; he bore a cardboard notice, stuck, by a felicitous stroke of fancy, into a cleft stick, on which was inscribed in unmistakable characters, '*Boot.*'

'I'm afraid that must be for me,' said William.

'There's a whole lot of them.'

The train seemed likely to start. William took the telegrams and opened them in the carriage, under the curious eyes of his fellow travellers.

PERSONALLY GRATIFIED YOUR SAFE RETURN COPPER.

BEAST REPRESENTATIVE WILL MEET YOU VICTORIA STOP PLEASE REPORT HERE IMMEDIATELY YOU RETURN STOP TALK BUSINESS NO ONE SALTER.

WILL YOU ACCEPT FIVE YEAR CONTRACT FIVE THOUSAND YEAR ROVING CORRESPONDENT EDITOR BRUTE.

PLEASE WIRE AUTHORITY NEGOTIATE BOOK SERIAL CINEMA RIGHTS AUTOBIOGRAPHY PAULS LITERARY AGENCY.

There were others, similarly phrased. William released them, one by one as he read them, at the open window. The rush of air whirled them across the charred embankment to the fields of stubble and stacked corn beyond.

At Victoria it was, once again, William's luggage which betrayed him. As he stood among the crates and bundles waiting for a taxi, a very young man approached him and said, 'I say, please, are you William Boot?' He had a pimply, eager face.

'Yes.'

'I'm from the *Beast*. They sent me to meet you. Mr Salter did.'

'Very kind of him.'

'I expect you would like a drink after your journey.'

'No, thank you.'

'Mr Salter said I was to ask you.'

'Very kind of him.'

'I say, please have a drink. Mr Salter said I could put it down as expenses.'

The young man seemed very eager.

'All right,' said William.

'You wouldn't know me,' said the young man as they walked to the buffet. 'I'm Bateson. I've only been on the paper three weeks. This is the first time I've charged anything on expenses. In fact it is the first time I've drawn any money from the *Beast* at all. I'm "on space", you see.'

'Ah.'

They reached the buffet and Bateson bought some whisky. 'I say,' he said, 'would you think it awful cheek if I asked you to do something?'

'What?'

'It's your big story. I've got a first edition of it.' He drew a grubby newspaper from his pocket. 'Would you sign for me?'

William signed.

'I say, thanks awfully. I'll get it framed. I've been carrying it about ever since it appeared – studying it, you know. That's the way they told me in the Correspondence School. Did you ever take a Correspondence School?'

'No.'

Bateson looked disappointed. 'Oh, dear, aren't they a good thing? They're terribly expensive.'

'I expect they are a very good thing.'

'You do think so, don't you? I'm a graduate of the Aircastle School. I paid fifteen shillings a month and I got a specially recommended diploma. That's how I got taken on the *Beast*. It's a great chance, I know. I haven't had anything in the paper yet. But one has to start sometime. It's a great profession, isn't it?'

'Yes, I suppose in a way it is.'

'It must be wonderful to be like you,' said Bateson wistfully. 'At the top. It's been a great chance my meeting you like this. I could hardly believe it when Mr Salter picked me to come. "Go and greet Boot," he said. "Give him a drink. Get him here before he signs on with the *Brute*." You wouldn't want to sign on with the *Brute*, would you?'

'No.'

'You do think the *Beast* is the leading paper, don't you? I mean it's the greatest chance you can have working for the *Beast*?'

'Yes.'

'I *am* glad. You see it's rather depressing sometimes, day after day and none of one's stories getting printed. I'd like to be a foreign correspondent like you. I say, would you think it awful cheek if I showed you some of the stuff I write? In my spare time I do it. I imagine some big piece of news and then I see how I should handle it. Last night in bed I imagined an actress with her throat cut. Shall I show it to you?'

'Please do,' said William, 'some time. But I think we ought to be going now.'

'Yes, I suppose we should. But you do think it's a good way of training oneself – inventing imaginary news?'

'None better,' said William.

They left the bar. The porter was keeping guard over the baggage. 'You'll need two cabs,' he said.

'Yes . . . Suppose you take the heavy stuff in one, Bateson, I'll follow with my own bags in the other.' He packed the young man in among the tropical equipment. 'Give them to Mr Salter and say I shan't need them any more.'

'But you're coming too?'

'I'm taking the cab behind,' said William.

They drove off down Victoria Street. When Bateson's cab was some distance ahead, William leant through the window and said, 'I've changed my mind. Go to Paddington instead.'

There was time before his train to telegraph to Boot Magna. '*Returning tonight William.*'

'Boot said he didn't want these any more.'

'No,' said Mr Salter, surveying with distaste the heap of travel-worn tropical equipment which encumbered his room. 'No, I suppose not. And where is Boot?'

'Just behind.'

'You ought to have stayed with him.'

'I'm sorry, Mr Salter.'

'There's no need for you to wait.'

'All right.'

'Well, what are you waiting for?'

'I was wondering, would you think it awful cheek if I asked for a souvenir.'

'Souvenir?'

'Of my meeting with Boot. Could you spare one of those sticks?'

'Take the lot.'

'I say, may I really. I say, thank you ever so much.'

'That boy, Bateson. Is he balmy or something?'

'I daresay.'

'What's he doing here?'

'He comes from the Aircastle Correspondence School. They guarantee a job to all their star pupils. They've a big advertising account with us, so we sometimes take one of their chaps "on space" for a bit.'

'Well, he's lost Boot. I suppose we can fire him now?'

'Surely.'

The harvest moon hung, brilliant and immense, over the elm trees. In the lanes around Boot Magna motor-cycles or decrepit cars travelled noisily home from the village whist drive; Mr Atwater, the bad character, packed his pockets for the night's sport; the smell of petrol hung about the hedges but inside the park everything was sweet and still. For a few feet ahead the lights of the car shed a feeble, yellow glow; beyond, the warm land lay white as frost, and, as they emerged from the black tunnel of evergreen around the gates into the open pasture, the drive with its sharply defined ruts and hollows might have been a strip of the moon itself, a volcanic field cold since the creation.

A few windows were alight; only Uncle Theodore was still up. He opened the door to William.

'Ah,' he said, 'train late?'

'I don't think so.'

'Ah,' he said. 'We got your telegram.'

'Yes.'

'Had a good time?'

'Yes, fairly.'

'You must tell us all about it tomorrow. Your grand-mother will want to hear, I know. Had any dinner?'

'Yes, thank you, on the train.'

'Good. We thought you might. We didn't keep any-thing hot. Rather short-handed at the moment. James hasn't been at all well, getting too old for his work – but there are some biscuits in the dining-room.'

'Thanks very much,' said William. 'I don't think I want anything.'

'No. Well, I think I'll be going along. Glad you've had such a good time. Don't forget to tell us about it. Can't say I read your articles. They were always cut out by the time I got the paper. Nannie Price disapproved of them. I must get hold of them, want to read them very much. . . .' They were walking upstairs together; they reached the landing where their ways diverged. William carried his bag to his own room and laid it on the bed. Then he went to the window and, stooping, looked out across the moonlit park.

On such a night as this, not four weeks back, the tin roofs of Jacksonburg had laid open to the sky, a three-legged dog had awoken, started from his barrel in Frau Dressler's garden, and all over the town, in yards and refuse heaps, the pariahs had taken up his cries of protest.

4

'Well,' said Mr Salter, 'I've heard from Boot.'

'Any good?'

'No. No good.'

He handed the News Editor the letter that had arrived that morning from William.

Dear Mr Salter, it ran,

Thank you very much for your letter and the invitation. It is very kind of Lord Copper, please thank him, but if you don't mind I think I won't come to the banquet. You see it is a long way and there is a great deal to do here and I can't make speeches. I have to every now and then for things in the village and they are bad enough – a banquet would be worse.

I hope you got the tent and things. Sorry about the canoe. I gave it to a German, also the Xmas dinner. I still have some of your money left. Do you want it back? Will you tell the other editor that I shall be sending him Lush Places on Wednesday.

Yours ever,

William Boot.

P.S. – Sorry. They forgot to post this. Now it's Saturday, so you won't get it till Monday.

'You think he's talking turkey with the *Brute*.'

'If he's not already signed up.'

'Ours is a nasty trade, Salter. No gratitude.'

'No loyalty.'

'I've seen it again and again since I've been in Fleet Street. It's enough to make one cynical.'

'What does Lord Copper say?'

'He doesn't know. For the moment, fortunately, he seems to have forgotten the whole matter. But he may raise it again at any moment.'

He did, that morning.

'. . . ah, Salter, I was talking to the Prime Minister last night. The honours list will be out on Wednesday. How are the preparations going for the Boot banquet? It's on the Thursday, I think.'

'That *was* the date, Lord Copper.'

'Good. I shall propose the health of our guest of honour. By the way, did Boot ever come and see me?'

'No, Lord Copper.'

'But I asked for him.'

'Yes, Lord Copper.'

'Then, why was he not brought? Once and for all,

Salter, I will not have a barrier erected between me and my staff. I am as accessible to the humblest' . . . Lord Copper paused for an emphatic example . . . 'the humblest book reviewer as I am to my immediate entourage. I will have no cliques in the *Beast*, you understand me?'

'Definitely.'

'Then bring Boot here.'

'Yes, Lord Copper.'

It was an inauspicious beginning to Mr Salter's working day; worse was to come.

That afternoon he was sitting disconsolately in the News Editor's room when they were interrupted by the entry of a young man whose face bore that puffy aspect, born of long hours in the golf-house, which marked most of the better paid members of the *Beast* staff on their return from their summer holidays. Destined by his trustees for a career in the Household Cavalry, this young man had lately reached the age of twenty-five and plunged into journalism with a zeal which Mr Salter found it difficult to understand. He talked to them cheerfully for some time on matters connected with his handicap. Then he said:

'By the way, I don't know if there's a story in it, but I was staying last week with my Aunt Trudie. John Boot was there among other people – you know, the novelist. He'd just got a letter from the King or someone like that, saying he was going to be knighted.' The look of startled concern on the two editors' faces checked him. 'I see you don't think much of it. Oh, well, I thought it might be worth mentioning. You know. "Youth's Opportunity in New Reign", that kind of thing.'

'*John* Boot – the novelist.'

'Yes. Rather good – at least I always read him. But it seemed a new line for the Prime Minister . . .'

'No,' said the Prime Minister with unusual finality.

'No?'

'No. It would be utterly impossible to change the list

now. The man has been officially notified. And I could not consider knighting two men of the same name on the same day. Just the kind of thing the Opposition would jump on. Quite rightly. Smacks of jobbery, you know.'

'*Two Boots.*'
'Lord Copper must know.'
'Lord Copper must never know. . . . There's only one comfort. We haven't committed ourselves to which Boot we are welcoming on Thursday or where he's come from.' He pointed to the engraved card which had appeared, during the week-end, on the desks of all the four-figure men in the office.

VISCOUNT COPPER
and

the Directors of the Megalopolitan Newspaper Company request the honour of your company to dinner on Wednesday, September 16th, at the Braganza Hotel, to welcome the return of

BOOT of THE BEAST
7.45 for 8 o'clock.

'We had a row with the social secretary about that. He said it wasn't correct. Lucky how things turned out.'
'It makes things little better.'
'A little.'
'Salter, this is a case for personal contact. We've got to sign up this new Boot and any other Boot that may be going and one of them has got to be welcomed home on Thursday. There's only one thing for it, Salter, you must go down to the country and see Boot. I'll settle with the other.'
'To the country?'
'Yes, tonight.'
'Oh, but I couldn't go tonight.'
'Tomorrow, then.'
'You think it is really necessary?'

'Either that, or we must tell Lord Copper the truth.'

Mr Salter shuddered. 'But wouldn't it be better,' he said, 'if *you* went to the country?'

'No. I'll see this novelist and get him signed up.'

'And sent away.'

'Or welcomed home. And you will offer the other Boot any reasonable terms to lie low.'

'Any reasonable terms.'

'Salter, old man, what's come over you? You keep repeating things.'

'It's nothing. It's only . . . travelling . . . always upsets me.'

He had a cup of strong tea and later rang up the Foreign Contacts Adviser to find how he could best get to Boot Magna.

TWO

I

AT the outbreak of the war of 1914 Uncle Roderick had declared for retrenchment. 'It's up to all of us who are over military age to do what we can. All unnecessary expenses must be cut down.'

'Why?' asked Great Aunt Anne.

'It is a question of national emergency and patriotism.'

'How will our being uncomfortable hurt the Germans? It's just what they want.'

'Everything is needed at the front,' explained William's mother.

Discussion had raged for some days; every suggested economy seemed to strike invidiously at individual members of the household. At last it was decided to give up the telephone. Aunt Anne sometimes spoke bitterly of the time when 'my nephew Roderick won the war by cutting me off from my few surviving friends,' but the service had

never been renewed. The antiquated mahogany box still
stood at the bottom of the stairs, dusty and silent, and
telegrams which arrived in the village after tea were
delivered next day with the morning post. Thus, William
found Mr Salter's telegram waiting for him on the breakfast table.

His mother, Priscilla, and his three uncles sat round
the table. They had finished eating and were sitting there,
as they often sat for an hour or so, doing nothing at all.
Priscilla alone was occupied, killing wasps in the honey
on her plate.

'There's a telegram for you,' said his mother. 'We were
wondering whether we ought to open it or send it up to
you.'

It said: MUST SEE YOU IMMEDIATELY URGENT
BUSINESS ARRIVING BOOT MAGNA HALT TO-
MORROW AFTERNOON 6.10 SALTER.

The message was passed from hand to hand around the
table.

Mrs Boot said, 'Who is Mr Salter, and what urgent
business can he possibly have here?'

Uncle Roderick said, 'He can't stay the night. Nowhere
for him to sleep.'

Uncle Bernard said, 'You must telegraph and put him
off.'

Uncle Theodore said, 'I knew a chap called Salter
once, but I don't suppose it's the same one.'

Priscilla said, 'I believe he means to come today. It's
dated yesterday.'

'He's the foreign editor of the *Beast*,' William explained.
'The one I told you about who sent me abroad.'

'He must be a very pushful fellow, inviting himself here
like this. Anyway, as Roderick says, we've no room for
him.'

'We could send Priscilla to the Caldicotes for the
night.'

'I like that,' said Priscilla, adding illogically, 'Why
don't you send William, it's his friend.'

'Yes,' said Mrs Boot. 'Priscilla could go to the Caldicotes.'

'I'm cubbing tomorrow,' said Priscilla, 'right in the other direction. You can't expect Lady Caldicote to send me thirty miles at eight in the morning.'

For over an hour the details of Priscilla's hunt occupied the dining-room. Could she send her horse overnight to a farm near the meet; could she leave the Caldicotes at dawn, pick up her horse at Boot Magna, and ride on; could she borrow Major Watkins's trailer and take her horse to the Caldicotes for the night, then as far as Major Watkins's in the morning and ride on from there; if she got the family car from Aunt Agnes and Major Watkins's trailer, would Lady Caldicote lend her a car to take it to Major Watkins's; would Aunt Anne allow the car to stay the night; would she discover it was taken without her permission? They discussed the question exhaustively, from every angle; Troutbeck twice glowered at them from the door and finally began to clear the table; Mr Salter and the object of his visit were not mentioned.

2

That evening, some time after the advertised hour, Mr Salter alighted at Boot Magna Halt. An hour earlier, at Taunton, he had left the express, and changed into a train such as he did not know existed outside the imagination of his Balkan correspondents; a single tram-like, one-class coach, which had pottered in a desultory fashion through a system of narrow, under-populated valleys. It had stopped eight times, and at every station there had been a bustle of passengers succeeded by a long, silent pause, before it started again; men had entered who, instead of slinking and shuffling and wriggling themselves into corners and decently screening themselves behind newspapers, as civilized people should when they travelled by train, had sat down squarely quite close to Mr

Salter, rested their hands on their knees, stared at him
fixedly and uncritically and suddenly addressed him on
the subject of the weather in barely intelligible accents;
there had been very old, unhygienic men and women,
such as you never saw in the Underground, who ought
long ago to have been put away in some public institu-
tion; there had been women carrying a multitude of
atrocious little baskets and parcels which they piled on
the seats; one of them had put a hamper containing a live
turkey under Mr Salter's feet. It had been a horrible
journey.

At last, with relief, Mr Salter alighted. He lifted his
suitcase from among the sinister bundles on the rack and
carried it to the centre of the platform. There was no one
else for Boot Magna. Mr Salter had hoped to find
William waiting to meet him, but the little station was
empty except for a single porter who was leaning against
the cab of the engine engaged in a kind of mute, tele-
pathic converse with the driver, and a cretinous native
youth who stood on the further side of the paling, leant
against it and picked at the dry paint-bubbles with a toe-
like thumb nail. When Mr Salter looked at him, he
glanced away and grinned wickedly at his boots.

The train observed its customary two minutes' silence
and then steamed slowly away. The porter shuffled across
the line and disappeared into a hut labelled 'Lamps'. Mr
Salter turned towards the palings; the youth was still
leaning there, gazing; his eyes dropped; he grinned.
Three times, shuttlecock fashion, they alternately glanced
up and down till Mr Salter, with urban impatience, tired
of the flirtation and spoke up.

'I say.'

'Ur.'

'Do you happen to know whether Mr Boot has sent a
car for me?'

'Ur.'

'He has?'

'Noa. She've a taken of the harse.'

'I am afraid you misunderstand me.' Mr Salter's voice sounded curiously flutey and querulous in contrast to the deep tones of the moron. 'I'm coming to visit Mr Boot. I wondered if he had sent a motor-car for me.'

'He've a sent me.'

'With the car?'

'Noa. Motor-car's over to Lady Caldicote's taking of the harse. The bay,' he explained, since Mr Salter seemed not to be satisfied with this answer. 'Had to be the bay for because the mare's sick . . . The old bay's not up yet,' he added as though to make everything perfectly clear.

'Well, how am I to get to the house?'

'Why, along of me and Bert Tyler.'

'Has this Mr Tyler got a car, then?'

'Noa. I tell e car's over to Lady Caldicote's along of Miss Priscilla and the bay . . . Had to be the bay,' he persisted, 'because for the mare's sick.'

'Yes, yes, I quite appreciate that.'

'And the old bay's still swole up with grass. So you'm to ride along of we.'

'Ride?' A hideous vision rose before Mr Salter.

'Ur. Along of me and Bert Tyler and the slag.'

'Slag?'

'Ur. Mr Roderick's getting in the slag now for to slag Westerheys. Takes a tidy bit.'

Mr Salter was suffused with relief. 'You mean that you have some kind of vehicle outside full of slag?'

'Ur. Cheaper now than what it will be when Mr Roderick wants it.'

Mr Salter descended the steps into the yard where, out of sight from the platform, an open lorry was standing; an old man next to the driving seat touched his cap; the truck was loaded high with sacks; bonnet and back bore battered learner plates. The youth took Mr Salter's suitcase and heaved it up among the slag. 'You'm to ride behind,' he said.

'If it's all the same to you,' said Mr Salter rather sharply, 'I should prefer to sit in front.'

'It's all the same to *me*, but I durstn't let you. The police would have I.'

'Good gracious, why?'

'Bert Tyler have to ride along of me, for because of the testers.'

'Testers?'

'Ur. Police don't allow for me to drive except along of Bert Tyler. Bert Tyler he've a had a licence twenty year. There wasn't no testers for Bert Tyler. But police they took and tested I over to Taunton.'

'And you failed?'

A great grin spread over the young man's face. 'I busted tester's leg for he,' he said proudly. 'Ran he bang into the wall, going a fair lick.'

'Oh, dear. Wouldn't it be better for your friend Tyler to drive us?'

'Noa. He can't see for to drive, Bert Tyler can't. Don't e be afeared. I can *see* all right. It be the corners do for I.'

'And are there many corners between here and the house?'

'Tidy few.'

Mr Salter, who had had his foot on the hub of the wheel preparatory to mounting, now drew back. His nerve, never strong, had been severely tried that afternoon; now it failed him.

'I'll walk,' he said. 'How far is it?'

'Well, it's all according as you know the way. We do call it three mile over the fields. It's a tidy step by the road.'

'Perhaps you'll be good enough to show me the field path.'

'Tain't exactly what you could call a path. E just keeps straight.'

'Well, I daresay I shall find it. If . . . if by any chance you get to the house before me, will you tell Mr Boot that I wanted a little exercise after the journey?'

The learner-driver looked at Mr Salter with undis-

guised contempt. 'I'll tell e as you was afeared to ride
along of me and Bert Tyler,' he said.

Mr Salter stepped back into the station porch to avoid
the dust as the lorry drove away. It was as well that he
did so, for, as he mounted the incline, the driver mis-
takenly changed into reverse and the machine charged
precipitately back in its tracks, and came noisily to rest
against the wall where Mr Salter had been standing. The
second attempt was more successful and it reached the
lane with no worse damage than a mudguard crushed
against the near gatepost.

Then with rapid, uncertain steps Mr Salter set out on
his walk to the house.

3

It was eight o'clock when Mr Salter arrived at the
front door. He had covered a good six miles tacking from
field to field under the setting sun; he had scrambled
through fences and ditches; in one enormous pasture a
herd of cattle had closed silently in on him and followed
at his heels – the nearest not a yard away – with lowered
heads and heavy breath; Mr Salter had broken into a
run and they had trotted after him; when he gained the
stile and turned to face them, they began gently grazing
in his tracks; dogs had flown at him in three farmyards
where he had stopped to ask the way, and to be misdirec-
ted; at last, when he felt he could go no further but must
lie down and perish from exposure under the open sky,
he had stumbled through an overgrown stile to find himself
in the main road with the lodge gates straight ahead; the
last mile up the drive had been the bitterest of all.

And now he stood under the porch, sweating, blistered,
nettlestung, breathless, parched, dizzy, dead-beat and
dishevelled, with his bowler hat in one hand and umbrella
in the other, leaning against a stucco pillar waiting for

someone to open the door. Nobody came. He pulled
again at the bell; there was no answering ring, no echo
in the hall beyond. No sound broke the peace of the
evening save, in the elms that stood cumbrously on every
side, the crying of the rooks, and, not unlike it but nearer
at hand, directly it seemed over Mr Salter's head, a
strong baritone decanting irregular snatches of sacred
music.

'In Thy courts no more are needed, sun by day nor
moon by night,' sang Uncle Theodore blithely, stepping
into his evening trousers; he remembered it as a treble
solo rising to the dim vaults of the school chapel, touching
the toughest adolescent hearts; he remembered it imperfectly but with deep emotion.

Mr Salter listened, unmoved. In despair he began to
pound the front door with his umbrella. The singing
ceased and the voice in fruity, more prosaic tones demanded, 'What, ho, without there?'

Mr Salter hobbled down the steps, clear of the porch,
and saw framed in the ivy of a first-floor window, a ruddy,
Hanoverian face and plump, bare torso. 'Good-evening,'
he said politely.

'Good-evening.' Uncle Theodore leaned out as far as
he safely could and stared at Mr Salter through a monocle.
'From where you are standing,' he said, 'you might easily
take me to be totally undraped. Let me hasten to assure
you that such is not the case. Seemly black shrouds me
from the waist down. No doubt you are the friend my
nephew William is expecting?'

'Yes ... I've been ringing the bell.'

'It sounded to me,' said Uncle Theodore severely, 'as
though you were hammering the door with a stick.'

'Yes, I was. You see ...'

'You'll be late for dinner, you know, if you stand out
there kicking up a rumpus. And so shall I if I stay talking
to you. We will meet again shortly in more conventional
circumstances. For the moment – *a rivederci*.'

The head withdrew and once more the melody rose

into the twilight, mounted to the encircling tree-tops and joined the chorus of the homing rooks.

Mr Salter tried the handle of the door. It opened easily. Never in his life had he made his own way into anyone else's house. Now he did so and found himself in a lobby cluttered with implements of sport, overcoats, rugs, a bicycle or two and a stuffed bear. Beyond it, glass doors led into the hall. He was dimly aware of a shadowy double staircase which rose and spread before him, of a large, carpetless chequer of black and white marble pavings, of islands of furniture and some potted palms. Quite near the glass doors stood a little arm-chair where no one ever sat; there Mr Salter sank and there he was found twenty minutes later by William's mother when she came down to dinner. His last action before he lapsed into coma had been to remove his shoes.

Mrs Boot surveyed the figure with some distaste and went on her way to the drawing-room. It was one of the days when James was on his feet; she could hear him next door rattling the silver on the dining-room table. 'James,' she called, through the double doors.

'Yes, madam.'

'Mr William's friend has arrived. I think perhaps he would like to wash.'

'Very good, madam.'

Mr Salter was not really asleep; he had been aware, remotely and impersonally, of Mrs Boot's scrutiny; he was aware, now, of James's slow passage across the hall.

'Dinner will be in directly, sir. May I take you to your room?'

For a moment Mr Salter thought he would be unable ever to move again; then, painfully, he rose to his feet. He observed his discarded shoes; so did James; neither of them felt disposed to stoop; each respected the other's feeling; Mr Salter padded upstairs beside the footman.

'I regret to say, sir, that your luggage is not yet available. Three of the outside men are delving for it at the moment.'

'Delving?'

'Assiduously, sir. It was inundated with slag at the time of the accident.'

'Accident?'

'Yes, sir, there has been a misadventure to the farm lorry that was conveying it from the station; we attribute it to the driver's inexperience. He overturned the vehicle in the back drive.'

'Was he hurt?'

'Oh, yes, sir; gravely. Here is your room, sir.'

An oil lamp, surrounded by moths and autumnal beetles, burned on Priscilla's dressing-table, illuminating a homely, girlish room. Little had been done, beyond the removal of loofah and nightdress, to adapt it for male occupation. Twenty or thirty china animals stood on brackets and shelves, together with slots of deer, brushes of foxes, pads of otters, a horse's hoof, and other animal trophies; a low, bronchial growl came from under the bed.

'Miss Priscilla hoped you would not object to taking charge of Amabel for the night, sir. She's getting an old dog now and doesn't like to be moved. You'll find her perfectly quiet and good. If she barks in the night, it is best to feed her.'

James indicated two saucers of milk and minced meat which stood on the bed table that had already attracted Mr Salter's attention.

'Would that be all, sir?'

'Thank you,' said Mr Salter, weakly.

James left, gently closing the door which, owing to a long-standing defect in its catch, as gently swung open again behind him.

Mr Salter poured some warm water into the prettily flowered basin on the washhand stand.

James returned. 'I omitted to tell you, sir, the lavatory on this floor is out of order. The gentlemen use the one opening on the library.'

'Thank you.'

James repeated the pantomime of shutting the door.

Nurse Grainger was always first down in the drawing-room. Dinner was supposed to be at quarter past eight, and for fifteen years she had been on time. She was sitting there, stitching a wool mat of modernistic design, when Mrs Boot first entered. When Mrs Boot had given her order to James, she smiled at her and said, 'How is your patient tonight, nurse?' and Nurse Grainger answered as she had answered nightly for fifteen years, 'A little low-spirited.'

'Yes,' said Mrs Boot, 'she gets low-spirited in the evenings.'

The two women sat in silence, Nurse Grainger snipping and tugging at the magenta wool; Mrs Boot reading a gardening magazine to which she subscribed. It was not until Lady Trilby entered the room that she expressed her forebodings.

'The boys are late,' said Lady Trilby.

'Aunt Agnes,' said Mrs Boot gravely, 'William's friend has arrived in a *most peculiar condition*.'

'I know. I watched him come up the drive. Reeling all over the shop.'

'He let himself in and went straight off to sleep in the hall.'

'Best thing for him.'

'You mean ... You don't think he could have been ... ?'

'The man was squiffy,' said Aunt Agnes. 'It was written all over him.'

Nurse Grainger uttered a knowing little cluck of disapproval.

'It's lucky Priscilla isn't here. What had we better do?'

'The boys will see to him.'

'Here is Theodore. I will ask him at once. Theodore, William's friend from London has arrived, and Aunt Agnes and I very much fear that he has taken too much.'

'Has he, by Jove,' said Uncle Theodore, rather enviously. 'Now you mention it, I shouldn't be at all surprised. I talked to the fellow out of my window. He was pounding the front door fit to knock it in.'

'What ought we to do?'

'Oh, he'll sober up,' said Uncle Theodore, from deep experience. Uncle Roderick joined them. 'I say, Rod, what d'you think? That journalist fellow of William's – he's sozzled.'

'Disgusting. Is he fit to come into dinner?'

'We'd better keep an eye on him to see he doesn't get any more.'

'Yes. I'll tell James.'

Uncle Bernard joined the family circle. 'Good evening, good evening,' he said in his courtly fashion. 'I'm nearly the last, I see.'

'Bernard, we have something to tell you.'

'And I have something to tell *you*. I was sitting in the library not two minutes ago when a dirty little man came prowling in – without any shoes on.'

'Was he tipsy?'

'I dare say . . . now you mention it, I think he was.'

'That's William's friend.'

'Well, he should be taken care of. Where is William?'

William was playing dominoes with Nannie Bloggs. It was this custom of playing dominoes with her from six till seven every evening which had prevented him meeting Mr Salter at the station. On this particular evening the game had been prolonged far beyond its usual limit. Three times he had attempted to leave, but the old woman was inflexible. 'Just you stay where you sit,' she said. 'You always were a headstrong, selfish boy. Worse than your Uncle Theodore. Gallivanting about all over Africa with a lot of heathens, and now you *are* home you don't want to spend a few minutes with your old Nannie.'

'But, Nannie, I've got a guest arriving.'

'*Guest*. Time enough for him. It's not *you* he's after, I'll be bound. It's my pretty Priscilla. You leave them be . . . I'll make it half a sovereign this time.'

Not until the gong sounded for dinner would she let him go. 'Wash your hands,' she said, 'and brush your

hair nicely. I don't know what your mother will say at
you going down to dinner in your flannels. And mind you
bring Priscilla's young man up afterwards and we'll have
a nice game of cards. It's thirty-three shillings you owe
me.'

Mr Salter had no opportunity of talking business at
dinner. He sat between Mrs Boot and Lady Trilby; never
an exuberant man, he now felt subdued almost to extinc-
tion and took his place glumly between the two formidable ladies; he might feel a little stronger, he hoped, after
a glass of wine.

James moved heavily round the table with the decan-
ters; claret for the ladies, William and Uncle Bernard,
whisky and water for Uncle Theodore, medicated cider
for Uncle Roderick. 'Water, sir?' said a voice in Mr Salter's ear.

'Well, I think perhaps I would sooner . . .' A clear and
chilling cascade fell into his tumbler and James returned
to the sideboard.

William, noticing a little shudder pass over his guest,
leaned forward across the table. 'I say, Salter, haven't
they given you anything to drink?'

'Well, as a matter of fact . . .'

Mrs Boot frowned at her son – a frown like a sudden
spasm of pain. 'Mr Salter *prefers* water.'

'Nothing like it,' said Uncle Theodore. 'I respect him
for it.'

'Well, as a matter of fact . . .'

Both ladies addressed him urgently and simultaneously;
'You're a great walker, Mr Salter,' in challenging tones
from Lady Trilby; 'It is quite a treat for you to get away
from your work into the country,' more gently from Mrs
Boot. By the time that Mr Salter had dealt civilly with
these two mis-statements, the subject of wine was closed.

Dinner was protracted for nearly an hour, but not by
reason of any great profusion or variety of food. It was
rather a bad dinner; scarcely better than he would have

got at Lord Copper's infamous table; greatly inferior to
the daintily garnished little dishes which he enjoyed at
home. In course of time each member of the Boot family
had evolved an individual style of eating; before each
plate was ranged a little store of seasonings and delica-
cies, all marked with their owner's initials – onion salt,
Bombay duck, gherkins, garlic vinegar, Dijon mustard,
pea-nut butter, icing sugar, varieties of biscuit from Bath
and Tunbridge Wells, Parmesan cheese, and a dozen
other jars and bottles and tins mingled incongruously
with the heavy, Georgian silver; Uncle Theodore had a
little spirit lamp and chafing dish with which he concoc-
ted a sauce. The dishes as sent in from the kitchen were
rather the elementary materials of dinner than the dinner
itself. Mr Salter found them correspondingly dull and
unconscionably slow in coming. Conversation was
general and intermittent.

Like foreign news bulletins, Boot family table talk took
the form of antithetical statements rather than of free
discussion.

'Priscilla took Amabel with her to the Caldicotes,' said
Lad·· Trilby.

'She left her behind,' said Mrs Boot.

'A dirty old dog,' said Uncle Bernard.

'Too old to go visiting,' said Uncle Roderick.

'Too dirty.'

'Mr Salter is having Amabel to sleep with him,' said
Mrs Boot.

'Mr Salter is very fond of her,' said Lady Trilby.

'He doesn't know her,' said Uncle Bernard.

'He's very fond of all dogs,' said Mrs Boot.

There was a pause in which James announced: 'If you
please, madam, the men have sent up to say it is too dark
to go on moving the slag.'

'Very awkward,' said Uncle Roderick. 'Blocks the back
drive.'

'And Mr Salter will have no things for the night,' said
Mrs Boot.

'William will lend him some.'
'Mr Salter will not mind. He will understand.'
'But he is sorry to have lost his things.'

Presently Mr Salter got the hang of it. 'It is a long way from the station,' he ventured.
'You stopped on the way.'
'Yes, to ask ... I was lost.'
'You stopped several times.'

At last dinner came to an end.
'He got better towards the end of dinner,' said Lady Trilby in the drawing-room.
'He is practically himself again,' said Mrs Boot.
'Roderick will see that he does not get at the port.'

'You won't take port,' said Uncle Roderick.
'Well, as a matter of fact ...'
'Push it round to Bernard, there's a good fellow.'
'You and William have business to discuss.'
'Yes,' said Mr Salter eagerly. 'Yes, it's most important.'
'You could go to the library.'
'Yes.'
William led his guest from the table and out of the room.
'Common little fellow,' said Uncle Roderick.
'It's a perfectly good name,' said Uncle Bernard. 'An early corruption of saltire, which no doubt he bears on his coat. But of course it may have been assumed irregularly.'
'Can't hold it,' said Uncle Theodore.
'I always understood that the true Salters became extinct in the fifteenth century ...'

In the library William for the first time had the chance of apologizing for the neglect of his guest.
'Of course, of course. I quite understand that living where you do, you are naturally distracted ... I would not have intruded on you for the world. But it was a mat-

ter of first-rate importance – of Lord Copper's personal wishes, you understand.

'There are two things. First, your contract with us . . . Boot,' said Mr Salter earnestly, 'you won't desert the ship.'

'Eh?'

'I mean it was the *Beast* that gave you your chance. You mustn't forget that!'

'No.'

'I suppose the *Brute* have made a very attractive offer. But believe me, Boot, I've known Fleet Street longer than you have. I've seen several men transfer from us to them. They thought they were going to be better off, but they weren't. It's no life for a man of individuality, working for the *Brute*. You'd be selling your soul, Boot . . . You haven't by the way, sold it?'

'No. They did send me a telegram. But to tell you the truth I was so glad to be home that I forgot to answer it.'

'Thank heaven. I've got a contract here, ready drawn up. Duplicate copies. They only need your signature. Luckily I did not pack them in my suitcase. A life contract for two thousand a year. Will you sign?'

William signed. He and Mr Salter each folded his copy and put it in his pocket; each with a feeling of deep satisfaction.

'And then there's the question of the banquet. There won't be any difficulty about that now. I quite understand that while the *Brute* offer was still in the air . . . Well, I'm delighted it's settled. You had better come up with me tomorrow morning. Lord Copper may want to see you beforehand.'

'No.'

'But, my dear Boot . . . You need have no worry about your speech. That is being written for you by Lord Copper's social secretary. It will be quite simple. Five minutes or so in praise of Lord Copper.'

'No.'

'The banquet will be widely reported. There may even be a film made of it.'

'No.'

'Really, Boot, I can't understand you at all.'

'Well,' said William with difficulty, 'I should feel an ass.'

'Yes,' said Mr Salter, 'I can understand that. But it's only for one evening.'

'I've felt an ass for weeks. Ever since I went to London. I've been treated like an ass.'

'Yes,' said Mr Salter sadly. 'That's what we are paid for.'

'It's one thing being an ass in Africa. But if I go to this banquet they may learn about it down here.'

'No doubt they would.'

'Nannie Bloggs and Nannie Price and everyone.'

Mr Salter was not in fighting form and he knew it. The strength was gone out of him. He was dirty and blistered and aching in every limb, cold sober and unsuitably dressed. He was in a strange country. These people were not his people nor their laws his. He felt like a Roman legionary, heavily armed, weighted with the steel and cast brass of civilization, tramping through forests beyond the Roman pale, harassed by silent, elusive savages, the vanguard of an advance that had pushed too far and lost touch with the base . . . or was he the abandoned rearguard of a retreat; had the legions sailed?

'I think,' he said, 'I'd better ring up the office and ask their advice.'

'You can't do that,' said William cheerfully. 'The nearest office is three miles away; there's no car; and anyway it shuts at seven.'

Silence fell in the library. Once more Mr Salter rallied to the attack. He tried sarcasm.

'These ladies you mention; no doubt they are estimable people, but surely, my dear Boot, you will admit that Lord Copper is a little more important.'

'No,' said William gravely 'Not down here.'

They were still sitting in silence when Troutbeck came to them, ten minutes later.

'Miss Price says she is expecting you upstairs to play cards.'

'You don't mind?' William asked.

Mr Salter was past minding anything. He was led upstairs, down long lamp-lit corridors, through doors of faded baize to Nannie Price's room. Uncle Theodore was already there arranging the card table beside her bed. 'So this is him,' she said. 'Why hasn't he got any shoes?'

'It's a long story,' said William.

The beady old eyes studied Mr Salter's careworn face; she put on her spectacles and looked again. 'Too old,' she said.

Coming from whom it did, this criticism seemed a bit thick; even in his depressed condition, Mr Salter was roused to resentment. 'Too old for what?' he asked sharply.

Nannie Price, though hard as agate about matters of money and theology, had, in old age, a soft spot for a lover. 'There, there, dearie,' she said. 'I don't mean anything. There's many a young heart beats in an old body. Sit down. Cut the cards, Mr Theodore. You've had a disappointment, I know, her being away. She always was a contrary girl. The harder the wooing the sweeter the winning, they say — two spades — and there's many a happy marriage between April and December — don't go peeping over my hand, Mr Theodore — and she's a good girl at heart, though she does forget her neck sometimes — three spades — comes out of the bath as black as she went in. I don't know what she does there...'

They played three rubbers and Mr Salter lost twenty-two shillings. As they rose to leave, Nannie Price, who had from long habit kept up a more or less continuous monologue during the course of the game, said, 'Don't give up, dearie. If it wasn't that your hair was thinning you mightn't be more than thirty-five. She doesn't know her own mind yet, and that's the truth.'

They left. William and Uncle Theodore accompanied
Mr Salter to his room. William said 'Good night.' Uncle
Theodore lingered.

'Pity you doubled our hearts,' he said.

'Yes.'

'Got you down badly.'

'Yes.'

A single candle stood on the table by the bed. In its
light Mr Salter saw a suit of borrowed pyjamas laid out.
Sleep was coming on him like a vast, pea-soup fog, rolling
down Fleet Street from Ludgate Hill. He did not want to
disc.ss their game of bridge.

'We had all the cards,' said Uncle Theodore mag-
nanimously, sitting down on the bed.

'Yes.'

'I expect you keep pretty late hours in London.'

'Yes...no...that is to say, sometimes.'

'Hard to get used to country hours. I don't suppose you
feel a bit sleepy?'

'Well, as a matter of fact...'

'When I lived in London,' began Uncle Theodore...
The candle burned low.

'Funny thing that...'

Mr Salter awoke with a start. He was sitting in Priscilla's chintz-covered arm-chair; Uncle Theodore was
still on the bed, reclining now like a surfeited knight of
the age of Heliogabalus...

'Of course you couldn't print it. But I've quite a number of stories you *could* print. Hundreds of 'em. I was
wondering if it was the kind of thing your newspaper...'

'Quite outside my province, I'm afraid. You see, I'm
the Foreign editor.'

'Half of them deal with Paris; *more* than half. For
instance...'

'I should love to hear them, *all* of them, sometime,
later, not now...'

'You pay very handsomely, I believe, on the *Beast*.'

'Yes.'

'Now suppose I was to write a series of articles . . .'

'Mr Boot,' said Mr Salter desperately, 'let us discuss it in the morning.'

'I'm never in my best form in the morning,' said Uncle Theodore doubtfully. 'Now after dinner I can talk quite happily until *any* time.'

'Come to London. See the features editor.'

'Yes,' said Uncle Theodore. 'I will. But I don't want to shock him; I should like your opinion first.'

The mists rose in Mr Salter's brain; a word or two loomed up and was lost again . . . 'Willis's rooms . . . "Pussy" Gresham . . . Romano's . . . believe it or not, fifteen *thousand* pounds . . .' Then all was silence.

When Mr Salter awoke he was cold and stiff and fully dressed except for his shoes; the candle was burned out. Autumnal dawn glimmered in the window, and Priscilla Boot, in riding habit, was ransacking the wardrobe for a lost tie.

4

The managing editor of the *Beast* was not easily moved to pity. 'I say, Salter,' he said, almost reverently, 'you look terrible.'

'Yes,' said Mr Salter, lowering himself awkwardly into a chair, 'that's the only word for it.'

'These heavy drinking country squires, eh?'

'No. It wasn't *that*.'

'Have you got Boot?'

'Yes and no. Have you?'

'Yes and no. He signed all right.'

'So did mine. But he won't come to the banquet.'

'I've sent my Boot off to the Antarctic. He said he had to go abroad at once. Apparently some woman is pursuing him.'

'Mr Boot,' said Mr Salter, 'is afraid of losing the esteem of his old nurse.'

'*Women*,' said the managing editor.

One thought was in both men's minds. 'What are we going to say to Lord Copper?'

The social secretary, whom they went to consult, was far from helpful.

'Lord Copper is looking forward very much to his speech,' she said. 'He has been rehearsing it all the afternoon.'

'You could rewrite it a little,' said the managing editor. '"Even in the moment of triumph, duty called. Here today, gone tomorrow ... honouring the empty chair ... the high adventure of modern journalism ..."' But even as he spoke, his voice faltered.

'No,' said the social secretary. 'That is not the kind of speech Lord Copper intends to make. You can hear him, in there, now.' A dull booming sound, like breakers on shingle, rose and fell beyond the veneered walnut doors. 'He's getting it by heart,' she added.

The two editors went sadly back to their own quarters.

'I've worked with the Megalopolitan, one way and another, for fifteen years,' said Mr Salter. 'I've got a wife to consider.'

'You at least might get other employment,' said the managing editor. 'You've been educated. There's nothing in the world I'm fit to do except edit the *Beast*.'

'It was your fault in the first place for engaging Boot at all. He wasn't a foreign page man.

'You sent him to Ishmaelia.'

'*I* wanted to sack him. You made him a hero. You made a monkey of him. It was you who thought of that article which upset him.'

'You encouraged Lord Copper to give him a knighthood.'

'You encouraged the banquet.'

'We were both at fault,' said the managing editor. 'But there's no point in our both suffering. Let's toss for who takes the blame.'

The coin spun in the air, fell and rolled away out of

sight. Mr Salter was on his knees, searching, when the features editor looked in.

'Do either of you know anything about an old chap called Boot?' he asked. 'I can't get him out of my room. He's been sitting there telling me dirty stories since I got back from lunch. Says Salter sent him.'

THREE

I

LORD COPPER quite often gave banquets; it would be an understatement to say that no one enjoyed them more than the host, for no one else enjoyed them at all, while Lord Copper positively exulted in every minute. For him they satisfied every requirement of a happy evening's entertainment; like everything that was to Lord Copper's taste, they were a little over life-size, unduly large and unduly long; they took place in restaurants which existed solely for such purposes, amid decorations which reminded Lord Copper of his execrable country seat at East Finchley; the provisions were copious, very bad and very expensive; the guests were assembled for no other reason than that Lord Copper had ordered it; they did not want to see each other; they had no reason to rejoice on the occasions which Lord Copper celebrated; they were there either because it was part of their job or because they were glad of a free dinner. Many were already on Lord Copper's pay roll and they thus found their working day prolonged by some three hours without recompense – with the forfeit, indeed, of the considerable expenses of dressing up, coming out at night, and missing the last train home; those who were normally the slaves of other masters were, Lord Copper felt, his for the evening. He had bought them and bound them, hand and

foot, with consommé and cream of chicken, turbot and
saddle, duck and pêche melba; and afterwards, when the
cigars had been furtively pocketed and the brandy glasses
filled with the horrible brown compound for which Lord
Copper was paying two pounds a bottle, there came the
golden hour when he rose to speak at whatever length he
liked and on whatever subject, without fear of rivalry or
interruption.

Often the occasion was purely contingent on Lord
Copper's activities – some reshuffling of directorships, an
amalgamation of subsidiary companies, or an issue of new
stocks; sometimes some exhausted and resentful celebrity
whom the *Beast* had adopted sat on Lord Copper's right
hand as the guest of honour, and there, on this particular
evening, at half-past eight, sat Mr Theodore Boot; he had
tucked up his coat tails behind him, spread his napkin
across his knees and, unlike any of Lord Copper's guests
of honour before or since, was settling down to enjoy
himself.

'Don't think I've ever been to this place before,' he
began.

'No,' said Lord Copper. 'No, I suppose not. It is, I
believe, the best place of its kind.'

'Since my time,' said Uncle Theodore tolerantly. 'New
places always springing up. Other places closing down.
The old order changeth, eh?'

'Yes,' said Lord Copper coldly.

It was not thus that he was accustomed to converse
with junior reporters, however promising. There was a
type, Lord Copper had learned, who became presump-
tuous under encouragement. Uncle Theodore, it was
true, did not seem to belong to this type; it was hard to
know exactly what type Uncle Theodore did belong
to.

Lord Copper turned away rather petulantly and engaged his other neighbour – a forgotten and impoverished
ex-Viceroy who for want of other invitations spent three
or four evenings a week at dinners of this kind – but his

mind was not in the conversation; it was disturbed. It had
been disturbed all the evening, ever since, sharp on time,
he had made his entrance to the inner reception room
where the distinguished guests were segregated. Uncle
Theodore had been standing there between Mr Salter
and the Managing Editor. He wore a tail coat of obsolete
cut, a black waistcoat, and a very tall collar; his purplish
patrician face had beamed on Lord Copper, but there
had been no answering cordiality in Lord Copper's greeting. Boot was a surprise. Images were not easily formed
or retained in Lord Copper's mind, but he had had quite
a clear image of Boot, and Uncle Theodore did not con-
form to it. Was *this* Mrs Stitch's protégé? Was this the
youngest K.C.B.? Had Lady Cockpurse commended *this*
man's style? And – it gradually came back to him – was
this the man he had himself met not two months back,
and speeded on his trip to Ishmaelia? Lord Copper took
another look and encountered a smile so urbane, so
patronizing, so intolerably knowing, that he hastily
turned away.

Someone had blundered.

Lord Copper turned to the secretary who stood, with
the toast master, behind his chair.

'Wagstaff.'

'Yes, Lord Copper.'

'Take memo for tomorrow. "See Salter".'

'Very good, Lord Copper.'

The banquet must go on, thought Lord Copper.

The banquet went on.

The general hum of conversation was becoming louder.
It was a note dearer to Lord Copper than the tongue of
hounds in covert. He tried to close his mind to the enigmatic and, he was inclined to suspect, obnoxious presence
on his right. He heard the unctuous voice rising and
falling, breaking now and then into a throaty chuckle.
Uncle Theodore, after touching infelicitously on a variety
of topics, had found common ground with the distin-

guished guest on his right; they had both, in another age,
known a man named Bertie Wodehouse-Bonner.

Uncle Theodore enjoyed his recollection and he enjoyed his champagne, but politeness at last compelled
him reluctantly to address Lord Copper – a dull dog,
but his host.

He leant nearer to him and spoke in a confidential
manner.

'Tell me,' he asked, 'where does one go on to nowadays?'

'I beg your pardon.'

Uncle Theodore leered. 'You know. To round off the
evening?'...

'Personally,' said Lord Copper, 'I intend to go to bed
without any delay.'

'*Exactly*. Where's the place, nowadays?'

Lord Copper turned to his secretary.

'Wagstaff.'

'Yes, Lord Copper.'

'Memo for tomorrow. "Sack Salter".'

'Very good, Lord Copper.'

Only once did Uncle Theodore again tackle his host.
He advised him to eat mustard with duck for the good of
his liver. Lord Copper seemed not to hear. He sat back
in his chair, surveying the room – for the evening, *his*
room. The banquet must go on. At the four long tables
which ran at right angles to his own the faces above the
white shirt fronts were growing redder; the chorus of
male conversation swelled in volume. Lord Copper began
to see himself in a new light, as the deserted leader,
shouldering alone the great burden of Duty. The thought
comforted him. He had made a study of the lives of other
great men; loneliness was the price they had all paid.
None, he reflected, had enjoyed the devotion they
deserved; there was Caesar and Brutus, Napoleon and
Josephine, Shakespeare and – someone, he believed, had
been disloyal to Shakespeare.

The time of his speech was drawing near. Lord Copper
felt the familiar, infinitely agreeable sense of well-being
which always preceded his after-dinner speeches; his was
none of the nervous inspiration, the despair and exalta-
tion of more ambitious orators; his was the profound,
incommunicable contentment of monolocution. He felt
himself suffused with a gentle warmth; he felt mag-
nanimous.

'Wagstaff.'

'Lord Copper?'

'What was the last memo I gave you?'

'"Sack Salter", Lord Copper.'

'Nonsense. You must be more accurate. I said "Shift
Salter."'

At last the great moment came. The toast master
thundered on the floor with his staff and his tremendous
message rang through the room.

'My Lords and Gentlemen. Pray silence for the Right
Honourable the Viscount Copper.'

Lord Copper rose and breasted the applause. Even the
waiters, he noticed with approval, were diligently clapping. He leant forwards on his fists, as it was his habit to
stand on these happy occasions, and waited for silence.
His secretary made a small, quite unnecessary adjust-
ment to the microphone. His speech lay before him in a
sheaf of typewritten papers. Uncle Theodore murmured
a few words of encouragement. 'Cheer up,' he said. 'It
won't last long.'

'Gentlemen,' he began, 'many duties fall to the lot of a
man of my position, some onerous, some pleasant. It is a
very pleasant duty to welcome tonight a colleague who
though – ' and Lord Copper saw the words 'young in
years' looming up at him; he swerved – 'young in his
service to Megalopolitan Newspapers, has already added
lustre to the great enterprise we have at heart – Boot of
the *Beast*.'

Uncle Theodore, who had joined the staff of the *Beast*

less than six hours ago, smirked dissent and began to revise his opinion of Lord Copper; he was really an uncommonly civil fellow, thought Uncle Theodore.

At the name of Boot applause broke out thunderously, and Lord Copper, waiting for it to subside, glanced grimly through the pages ahead of him. For some time now his newspapers had been advocating a new form of driving test, by which the applicant for a licence sat in a stationary car while a cinema film unfolded before his eyes a nightmare drive down a road full of obstacles. Lord Copper had personally inspected a device of the kind and it was thus that his speech now appeared to him. The opportunities and achievements of youth had been the theme. Lord Copper looked from the glowing sentences to the guest of honour beside him (who at the moment had buried his nose in his brandy glass and was inhaling stertorously) and he rose above it. The banquet must go on.

The applause ended and Lord Copper resumed his speech. His hearers sank low in their chairs and beguiled the time in a variety of ways; by drawing little pictures on the menu, by playing noughts and crosses on the table-cloth, by having modest bets as to who could keep the ash longest on his cigar; and over them the tropic tide of oratory rose and broke in foaming surf, over the bowed, bald head of Uncle Theodore. It lasted thirty-eight minutes by Mr Salter's watch.

'Gentlemen,' said Lord Copper at last, 'in giving you the toast of Boot, I give you the toast of the Future...'

The Future... A calm and vinous optimism possessed the banquet...

A future for Lord Copper that was full to surfeit of things which no sane man seriously coveted – of long years of uninterrupted oratory at other banquets in other causes; of yearly, prodigious payments of super-tax crowned at their final end by death duties of unprecedented size; of a deferential opening and closing of doors, of muffled telephone bells and almost soundless type-writers.

A future for Uncle Theodore such as he had always at heart believed to be attainable. Two thousand a year, shady little gentlemen's chambers, the opportunity for endless reminiscence; sunlit morning saunterings down St James's Street between hatter and boot-maker and club; feline prowlings after dark; a buttonhole, a bowler hat with a curly brim, a clouded malacca cane, a kindly word to commissionaires and cab drivers.

A future for Mr Salter as art editor of *Home Knitting;* punctual domestic dinners; Sunday at home among the crazy pavements.

A future for Sir John Boot with the cropped amazons of the Antarctic.

A future for Mrs Stitch heaped with the spoils of every continent and every century, gadgets from New York and bronzes from the Aegean, new entrées and old friends.

A future for Corker and Pigge; they had travelled six hundred miles by now and were nearing the Sudanese frontier. Soon they will be kindly received by a District Commissioner, washed and revictualled and sent on their way home.

A future for Kätchen. She was sitting, at the moment, in the second class saloon of a ship bound for Madagascar, writing a letter:

Darling William,

We are going to Madagascar. My husband used to have a friend there and he says it is more comfortable than to come to Europe so will you please send us the money there. Not care of the consul because that would not be comfortable but poste restante. My husband says I should not have sold the specimens but I explained that you would pay what they are worth so now he does not mind. They are worth £50. It will be better if you will buy francs because he says you will get more than we should.

*We look forward very much to getting the money, so please send it
by the quickest way. The boat was not worth very much money
when we got to French territory. I am very well.*

Ever your loving,
Kätchen.

A future for William . . .

. . . *the waggons lumber in the lane under their golden glory
of harvested sheaves,* he wrote; *maternal rodents pilot their furry
brood through the stubble ;* . . .

He laid down his pen. *Lush Places* need not be finished
until tomorrow evening.

The rest of the family had already gone up. William
took the last candle from the table and put out the lamps
in the hall. Under the threadbare carpet the stair-boards
creaked as he mounted to his room.

Before getting into bed he drew the curtain and threw
open the window. Moonlight streamed into the room.

Outside the owls hunted maternal rodents and their
furry brood.

THE STORY OF PENGUIN CLASSICS

Before 1946 ...'Classics' are mainly the domain of academics and students, without readable editions for everyone else. This all changes when a little-known classicist, E. V. Rieu, presents Penguin founder Allen Lane with the translation of Homer's *Odyssey* that he has been working on and reading to his wife Nelly in his spare time.

1946 *The Odyssey* becomes the first Penguin Classic published, and promptly sells three million copies. Suddenly, classic books are no longer for the privileged few.

1950s Rieu, now series editor, turns to professional writers for the best modern, readable translations, including Dorothy L. Sayers's *Inferno* and Robert Graves's *The Twelve Caesars*, which revives the salacious original.

1960s The Classics are given the distinctive black jackets that have remained a constant throughout the series's various looks. Rieu retires in 1964, hailing the Penguin Classics list as 'the greatest educative force of the 20th century'.

1970s A new generation of translators arrives to swell the Penguin Classics ranks, and the list grows to encompass more philosophy, religion, science, history and politics.

1980s The Penguin American Library joins the Classics stable, with titles such as *The Last of the Mohicans* safeguarded. Penguin Classics now offers the most comprehensive library of world literature available.

1990s The launch of Penguin Audiobooks brings the classics to a listening audience for the first time, and in 1999 the launch of the Penguin Classics website takes them online to a larger global readership than ever before.

The 21st Century Penguin Classics are rejacketed for the first time in nearly twenty years. This world famous series now consists of more than 1300 titles, making the widest range of the best books ever written available to millions – and constantly redefining the meaning of what makes a 'classic'.

The Odyssey continues ...

The best books ever written

PENGUIN CLASSICS

SINCE 1946

Find out more at www.penguinclassics.com